Summer at Sunset

Beth Labonte

For Karyn & Steve, who let me drive their golf cart

"I'm not absolutely certain of the facts, but I rather fancy it's Shakespeare who says that it's always just when a fellow is feeling particularly braced with things in general that Fate sneaks up behind him with a bit of lead piping."

P.G. Wodehouse

SUMMER

We're engaged!

What do you mean *who?*

Us. Summer Eve Hartwell and Graham Michael Blenderman. You may remember us from such fiascos as Cruising to Bermuda with Summer's Wackadoodle Parents and, well, I guess that's probably all you may remember us from. We've been living a relatively quiet existence for the past two years.

Anyway, it was all very romantic. It was the morning after my brother Eric's wedding, and Graham and I were sipping mimosas over breakfast on the veranda of the Boston Park Plaza. Sure, Mom and Dad were also there—sitting across the table, sipping decaf coffee, and obsessing over the likelihood of developing skin cancer after fifteen minutes exposure to early morning sunlight—but I hardly even noticed them.

All I noticed was Graham suddenly putting his fork down, pushing his chair back, and getting down on one knee beside me. As I quickly tried to swallow the last forkful of bacon and eggs I'd shoveled into my mouth, Graham told me that I was his one true love, the Arwen to his Aragorn, the Rose to his Doctor, the Khaleesi to his Khal Drogo—I admit that I may have imagined some of those—and asked me to marry him!

Then he slid the most gorgeous, sparkling, must-have-sold-a-*lot*-of-iPhone-apps diamond ring onto my finger, while Mom and Dad sat across the table looking completely stunned. I mean, they would not have looked any more stunned had Abe Lincoln Vampire Slayer just lopped off both of our heads with an axe. But we didn't have our heads lopped off, we got engaged!

Once Mom and Dad snapped out of it, they went nuts hugging and kissing us and trying to take pictures with Dad's new smartphone. Then people at the other tables started clapping, and the hotel even sent over a bottle of complimentary champagne. It was like something out of a movie.

And even though Dad announced, about four minutes after the ring was nestled snugly onto my finger, that he had to find a men's room due to his Irritable Bowel Syndrome, it was truly the most magical moment of my life.

Truly.

It's funny how a mere twelve months after the most magical moment of my life, I could so desperately wish that I'd never been born.

1

When I say that it's funny, I don't mean that it's *ha ha* funny.

I mean it's funny like when you get a pedicure and then immediately drop a book on your big toe after leaving the nail salon. Trust me, it's happened. And right now my life is my big toe, and all of *this* is one big, heavy, *Harry Potter and the Deathly Hallows*-sized book waiting to drop and mess everything up.

It's too early to think about any of that, though. All I can think about right now is the fact that it can't possibly be six o'clock already. I feel like I slid into bed mere minutes ago. It can't have been more than a millisecond since my head sank into the pillow and I blissfully lost consciousness. I would give anything to be able to hit the snooze button right now. *Anything.* But I can't.

Would you like to know why?

Because instead of a simple alarm going off—one that I could smash with the palm of my hand, and then roll over into a deep, glorious slumber—I have Graham's mother pounding on my bedroom door. She's pounding on it, and she's *singing*.

Good morning! Good morning! Good morning to you!

The woman is completely insane. I mean, I love her and can't wait to be a part of the family and all that. But let's face it, she's nuts.

I really hope Graham is enjoying himself, sound asleep in the other guest bedroom. He started sleeping over there after the first time his mother bull-horned the both of us out of bed for a seven a.m. Zumba class. As chipper as Graham can be, he's actually not much of a morning person. After attending one class, he decided that Zumba should be a mother and daughter-in-law bonding event, and politely bowed out.

I should mention that these early mornings always occur after several consecutive nights of drinking and dancing on the town common. Let me tell you, the old people here are completely out of their minds. How they are managing to see eighty and ninety years old with this kind of lifestyle is seriously baffling. I mean, here I am—twenty-eight years old—and after only a few weeks at this place I feel as if I've got one foot in the grave.

Bang! Bang! Bang!

"Summer? Are you up? We want to make sure we get a spot in the front row!"

"Yes, yeah…I'm up," I mumble into my pillow.

"Summer?"

Bang! Bang! Bang!

"Yes! Yes! I'm *up!*" I scream, before she has a chance to start banging again. Or worse yet, singing.

Yes, I'm up. At least I don't have to shower. Zumba class at Sunset Havens doesn't exactly require one to look her best. That's where Graham and I are right now—Sunset Havens, or "The Havens," as it's fondly known to its residents. Sunset

Havens is one of Florida's largest retirement communities, with a population of over one hundred thousand and a black market for Viagra. They even have swingers.

No, not *golfers*. Why would I point out something as mundane as golfers? Every retirement community has golfers. No, I'm talking about the *other* kind of swingers. Gross, I know. Believe me, it didn't become any less gross when four of Babette Blenderman's elderly girlfriends described a swingers party to me in great detail. Babette swore up and down that she and Graham's dad aren't involved in that kind of thing, but I'm pretty sure I saw a twinkle in her eye. I have to remember to bring that up with Graham, actually.

I grab a pair of yoga pants and a t-shirt from the dresser and head into the bathroom. I wash my face, put in my contact lenses, and throw my hair into a who-cares-I'm-doing-Zumba-with-my-mother-in-law sort of ponytail. Done and done. I follow the smell of coffee into the kitchen and take a seat at the island. Babette is whizzing around in her purple spandex workout gear, her shoulder length blonde hair pulled back into a ponytail by a purple satin scrunchie. Scrunchies are still in style here at The Havens, as are shorts with sandals and black knee socks. She slides a plate of egg whites and wilted kale in front of me.

"Thanks," I say, picking up the saltshaker and sprinkling a liberal amount over my food. Babette's become a bit of a health nut since moving here. I think she's trying to counteract all of the drinking and sun exposure by overdosing on beta-carotene and Vitamin K. Will it work? Nobody knows. What I do know is that if we were staying at my parents' house, I'd be eating an

Egg McMuffin and hash browns right now. I sigh and take a bite of kale. Sometimes I miss my parents.

"What time do you expect your parents to get here?" asks Babette, pouring us two cups of coffee. Babette drinks hers black. I dump two teaspoons of sugar into mine.

"I'm not sure," I say, a small pit forming in the bottom of my stomach. "They stayed last night in Georgia, so probably later this afternoon. Eric's going to call me once they're close."

Did I say that I missed my parents? Well, fortunately, I don't have long to wait. You see, Graham and I are getting married in one week, right here in Florida.

Right here in Florida…at a retirement community.

Yes, you heard right. And yes, it's all my fault.

We were down here for a visit shortly after our engagement, when Babette and I attended a bridal show at the Sunset Havens function hall called The Lakeview. I'd been having anxiety over the thought of planning a wedding with my mother—surely wedding planning involved more nervous breakdowns than she was equipped to handle. I mean, soon after our engagement, Mom gave me a lengthy dissertation on the cons of strapless wedding gowns (there were no pros). And so, after a few too many sample glasses of champagne, I had confided some of these fears in my future mother-in-law. I blame myself for not noticing the look of incredulous joy that had crept into Babette's eyes—a look that I now recognize as belonging to mothers of sons who, after years of Teenage Mutant Ninja Turtles, realize they might finally get the chance to do something girly.

About three seconds later, Babette found a contest to win an all expenses paid wedding at The Lakeview, and the two of us ceremoniously dropped my name and information into the entry box. After all of the champagne samples I'd consumed, the reality of what winning the contest might mean wasn't able to work itself into the proper parts of my brain. Besides, what were the odds?

Quite good, as it turns out. I won the contest.

After a minor freak-out—in which I repeated the words *what have I done* for about thirty minutes straight and in a variety of intonations and facial expressions—I decided that getting married at a retirement community would work out for the best.

First of all, it was too late to take the wedding away from Babette. She would have been completely heartbroken and have nothing girly to look forward to until Graham and I have children. And what if we have nothing but boys? I mean, within hours of winning, she had already started planning how I would arrive at The Lakeview via the Maid of the Havens tour boat. I'm not a monster. I couldn't disappoint her like that.

Second of all, when I got up the nerve to tell my mother about having the wedding in Florida, she told me that it was a "huge weight off of her shoulders." Granted, hearing one's mother describe her only daughter's wedding as a "huge weight" is a bit depressing. But that just proved my point. If I didn't want to run the risk of my wedding being called off every time a slight problem arose, I needed to take my mother out of the equation—even if that meant having my wedding at a retirement community.

So, you see, it all seemed like a win-win.

Graham continues to have a few reservations about the idea. He keeps telling me that I'm going to regret not planning the wedding with my mother, to which I simply reply, *Have you met my mother?*

Admittedly, it's been difficult planning a wedding from twelve hundred miles away. Not to mention that the guest list has had to be severely whittled down. The whole thing involves quite a lot of emails, quite a lot of phone calls, and quite a lot of trust in my future mother-in-law. And quite a lot of nervous breakdowns, to tell you the truth. But, it's my bed and I must lie in it.

Anyway, here we are.

With my school librarian job on summer break, and Graham able to build iPhone apps from anywhere he wants, we've already been down here for three weeks. Mom and Dad have refused to fly in for the wedding—citing the usual fears and phobias—and are instead being driven down the East Coast by Eric and his wife. They are arriving today and staying for the week, right here with us in the Blenderman house. That's right, there will be six of us crammed into a fifteen hundred square foot, three-bedroom, two-bathroom ranch. I can tell you that I am very much looking forward to Graham and I boarding that airplane and zipping off to our honeymoon in Jamaica.

But, first thing's first.

***

Zumba class is taking place this morning at Redwood Corral—the Western themed town common here at The Havens. The town commons are where all of the shops and restaurants are located, and where hundreds of residents gather each night to listen to live music, drink, dance, and drink some more. Each town common is also filmed twenty-four hours a day by live web cams. I'm pretty certain that nobody in the world has ever tuned in to The Havens web cams, but still. It's very *1984*.

Babette and I are early enough to claim the last two spots directly in front of the bandstand, but the common is filling up fast. Golf carts are pouring in, vying for parking spaces. Somebody lays on their horn. I look up to see a golf cart moving timidly off down the street, while another cart, with pink and purple feather boas wound all around the frame, turns roughly into a parking space.

I clench my fists as two women get out of the cart and make their way across the common toward us. Let's just say that Graham has a bit of a history with these two. Let's also just say that they make my skin crawl.

The one on the left is Francine—short, dyed jet black hair, with a smoker's cough. Today she's wearing turquoise terrycloth pants, and a t-shirt that says *Co-ed Naked Shuffleboard*. Next to her is Janice—tall, blonde, and with what I can only assume are Jessica Simpson hair extensions. She's wearing black spandex bicycle shorts, and a pink t-shirt that says *Sunset Havens Twirlers*.

"Hi, Summer," says Francine, poking me in the back. "Babette."

"Hello, girls," says Babette. "Nice to see you up so early. I like what you've done with your hair, Francine. Very *natural*."

"My hairdresser says that black is the new blonde." Francine gives Janice a smug look.

"It's a shame you didn't have enough time to do your makeup this morning," says Janice, inspecting her nails.

"Looks like you two girls got the last spots in the front row," says Francine, ignoring Janice. She gives us an exaggerated wink.

I look in the direction of the live web cam, and roll my eyes. I find myself doing that a lot here. I know nobody can actually see my individual facial expressions, but it's fun to imagine. I feel like I'm the star of my own crazy reality show.

Summer At Sunset.

It's got a bit of a ring to it.

2

Front row. Big deal. The reason there is such competition for the front row is ridiculous. There is this instructor named Flavio, and he is straight out of a nineteen-eighties aerobics video—including a neon spandex bodysuit, terrycloth headband, and mullet. The old ladies go absolutely crazy for him. Being in the front row means there is a higher chance that he will toss his sweaty towel at you at the end of class. He throws his sweaty, summer-in-Florida workout towel at somebody in the front row at the end of every class, and they *love* it.

After my first class—the one that Graham and I attended together—Flavio threw the towel to *me* and I completely freaked out. I flung it on the ground and screamed as if he'd thrown a squirrel in my face. The ladies took it as a personal insult, as if I thought myself too good for their precious Flavio. I'm pretty sure they held a committee meeting before agreeing to let me back into the front row. Believe me, I would have been thrilled to be permanently relegated to the way back, but apparently it means a lot to Babette that we Merengue directly next to one another.

So, here I am, on my best behavior.

The music starts, and Flavio bounds up the steps of the bandstand, dressed to the nines in his signature outfit. The spandex bodysuit is green today, with a large yellow triangle down the front. The crowd goes wild and the next thirty minutes are nothing but a blur of Latin dance moves and bad Gloria Estefan remixes.

Man, it's hot out here. The sun is barely up and I'm already sweating bullets. The idea that I have to wear a wedding gown in a week is somewhat concerning. At least it's sleeveless and fairly lightweight. Mom and Dad offered to drive it down with them so I wouldn't have to bring it on the airplane, and I agreed. Despite the heat, I smile when I think about finally being able to try it on later.

I can't believe that in one week I'm going to be Mrs. Summer Blenderman. Whenever I say my new name I picture a cheerful man with a blender mixing up colorful frozen cocktails. What's better than that?

Air conditioning, I suppose. And water. I turned down Babette's offer of a bottle of Indonesian coconut water before we left the house this morning, and then I forgot to bring any of my own. Now all I can think about are those ice cold, frozen cocktails, and the fact that my cells probably look like shriveled old raisins rolling around inside my body. Maybe that's why my side hurts. No, that's just a stitch. Flavio is really killing us today. You'd think doing Zumba for the past few weeks would have whipped me into some sort of shape, but no. These old ladies still put me to shame every single time. Whatever. Shame accepted. I need water.

I smile apologetically at Babette and excuse myself to go and find something to drink. I don't know how these women do it. Some of them are wearing long sleeves. One's wearing a black nylon windbreaker. I take my time crossing the street to Dunkin Donuts and order myself a lemonade. The air conditioning is absolutely cranking in here, and I can only sit inside for about three minutes before feeling the need to warm up again. I feel like that should be Florida's slogan—*Too Hot Outside, Too Cold Inside.*

I arrive back at the common just in time to see Flavio whip his sweaty towel into the second row. Francine elbows Janice out of the way, and catches the towel tightly in her hands. She brings it to her lips, *kisses it*—I'm trying hard not to gag at this point—and stretches it up and over her head.

"Nice try, sister!" screams Janice, flying in from the side and knocking Francine to the ground. She wrenches the towel from Francine's hand and twirls it around above her head, only to be hip-checked by some woman in the third row, and knocked down on top of Francine. Third-row-woman grabs the towel and holds it triumphantly up over her head as Flavio blows a kiss to the crowd and exits quickly down the back of the bandstand. He speeds away in his purple golf cart with the vanity plate *ZUMBA GOD.*

A class act, that one.

I wait for Babette by her golf cart. If she hurries, we can get out of here before Francine and Janice manage to pick themselves up off the ground. Otherwise, we're going to be here awhile. That's the thing about Sunset Havens, you can't just slip quietly in and out of a Zumba class. Everything here turns into a gossip hour.

Ah, yes. Here they all come. Janice has a straw wrapper stuck in her hair and the waistband of Francine's pants have done almost a complete three-sixty.

"What are you two broads up to tonight?" asks Francine, adjusting her pants and lighting up a cigarette. She takes a long drag.

"Summer's parents are arriving today for the wedding!" says Babette in a singsong voice. She puts her arm around my shoulder and gives it a firm squeeze. "We're going to take them out on the town tonight and give them a proper Havens welcome!"

"Oh, that's right. The *wedding*," says Francine, as if this is the first she's heard of it. She takes another puff and looks me slowly up and down. Unflinching, I look her up and down right back.

"Will you be taking them to Rosa Lee's?" asks Janice.

"Where else?"

I cringe. Rosa Lee's is a resident-only saloon-style restaurant and dance club—the antithesis of where I would want to bring my parents on their first night here. Or, to be honest, on any night anywhere.

"We'll come by," says Francine. "I can't wait to see that son of yours again. He left us girls high and dry yesterday after karaoke. He had to rush off to meet *someone*." Francine glances in my direction.

So, here's the other thing about Sunset Havens. Graham has always been very attractive to women that are ten to twenty years older than him. A cougar magnet, if you will. You may remember this phenomenon from such incidents as Lana the Former Hooter's Waitress. Well, if middle-aged women think of Graham as a piece of meat, down here at The Havens, amongst the over sixty-five crowd, he's the early bird special filet mignon. We can't even take a walk down the street without women popping out from behind shrubs and mailboxes to squeeze his biceps.

Graham's been coming down here for visits long before we started dating. These women look forward to his visits. I'll tell you one thing they were *not* looking forward to—me. Old people hate change. And what am I, if not a big, youthful heap of change that came prancing into town about to take their beloved Graham off the market?

So, yes, I am the *someone* that Francine speaks so kindly of. I am the *someone* that she has been making digs at ever since I stepped off the plane. I know that she, and Janice, and probably every other woman in this place, would love nothing more than to see Graham and I break up. The trouble is that nobody will back me up on this. Everybody thinks I'm overreacting—Graham, Babette, the kid that scoops ice cream at Ben & Jerry's (seriously, it's hard to find anyone young to speak with around here). Graham finds all of these women delightful. He thinks that they're sweet and innocent and that there's no harm in letting them squeeze his muscles once in a while if it's going to give them some enjoyment during the short time that they have left. Please. Some of these women have thirty more years.

"Sorry," I say. "Graham and I had a little date night planned. It was *so* romantic. We made out in our golf cart for, like, *ever*."

Babette shoots me a disgusted look, but I don't care. The look on Francine's face is priceless. For the record, Graham and I had an appointment at Mr. Tux, ate dinner at Taco Bell, and then drove directly home.

Before she can reply, Janice nudges Francine with an elbow.

An elderly man is shuffling by in a pair of cargo shorts, a blue polo shirt with the collar popped, and a floppy fishing hat.

"Gil, you old bastard!" calls out Francine.

I gasp, but Gil doesn't seem surprised. He gives Francine a feeble little wave, and continues shuffling toward the entrance of Dunkin Donuts. A woman meets him outside and hands him a cup of coffee.

"I see that Lorraine's gotten her hooks into Gil," says Francine, disapprovingly.

"For now," says Janice. "You know Gil. He's already got his collar popped."

"Mmm hmmm," agrees Babette.

"What? What's up with Gil?" I ask. "Why is his collar popped?"

The three women exchange knowing glances.

"Down here, a blue shirt with a popped collar means that a man has taken his Viagra," says Babette.

"Ew! Why would he need to announce that? Isn't he with *that* woman over there?" I ask.

"Gil never stays with one woman for very long," explains Francine. "He was with me last week. Until he stopped returning my calls." She throws her cigarette on the sidewalk, grinding it out with her turquoise tennis shoe.

Smart move, Gil.

"Lorraine is a fool," says Babette. "He'll probably have someone new by lunch."

"He'll probably have someone new *for* lunch," says Janice, and the three women roar with laughter.

"If he asks you to go for a ride in his golf cart," warns Babette, "you do *not* go."

"Are you serious?" I laugh. "That guy can barely walk."

"What that man can do in a golf cart does *not* require the use of his legs," says Babette, and all three women burst into a new wave of raucous laughter.

I raise my eyebrows at Babette. "And you know this *how*?"

She bats her hand at me and laughs. "Oh, you know. Word of mouth."

"That's right," says Francine. "*Orally*." She mutters the word out of the corner of her mouth and the three women break into laughter again.

"I think I'm going to be sick," I say, covering my eyes.

I sneak a look at Babette through my fingers, trying to see if that same twinkle in her eye is there—the one I thought I saw when she talked about the Sunset Havens swingers—but I can't tell. It has to be in my imagination. Graham's parents can't be *swingers*. Just because they live in a retirement paradise full of Viagra and alcohol and no consequences—

I crinkle up my nose.

I really ought to mention this to Graham.

3

It's another beautiful day here at Sunset Havens.

At least that's what the DJ keeps telling me through the loudspeakers that are stationed all around Duke's Landing. *It's another beautiful day here at Sunset Havens. Please enjoy these outdated songs that we shall play on a loop.* Duke's Landing is another of the three town commons, and was named for its founder, Fillmore W. Duke—a kooky old land speculator who settled the place back in nineteen twenty-six.

Yeah, not really.

Sunset Havens was actually founded in nineteen eighty-six by a regular, middle-aged businessman named Stuart Fogleman. But that's what they do down here—they make up history and stick make believe historical plaques on all of the buildings. For example, the Starbucks that we are about to go in, used to be called Ezekiel's Tavern and was a popular speak-easy during Prohibition.

"But it was built in two thousand and nine!" I say, stopping in front of the door and throwing my arms in the air.

"It's just part of the fun," says Graham, pulling the door open for me. "It's like those old-timey photos you get at amusement parks. Obviously I was never in the Union army, but now I have photos that say otherwise."

"But we're not *at* an amusement park," I argue. "This is where these people *live*. Putting on a costume for a photo isn't the same as making up history. I mean, what if they start pretending that the real history stuff never happened, just because it's unpleasant to think about? What if they forget about Hitler and the Kennedy assassination and Osama bin Laden? Then what?"

At the sound of the name Osama bin Laden, a few people turn their heads and give me looks of concern. See what I mean?

Graham shrugs. "I think that might actually be one of the selling points of this place."

We order our coffee and take a seat at a table. My parents aren't due in for a few more hours, so we've got some time to kill. Come to think of it, coffee probably wasn't the best idea for the state of my nerves, but I'm exhausted from Zumba class. How is it that I'm more exhausted by this retirement community than I am from anything back home?

"Hey," I say, leaning in across the table. "I meant to ask you something about your parents."

"What's that?"

"Well, it's just that your mom keeps saying things that seem a little odd. She always says she's joking afterwards, or she claims that she only knows certain things *from a friend*. But I swear I saw a twinkle in her eye."

"What kinds of things are we talking about?"

I clear my throat. "Like, you know, *sexual* stuff."

"My mom talks about sexual stuff with you?" says Graham, in the loudest voice ever. The Osama bin Laden people look over at us again.

"Not just with me!" I whisper. "With her friends. I just always have the misfortune of being there. You don't think your parents could be, you know…*swingers*, do you?"

Graham, who had been tilting his chair back, with one foot up on his knee, chokes on his latte and returns to an upright position.

"I really hope you're kidding. Any twinkle you may have seen in my mom's eye is probably from all the booze."

"But that's my point," I say. "Maybe they've gone overboard with their new lifestyle. I mean, it's *fine* if they did. They've worked hard and deserve to be able to do whatever weird things they want. But, what if they, like, try to get my parents into it?"

Graham lays his head down on the table and doesn't move until I shake him by the shoulders. He looks up at me and I see that same, Blenderman twinkle in his eye.

"I should have known that's where this was headed," he says. "First of all, my parents are not swingers. Why would my dad want to swap wives? My mom's hot."

I raise my eyebrows. "Okay, Oedipus, what's your next point?"

Graham laughs. "Second of all, if my parents *were* swingers and they took your parents to a swingers party, your parents wouldn't even know what was going on. They're too innocent."

"Oy, Richard!" I say, in my best Mom impersonation. "Why is everybody naked?"

Graham laughs. "Oy, Richard! Why are everybody's car keys in that filthy fish bowl?"

Now we're both cracking up and I realize how paranoid I've sounded since we walked into Starbucks. The stress of the wedding must finally be getting to me. I mean, not everybody is trying to erase Hitler, or corrupt my parents, or steal my fiancé. I really need to relax. I really need to—

Oh, great. Here we go again.

"We've got another one," I say. "Three o'clock."

"Another what?"

"Another one of your stalkers."

As I sat there trying to convince myself that all was right with the world, I noticed a woman in line staring at us. She's wearing a blue and white nautical themed outfit with a visor, gold anchor earrings, and about three hundred gold bracelets.

"I do not have stalkers," says Graham, a little too smugly.

"Of *course* you have stalkers," I say, taking a sip of coffee and glancing at the woman. "You have no idea what a guy like you does to these women. You volunteer at their swim aerobics classes, and their book club meetings, and you think that you're just being a good citizen. But do you know what you're *really* doing?"

Graham raises his eyebrows. "What's that?"

"You're getting them all hot and bothered with your tan and your muscles and your hair." I wave my hands around in the air to illustrate Graham's hair. "They want you, Graham. They can't get enough of you. And they want *me* out of the picture." I make a knife-across-the-throat motion and lean back in my chair, nodding in agreement with myself.

"Sounds like you have a little crush on me," says Graham. "Maybe we should get married."

I stick my tongue out. "I *was* considering it."

Graham reaches across the table and squeezes my hand. "You realize that you're taking all of this way too seriously, right? I mean, these women are like my grandmas."

"*You* may think that," I say, "but you should have seen the way Francine was looking me up and down today. You told me yourself that you took her to something called the Senior Prom and bought her a corsage and everything. I guarantee you there was nothing grandmotherly on her mind *that* night."

"Did you forget the part where I also told you Francine had just lost her husband? And the part where I told you I was helping her to get out of the house for the first time in a long time? She was practically agoraphobic."

I frown. Sometimes I have a selective memory.

"Okay, fine," I say, shaking my head. "But how about that time you took Lorraine to her grandson's piano recital, and she invited you back to her house for some May-December naughty time?"

Graham laughs. "That is *not* what happened. She wanted me to come over to watch *Downton Abbey*. She said she had tea and scones."

"I bet she did. I also bet she would have had you stripped down to your scones before the opening credits."

Graham reaches across the table and squeezes my other hand. "Please tell me you're not jealous of Lorraine?"

"Of course not. I just don't think you realize what a hot commodity you are. I don't think you realize what these women are capable of."

"What exactly do you think they're capable of?"

I stare at him for a few seconds. I've had these ideas running through my head for weeks, but now that I've been asked to verbalize them, I can't. They're just too stupid.

"Um, I don't know," I say, trying to pick out some of the less ridiculous sounding ones. "Kidnap me? Throw me off the Maid of the Havens into Lake Fillmore? Force me to overdose on Francine's thyroid medication?"

Okay, no. Those all sound pretty bad.

Graham slowly shakes his head. "You know, my mom told me that One-Eyed Hank asked you to fly away with him to his private island in the Caribbean the other night. Maybe I should be the one who's concerned."

"One-Eyed Hank doesn't have a private island," I say. "He has dementia. Is that the best you've got?"

"Yeah, that's it."

I roll my eyes and check the time. "We'd better get going. Eric and my parents should be arriving soon."

I'm gathering up my things to leave, when the woman that was staring at us in line appears next to our table, fumbling with her change purse. The next thing I know, there are coins rolling all over the floor.

"I am *so* sorry," she says. Then she gets on her hands and knees and crawls under our table.

"Let me get that," says Graham, starting to stand up. He stops mid-way. "I think you've got my leg, though."

"Don't get up!" calls the woman. "I'm just fine." A moment later, she emerges from Graham's side of the table—coming up right between his legs—and coils herself into his lap like a boa constrictor. I clamp a hand over my mouth.

"Gloria?" says Graham. "I didn't even recognize you!"

Oh my God, he actually knows her. Of *course* he knows her. He knows every woman down here.

"I just had my hair frosted," she says, patting the back of her head. "Do you like?"

"You look like a movie star," he says, giving me a wink. "Have you met my fiancée, Summer?"

"No, I don't think so," says Gloria, giving me the familiar once-over.

"Nice to meet you," I say, sticking out my hand. She doesn't take it as she's too busy combing her fingers through Graham's hair.

"You should consider getting yours frosted too," she says. "I think it's *such* a good look on a man."

"Graham's already blonde," I say, choking on my Frappuccino. "So, too bad."

"He could dye it black, and then bleach the tips for the wedding," says Gloria. "He would look just like that handsome boy, Lance Bass!"

I squeeze my cup so hard that the lid pops off. Gloria smiles at me.

"I really must be going," she says, sliding off of Graham's lap. "Will we be seeing you at Dirty Uno tomorrow night?"

Okay. I've crushed my cup. Frappuccino is leaking all over my hands.

"Dirty Uno?" I ask.

Graham clears his throat. "No, not this week, Glor. Lots of wedding stuff to get done."

"Shame," she says, giving me a look. Then she gives Graham a wink and walks out of the store.

"Dirty Uno?" I repeat. "Seriously?"

"There's actually nothing dirty about it," shrugs Graham. "It's just regular Uno, with a few rule changes. I was disappointed, to tell you the truth. Now Dirty Pinochle, that's another story."

I stare at him in awe. I really need to get him away from this place. Besides the weird card games, Graham has been a participant in three flash mobs since we've been here. And a few days ago I saw a picture of him on the Sunset Havens Facebook page leading a Conga line through Sunshine Springs. He denies that it was him. I will admit that the picture was a bit blurry, and that down here in Florida Graham may not be the only person to own a watermelon print Hawaiian shirt. But, I have a gut feeling.

4

Eric gave me the warning call as we were driving back from Starbucks. He, his wife Tanya, and my parents, should be pulling up to the Blenderman house at any moment.

To recap: Richard and Joan Hartwell will be arriving at Sunset Havens—the hedonistic retirement capital of the world—at any moment. Worlds are about to collide. Universes are on the verge of being blown apart. All of time and space shall momentarily cease to exist.

So, tell me…*how* is he so calm right now?

We're sitting in the driveway on plastic lawn chairs, while Graham plays a game on his phone, calm as can be. Classic Graham. Two years ago he literally thought that going on a cruise with my parents was going to be fun. And yes, I will admit that if we hadn't gone on that cruise we might not be engaged right now, but still. He somehow fails to see the impending disaster that is my parents and his parents living together under one roof.

It's true that after the Bermuda cruise, things at the Hartwell household changed for the better. Graham and I began dating, and I moved into my own apartment. Mom and Dad, no longer having my life to obsess over, started to actually go out and enjoy their retirement. They took up ballroom dancing. They started taking weekend trips, just the two of them, up to Maine and New Hampshire. Dad never did get back on a scooter, but he did convince Mom to buy one of those tandem bicycles, which they've occasionally ridden around Nantucket. I've actually come to view them not as the overbearing, anxiety-ridden stressors of my youth, but in the way that they've always appeared to others—as cute.

My parents are cute.

Graham's parents are cute too, just in a different way.

John Blenderman is a retired high school science teacher who began planning for retirement as soon as he started working at the age of twenty-five. He put in his thirty years of service, became well loved by the student population, and received several consecutive Teacher-of-the-Year awards. Then he promptly retired while he still had his youthful glow. He loves everything about Florida, and his mind is overflowing with ideas and projects that he wants to tackle in his golden years. He is a bit loud and a lot tanned, and when I look at him I see an older version of Graham in possession of a bucket list. He gives me quite a lot of anxiety, if we're being honest.

Babette, in her younger years, was a very successful real estate agent. Growing up, I was accustomed to seeing her smiling face plastered across For Sale signs all over the city. About ten years ago she moved into the high-end real estate market and made quite a hefty commission on a few waterfront properties. After that, it didn't take much convincing from her husband to pack it in and move down to Florida. Aside from becoming functioning alcoholics, they seem to have made the right decision.

All cute. All very nice people.

But throwing all of them together…*here*? I can't even wrap my head around it. I wonder if it's too late to find them a hotel? Believe me, I've suggested it many times, but Babette and John won't hear of it. They keep saying that you don't get the full Havens experience if you stay at a hotel.

Do you know who *is* staying at a hotel? My brother and his wife. That's right. In classic Eric style, he's going to toss Mom, Dad, and The Duffle out of the car and peel off to his relaxing hotel far, far away. I probably won't even see them again until the day of the wedding.

You know what? Screw the full Havens experience.

I take out my phone and start frantically searching for Holiday Inns, but my fingers are so jittery that I keep making typos and pulling up results for things like Hogwarts and the Holy Grail.

"Aaah!" I groan in frustration.

"What are you doing?" asks Graham, leaning over. "Why are you Googling Howard Stern?"

I turn off my phone.

"I *wasn't*. I was trying to find a hotel. Just in case things go horribly—"

"They're here!" shouts Graham.

Oh, God. He's right. Eric's Escalade is coming around the corner. Bass pumping. Spinning rims spinning. When did he get *those*? He really is a tool.

"Shhh!" I say to Graham.

"What?"

"We don't need everybody running out all at once, do we? It might be a bit overwhelming."

John and Babette are watching TV on the back porch, and I had been fantasizing about sneaking my parents in the front door and not bringing them out again until breakfast tomorrow.

"Of *course* everybody's going to run out all at once," he says. "This is a big deal. Mom! Dad! They're here!"

Graham jumps out of his chair and runs to the curb, flagging down the Escalade like he's hailing a cab in Times Square. As soon as Eric sees him, he lays on the horn.

BEEEEEP! BEEP! BEEP! BEEEEEEEEP!

Gray heads begin popping out of doors and windows up and down the street. The next-door neighbor's garage door goes up. A couple in a golf cart passes by and beeps back three times. Dogs bark.

So much for subtlety.

Eric pulls into the driveway and rolls down the window. Both the air conditioning and the radio are cranking at full blast.

"Hey, man. Good to see you!" he says, reaching out to shake hands with Graham. The silence is deafening when he turns off the engine.

"Hi, Graham! Hi, Summer!" Tanya leans over Eric's lap and waves to us from the passenger seat. She's got something of a feral look in her eyes, to be honest. Like somebody who just drove a great distance with her in-laws in the backseat.

"Hi, guys," I say, slowly approaching the vehicle. The windows are tinted, so I haven't been able to see Mom and Dad yet. They haven't made a peep. It's quite possible that Eric left them behind at the last rest area.

"Oy, Richard! I'm having a nervous breakdown!"

Nope. There they are.

I wrench open the back door and Dad almost falls out.

"Richard! Wake up! We're here!" Mom whacks him on the arm and he sits bolt upright.

My eyes widen at the sight of the backseat. Tissue boxes, napkins, umbrellas, tourist pamphlets, extra pairs of old-people sneakers, packets of emergency rain ponchos, and several thousand crumpled up fast food wrappers litter the floor. Defying all laws of physics, a lidless, nearly full cup of McDonald's coffee sits on the floor between Dad's feet. An Everest-sized pile of hats, jackets, and sweaters sits between them on the backseat, almost completely blocking Mom from view.

"Hi, Mom. Hi, Dad," I say. "How was the drive?"

"Great!" says Dad, moving his foot and kicking over the cup of coffee. "Eric took us to see the world's third largest ball of twine!"

"Oy, please," says Mom, waving her hand.

"What do you have against twine?" I ask, helping Dad down out of the car. I don't mention the coffee.

"Who needs that much twine?" asks Mom.

"Nobody was actually *using* the twine," snaps Eric. "It was just a—"

"Mom! Dad! They're *here!*" interrupts Graham, yelling in a voice loud enough to wake all the residents of Sunset Havens who have died over the past fifty years. Now John and Babette are running down the driveway, and everybody is hugging and shaking hands, and The Duffle is being unloaded from the trunk like a coffin from a hearse, and it's all really happening now.

I take a deep breath and watch everybody file into the house from the safety of the driveway. The front door shuts with a satisfying thud. I stand there alone for a good minute and a half, relishing the fact that they are all in there and I am alone out here. I glance longingly up the street. Maybe I should make a run for it. I could steal a golf cart and be at the airport in, like, three days.

The front door quietly re-opens. Graham pokes his head out.

"What are you doing out there, Sum? The party's in here!" He beckons to me with one of his irresistible Graham smiles. "Join us."

I melt a bit. Only Graham could consider this nightmare a party. He really is amazing. What am I worried about? With Graham by my side, I can do this. Of *course* I can do this. Graham was able to make a cruise with my parents enjoyable, why should this be any different? There's even a light at the end of the tunnel. In one short week, Graham and I will be husband and wife, and all of this will be behind us.

I smile back and follow him inside.

5

Okay, where the fuck is Graham?

We were inside the house for a whopping five minutes before Eric suggested that he and Graham go out on a beer run, and they've been gone *forever*. What do they need beer for, anyway? Babette's got enough booze in here to keep us all drunk for a very long time. Eric just couldn't take another second in close proximity with Mom and Dad, that's what happened. I saw the way he snapped at Mom about the twine. Not that I can blame him. If it'd been me who'd just driven them a thousand miles, I'd be out on a beer run too. I'd be out on a permanent beer run. But why did he have to go and take Graham with him?

Speaking of booze, while Graham and I were waiting outside, Babette was in here whipping up a batch of something she calls a Rusty Twizzler. Since moving to Sunset Havens, she fancies herself an amateur bartender. I don't know what exactly is in a Rusty Twizzler, but I can tell you three things: One, it tastes like a Twizzler, two, it's the color of a rusted out '57 Chevy, and three, one of them can knock me straight to the floor. On our first night here, Babette invited Francine and Janice over for drinks. The two of them had about six each and there I was, one Rusty Twizzler down, and Graham had to literally carry me off to bed. And they *laughed* at me. Two old ladies laughed at me because I couldn't hold my liquor. How will my parents—the people who think that having a second glass of Arbor Mist qualifies you as an alcoholic—be able to survive a week down here?

"Mom, Dad," I say, stepping in front of Babette as she comes out of the kitchen carrying a tray of the stuff. "Why don't I get you guys some lemonade?"

I turn around and sweep Babette back into the kitchen.

"You can't serve those things to my parents," I whisper. "Are you crazy?"

"Why not?" asks Babette. "They're delish! And we're having a celebration!" She does a little conga move and bumps me with her hip.

Why must all Blendermans think this is some sort of party? The real party will be at the end of the week—coincidentally, the same time that everybody is due to go home.

"They are delish," I say. "I'll give you that. But they're also potentially lethal. You need to ease people into them. Especially people like my parents. Trust me."

Babette makes a disappointed, pouty face.

"Okay, *fine*," she says. "We'll save them for after dinner." She returns the pitcher to the refrigerator, satisfied that an extra two hours should be sufficient to increase my parents' alcohol tolerance.

"So, tell us about your drive down," says Babette, after we've returned to the living room and served everyone their lemonade. "That must have been a fun experience for you two."

We all turn to Mom as she takes a sip of lemonade.

And three…two…one.

"Fun?" she says. "Oy, please. Let me tell you about the drive down…"

Twenty Minutes Later

"…stepped right in a pile of…told Eric to just go *around* New Jersey on the way back…thank God we had an extra pair of…hardly a single McDonald's in all of South Carolina…had to eat at something called a *Sonic*…totally undercooked…specifically asked for no mayonnaise…diarrhea *all* night…"

I take a deep breath and turn to Tanya.

"I am *so* sorry," I mumble.

She chokes back a laugh.

"Eric was losing it the whole way here," she whispers.

I take a sip of lemonade and smile at my sister-in-law. Tanya and I have become fairly close over the past two years, and she knows all about the resentment I harbored toward Eric when I was still living in my parents' basement. I say *harbored* since I like to think that I've developed a much healthier relationship with my brother after moving out on my own. For the most part. There are still times—like when Mom and Dad found a mysterious white powder between the pages of their Boston Globe, jumped to the conclusion that they had contracted Anthrax, and guilt-tripped me into spending an entire day with them at the emergency room—that the old bitterness rises back up like a phoenix from the ashes. (The powder, in case you were wondering, was tested and identified as $C_{12}H_{22}O_{11}$, a/k/a Hostess powdered donut. I will never get those twelve hours of my life back.)

"Why don't we show you to your room?" asks Babette, jumping up and glancing at her watch. "And then we can all freshen up for dinner!"

I know exactly what she's thinking. It's already three o'clock, and to get a good table at Rosa Lee's, we'll need to get there by four-thirty. We're in a retirement community after all. Mom and Dad look nothing like people who are ready for a night on the town. Mom's wearing this disheveled zippered thing, and her hair has a major cowlick in the back. Dad looks like he hasn't washed his hair in a week, and has this large, sort of Dorito-colored stain on his pants.

Babette leads the way down the small hallway to the guest bedroom, happily back in her element of showing people around their new homes. She flings open the door to reveal a queen-sized bed with a bright yellow comforter, tropically themed pillows, and an assortment of white wicker furniture. A vase of fresh flowers sits on the bureau. The room looks great—you would never know that Graham has been sleeping in here for the past few weeks.

John and Babette even went out and purchased window air conditioning units for the guest bedrooms, to make sure that everybody's comfortable. The rest of the house doesn't have central air, as John believes that you don't get the full Havens experience if you're not sweating your ass off on a daily basis.

"Oy," says Mom. She marches over to the air conditioner and

yanks the plug out of the wall. "That's better."

"What'd you do that for?" I ask, glancing at John and Babette.

"It's right next to the bed," says Mom. "We'll get a chill."

Right. Florida plus summertime equals chill.

"But that's why you have a comforter," I point out. "So you don't get cold." Honestly, do I really need to explain to them how beds work?

"It's not the temperature," says Mom. "It's the blowing." She makes blowing motions with her hands.

I roll my eyes. "Put it on low then. You know, John and Babette bought that special for you guys."

"No, no, no!" says Babette. "It's fine. We just want them to be comfortable. John and I don't use an air conditioner, either. We sleep in the buff! I highly recommend it!"

Oh.

My.

God.

Have Graham's parents been sleeping *naked* in the next room the entire time that we've been here? And now they're encouraging *my parents* to do the same? No. There's no way I can fall asleep knowing that I'm surrounded by nude parents. Just, no.

I walk over to the bed, and like a magician removing a tablecloth, yank the entire comforter out from under the pillows in one quick motion. I fold it up and put it in the closet.

"There," I say. "Now you just have a sheet. You'll be as cool as two pajama-wearing cucumbers."

"Nudity is nothing to be ashamed of, Summer," says Babette.

"You and Graham should try it. After you're married, of course." She gives me a wink.

If I could be granted one wish right now, it would be for immediate death. Painless, if possible, but beggars can't be choosers. I wait a moment, giving the angel of death one last chance to make an entrance, and then, accepting the fact that it is not yet my time to leave this Earth, turn and silently exit the room. I head straight to the refrigerator and pour myself a nice, tall glass of Rusty Twizzler.

I let out a loud belch as I walk back into the guest bedroom.

"So, did you bring your clubs?" asks John, clapping Dad hard on the shoulder.

"My...my clubs?"

"Golf clubs! You won't get the full Havens experience without putting in some time on the links!"

Here we go. Poor Dad. I'd almost rather go back to the nudity discussion. I hiccup.

"Oh," says Dad. "I, um, I never really got into the game. Unless you count the miniature kind, of course. I'm a whiz at the windmill." Dad mimes a golf swing and knocks a stack of bridal magazines off the nightstand.

"Oy, Richard!" says Mom. She bends down to pick up the magazines, pauses, and then dumps them into the trash.

"What'd you do that for?" I ask.

"They stink!" says Mom.

"It's just the perfume samples," I say. "They smell nice!"

"Who can sleep with that smell in the room?"

"You didn't have to throw them out!" I say, pulling them out of the trash. I have to steady myself against the wall because, well,

Rusty Twizzler. "I'll put them in the living room."

As I head out of the room I notice that John's face has turned solemn. He must still be thinking about Dad's lackadaisical attitude towards golf. Golf is serious business down here. Twelve championship courses, thirty-two executive courses, and as a resident you receive–

"– *free* lifetime membership in all of the country clubs," says John.

"Oh, my," says Dad. "That's really something."

"It *is* something," says John, nodding gravely. I can't tell if he's mad, or if he's just depressed to learn that there are still people in the world whose lives don't revolve around golf. John's not usually an angry kind of guy, so I'm guessing it's the latter. This place really does cut you off from reality.

"Well," says Dad, "not much to be done about it now. Like I said, I don't have any clubs."

"Don't you worry about clubs," says John. "You'll borrow my old set. We're teeing off tomorrow morning. Nine a.m."

"But I –"

"No buts."

"But –"

John claps Dad hard on the shoulder again. "*No* buts. You'll be one of us in no time. Now tell me, Richard, what's your favorite vodka?"

"Rich is more of a whiskey guy, isn't that right?" asks Graham, suddenly appearing in the room and clapping Dad on the other shoulder. He must have walked right past me and I didn't even notice. Like I said before…Rusty Twizzler.

"That's right," says Dad, jumping again, but quickly

regaining his composure. "I do enjoy a nice Manhattan."

"Just like J.P. Morgan," says Graham. "Did you know that he drank a Manhattan at the close of every trading day? No? I suppose that's not common knowledge. Oh, hey, Dad, did Rich happen to tell you about the time he crashed his motorcycle?"

John looks genuinely impressed, and Dad and I both smile gratefully at Graham. I reach over and squeeze his hand. I can do this.

6

I can't do this.

I'm sorry, but Francine and Janice are dressed like cheerleaders.

Granted, it's better than naughty police officers or, God forbid, schoolgirls, but still. They're wearing cowboy boots and mini skirts and more makeup than the cast of *Moulin Rouge*. They came to dinner straight from baton twirler practice, and in extreme disrespect to Mom, I've noticed Dad's eyes have been bugging out of his head. Even worse, every time Graham looks in her direction, Francine hikes her skirt up an extra couple of inches. He finds it all very amusing, but I'm extremely close to reminding her that it was well over forty years ago when she had her last chance with somebody like Graham.

I mean, I would say all that if only they weren't wielding batons.

"And this is what we call the helicopter!" shrieks Francine, twirling the baton up over her head and spinning around on one foot.

"I've been working on the splits," says Janice. "Watch this, Graham. And a one, and a two –"

"Your table is ready, ladies," interrupts the hostess.

Oh, thank God. Janice and Francine arrived to dinner too late to squeeze in with our already tight table for eight. So instead, they've been hanging around next to our table putting on their indecent little revue, and knocking into the waiters. I relax a bit as I watch the back of their heads retreat toward the far side of the restaurant.

"So," says Babette, taking a large gulp of wine, "what were we talking about before we were, um, interrupted?"

"The *wedding*," says Mom. "What else?"

"Oh, that's right," says Babette. "Summer, I'm dying to see your dress. You're trying it on for me first thing tomorrow morning. And then we have a meeting with Nadine, now that the mother of the bride is finally here."

"Sounds great," I lie.

Nadine is the wedding planner provided by The Lakeview, and also a long-time resident of Sunset Havens. Graham, naturally, has known her for years. In fact, he was once her date to something called the Twilight Cotillion—not to be confused with the Senior Prom, to which he was Francine's date. Bizarre does not even begin to describe this place. Also, I might be marrying Deuce Bigelow.

Anyway, Nadine is about eighty years old, and I'm fairly certain they dug her up special for the winner of the free wedding package. Like, literally dug her up. The first time we met, she kept saying something about Graham and I going into a room to consummate the marriage during the reception. I pressed the issue, only to learn that there's this ancient tradition where the bride and groom actually go off to some room and *do it*, while the rest of the wedding guests stand around drinking wine and listening to Michael Bublé. She said that she just naturally assumed we would be following tradition.

I told her to please never naturally assume anything again for the rest of her natural life. I also told her to please rip any pages out of her binder that concern trading me to Graham in exchange for livestock—and, I kid you not, she jotted down a note. Upon returning home, I performed a Google search in which I found out that not only was she never the high-end New York City wedding planner that she claimed to be, but that she used to be employed by a place called Bonita's Bridal Bonanza outside of Utica.

Of course, four weeks before my wedding was a tad too late to remedy the situation, so here we are.

I turn to Mom. "Speaking of my dress, where is it? I didn't see you guys carry it in when you got here."

"It's in The Duffle," says Mom.

"Excuse me?"

"It's in The Duffle."

My heart stops.

"What do you mean *it's in The Duffle*?"

As if anybody could possibly forget, The Duffle is the largest duffle bag ever created. It is six-feet long by three-feet wide, and was most likely manufactured for use by the mafia. Mom and Dad like to stuff it full of socks and underwear whenever they travel, and right now they are informing me that it also contains my wedding dress. My fingernails dig into Graham's thigh underneath the table.

"Why is it in The Duffle?" I ask, trying to keep my voice

even. Trying to remain calm. "It should be on a hanger in a garment bag, not rolling around with your Fruit of the Looms!" Graham pries my nails out of his leg and gives my hand a squeeze.

Mom gives me the look of death for a few seconds, before her face relaxes into a laugh.

"Just kidding."

"What?"

"I'm *kidding*," she says. "You should have seen your face. Do you really think I would throw your wedding dress into a giant duffle bag? Do you hear her, Richard? Oy, please!"

Mom's really laughing it up now, and Graham reaches across the table to give her a high five.

"Nice one, Joan," he says.

I give Graham a dirty look. Nice one, sure. I suppose it was a *bit* funny. But still, I never did see anybody carry my dress into the house. If it's not in The Duffle, it might very well be rolled up inside Dad's fanny pack.

"So, Babette," says Mom. "You and John are really enjoying all of *this*?" Mom waves her hand around, indicating the surrounding five square miles of Sunset Havens.

"Are you kidding?" asks Babette. "It's a dream come true! It's like we're on a vacation that never ends."

"Well, one day it'll end," mumbles Eric.

I laugh.

"Oh, stop," says Mom. "John and Babette are so young. They could live here for thirty more years."

"Amen," says John, holding his glass into the air. I can almost see tears in his eyes at the thought of thirty more years in this place.

"You and Richard should consider moving down," says Babette. "Especially with all the kids married off. What's left for you up north?"

"Snow," says Dad, staring morosely into his Manhattan.

"Don't miss that," says John.

"Richard, stop!" says Mom. "Just because the kids are married, doesn't mean they don't need us around anymore! It's lonely enough now that Summer's moved out of the house, I can't even imagine living thousands of miles away."

I look at Mom in surprise. Did she just say that it's been lonely since I moved out? I don't know why I'm so thrown by the idea, but I am. I always knew she'd be freaking out and worrying about me when the time came—but missing me? It hadn't even crossed my mind. I frown and take a sip of my drink.

"It was hard to downsize and move away from our Graham," agrees Babette. "But I tell you, it was worth it. We fly back every so often for visits, and Graham spends an *awful* lot of time visiting down here. I think it's the perfect balance."

"What about when you have grandchildren?" asks Mom. "Won't you want to see them?"

"Of course," says John. "But at our age, it's okay to be a little selfish. We've already raised our families. Summer and Graham are welcome to bring the kiddos down for a visit any time they want."

"And who knows," says Babette. "Maybe they'll decide to move to Florida." She gives me a wink.

Fat chance, Babette.

"I don't know," says Mom. "I plan to be *very* involved with my grandchildren."

It's funny how grandchildren are just assumed to be happening. I mean, I would love to have kids, but I don't think I've ever said as much to my mother. Also, what's this about being very involved? I take another sip of my drink as I picture two small children—one with my face, one with Graham's— being forced into sweaters and rubber overshoes. Maybe we *should* move to Florida.

"Who's to say they're even going to have children?" says Babette.

At that, Mom's face totally caves in.

"Of course we're going to have children!" I say, quickly. I probably should have kept my mouth shut, but Mom looked completely crushed. I had to say something.

Her face floods with relief. "Oh, thank God!" She raises both of her hands skyward, and—since we're eating dinner in a western style saloon—in the direction of a large, mounted buffalo head.

"You just shouldn't, you know, plan your whole retirement around Graham and I having kids," I say. "John's right, you guys should enjoy yourselves."

"We do plenty of things to enjoy ourselves," says Mom, a bit defensively. "Just this summer we bought a bicycle built for two."

"That sounds fun," says Babette. "That reminds me of the time John and I had a few too many cocktails at Allendale— that's our favorite of the country clubs. There are nine of them here, you know—"

"Ten," interrupts John.

"Sorry, *ten* country clubs. Anyway, when we came out after dinner, neither one of us could remember where we had parked the golf cart. So, we started walking, but then we saw this bicycle just *sitting* there. The next thing I know, John is pedaling and I'm riding on the handlebars!"

Eric chokes on his drink. "You guys *stole* a bike?"

"You *rode* on the *handlebars*?" asks Graham.

"We didn't steal it, we borrowed it. We returned it the next day." Babette looks lovingly at John. "We would never have done anything like that back in Massachusetts. But here, life just doesn't seem quite so serious."

No, life certainly doesn't seem very serious here. It almost seems like a bunch of college kids were suddenly told that there *is* no life after college, so they'd better just live it up now.

Dad is staring enviously at John and Babette, probably wondering why he and Mom have never done anything so crazy as stealing a bicycle. Mom is staring at them also, but with a look of absolute horror. I laugh as I picture Mom attempting to ride on a set of handlebars. I honestly don't even know how Babette managed it, especially with the two of them smashed out of their minds.

"To tell you the truth," says Babette, "riding that bicycle wasn't even the most climactic moment of the night." She gives John a wink.

"Oh, God," says Graham, dropping his fork. He may have missed out on the nudity conversation a few hours ago, but I'm willing to consider us even.

"Look," I say, never before so thrilled to see a tray of baked haddock bobbing its way through a crowd. "The food's here."

7

"Which of you assholes are ready to party?!"

I'm jolted out of my steak tips by an elderly man standing in front of our table and screaming. He's tall and tanned—what else is new?—and wearing a light blue polo shirt with the collar popped. His snow white hair is neatly combed, and he has a very expensive looking gold watch on his wrist. If he hadn't just swung down from the rafters like the Phantom of the Opera, and asked which one of us assholes was ready to party, I may have mistaken him for a classy guy.

"Roger!" says John, standing up and walking over to the deranged lunatic. "Great to see you!"

Is it, really? I put down my fork. Mom and Dad shoot each other nervous looks across their fish dinners.

"Everybody, this is Roger," says John. "He's a good golf buddy of mine. Summer, I don't think you two have met. Rog has been on vacation for the last few weeks."

That's the funny thing about Sunset Havens. The people that live here actually think that they need to take vacations from their permanent vacation.

"Nice to meet you," I say, standing up and leaning across the table to shake his hand. Roger whistles.

"Those are some juicy lookin' tips," he says. That's when I notice that his eyes aren't anywhere near my dinner plate. I clutch the neckline of my shirt tightly against my chest and sit back down.

"Well, well, well," he continues, walking over and standing behind Mom. "Who do we have here?"

"That's Summer's mother," says Babette. "Joan Hartwell."

If Roger were a cartoon character, his eyes would have turned into two red hearts, shooting from his head on springs.

"And her husband, Richard," she adds, quickly.

Dad sticks his hand out, but Roger ignores him. Instead, he kneels down next to Mom, his face creepily close to hers.

"Shall I compare thee to a summer's day?" he asks. "Thou art more lovely and more temperate."

"Oh," says Mom, looking at him out of the corner of her bifocals. "That's lovely."

I raise my eyebrows. I suppose she might just be paying Dad back for the way he was watching Francine and Janice twirl their batons earlier, but still. Gross.

Roger reaches out and takes Mom's hand. Then he kisses it. Wow. That's a bit much. I look around the table to gauge everybody else's reaction. Everybody has pretty much frozen with their forks halfway in their mouths.

"Thou's skin art the color of freshly squeezed milk," says Roger, doing a little Shakespearean ad-lib in regard to Mom's pasty New England flesh.

Eric lets out a loud snorting sound, which sets Graham and I off giggling as well.

"My," says Mom, blushing and looking down at Roger's completely opposite-colored skin. He looks like he just came back from a vacation on the sun. "Thank you. And yours is the color of...of..."

Please, Mom. Please don't say anything racist.

"Of an overcooked hot dog," she finishes.

Okay, weird. But not racist. Mom is making progress in her old age.

"So, who are you here with tonight, Roger?" asks Babette, which I believe is code for *Please go back to your own table*.

"Barbara," he says, turning and pointing to the poor woman sitting alone at a table across the room. "Second date. You know what that means." He gives us a wink and flicks his popped blue collar, which is code for *I'm going to do something later that you will never be able to erase from your imagination*.

On that note, Roger heads back to Barbara, and we all return to eating in awkward silence. I glance at Mom a few times, noticing that her skin, once the color of freshly squeezed milk, is now a tad closer to the color of overcooked hot dog. I can't believe she enjoyed that attention. Normally, Roger would have elicited nothing but an eye roll and an *Oy, please*. Mom's been at Sunset Havens for less than four hours and she's already getting hit on and enjoying it. What's going on? This does not bode well for the rest of the week.

By the time we finish dinner, the DJ has started his set, and people are making their way onto the dance floor for line dancing. Eric puts down his fork and proudly announces that he's been watching instructional videos on YouTube.

"He really has," says Tanya. "Every night. We've had to move furniture out of the living room and everything."

"You failed to tell me this," says Graham, his eyes lighting up.

"I wanted it to be a surprise," says Eric, holding his hand out as the music segues into "The Electric Slide." Graham grabs his hand and they twirl each other out onto the dance floor. I roll my eyes. Sometimes I wonder if I'm the Hartwell that Graham should be marrying.

"Come on, girls!" says Babette, motioning to me, Tanya, and to my horror, Mom. "If you visit The Havens, you have to line dance!"

"Oh, I think I'll just watch," says Mom. "I'm not finished eating yet." She starts nervously shoveling cold mashed potatoes into her mouth. Poor Mom.

"Don't tell me you don't know 'The Electric Slide'?" asks Babette.

Mom shrugs.

Babette's face changes into the same expression John's had when Dad said he didn't play golf. The same kind of expression I make when somebody tells me that they don't like to read— utter disbelieve, shock, and a pinch of revulsion. If I said that golf is serious business down here at Sunset Havens, then line dancing is a very close second.

Before I can intervene, Babette's physically dragged Mom out of her chair and off to a vacant corner of the dance floor where she begins instructing her on the proper steps. I glance at Dad and John. John's produced a golf course map from his pocket and has it spread out across the table. Dad's staring at it with a glazed look on his face. Tanya and I look at each other, shrug, and then head onto the dance floor.

Graham and Eric have been wedged apart by a woman that I recognize as Gil's girlfriend of the hour, Lorraine. She's wearing a pair of leopard print pants and seems about two drinks shy of throwing a lampshade on her head. They're flanked on either end by Francine and Janice. Only one of Francine's hands is visible. I don't feel the slightest bit of remorse as I shove her further down the line and squeeze in beside Graham.

"Hey," I say, smiling up at him.

"You made it," says Graham. He gives me a quick goose on the rear.

"There are so many evils in this place, the dance floor was actually the lesser of them all."

"I'm flattered. I can't believe you're dancing in front of your parents, by the way. Times have changed."

I laugh, thinking back to the time Graham made me look like a manic flamenco dancer in front of Mom and Dad on the cruise ship.

"I don't think either of them are watching me right now," I say. I glance around and see Dad still staring down at the golf map, and Mom—

Uh oh.

As we do a quarter turn to the right, I see that Babette has ended the lesson and pulled Mom onto the dance floor. I also see that Roger is back, circling Mom like a shark. He comes right up behind her and puts his hands on her hips, violating the first rule of line dancing which is to *remain in a line.* I look over at Dad again. Thankfully, he's still staring blankly down at John's golf map.

The Mom I used to know would have looked at Roger over

her shoulder, scrunched up her face as if she were performing the first incision of an alien autopsy, and told him to get lost. But this new, Sunset Havens Mom, looks like she's enjoying herself. They shimmy to the right. They take the requisite steps backward, and then they do three simultaneous lean-backs, snaps, and forward dips.

To be honest, Mom actually has some rhythm. If she didn't have a giant, white-haired parasite attached to her back, I might even enjoy watching her go.

That's when I notice Barbara, Roger's date, out on the dance floor too. She's coming quickly through the crowd, sneaking up from behind and carrying a glass of red wine. I've seen a few episodes of Dynasty in my day—I know what's about to happen, but there's nothing I can do.

Besides, what's the harm?

Barbara taps Roger on the shoulder, waits for him to turn around, and then flings the wine into his face. Then she slaps him. Nobody in the vicinity looks anything more than mildly interested. I get the feeling that this is a common occurrence at Sunset Havens.

Unfortunately for Mom, once she's no longer under the guiding hands of Roger, she completely loses her rhythm and is swept up by the unforgiving crowd of octogenarians. She tries to recover, but it's too late. She takes a bony elbow to the chest, and an arm whirl with a snap to the forehead.

And then, she's down.

"Mom!" I rush over to help.

"Joan!" shouts Roger, kneeling down beside her. "My darling! Speak to me!"

"Are you okay?" I ask, pushing Roger out of the way. "Watch

where you're going!" I shout the words into the crowd of surrounding feet. Nobody has even stopped dancing, they're just Electric Sliding right around us. I narrowly avoid being kicked by a pair of pink Crocs.

"I was assaulted," says Mom, weakly.

"You weren't *assaulted*," I say. "Unless you mean by this guy." I tilt my head toward Roger.

Roger cuts in front of me and slides an arm under Mom's shoulders, red wine dripping out of his hair and onto her face.

"Let me help you up," he says. With one arm under her shoulders, he slides his other arm under Mom's legs and attempts to lift her, like Superman. Only, he's far from being Superman, and also, he doesn't lift with his knees. Something cracks loudly from the vicinity of his spinal column, and Roger collapses onto the floor. Now the both of them are lying there next to each other, staring up at the ceiling. At least with two people down, the crowd is finally starting to thin.

"Joan?" yells Dad, pushing through the crowd and kneeling down beside Mom. "Oh my God! She's been shot!"

Somebody in the crowd screams and the house lights come up. The music stops.

"It's just red wine!" I say. "She's fine! Mom, tell Dad you're fine!"

"I was trampled," moans Mom.

Good enough. At the sound of her voice, Dad's face floods with relief.

"It's all my fault," says Roger, speaking to the ceiling. "I let go of her when I got slapped."

"It's my fault, too," I say. "I saw that he was about to get slapped and I didn't do anything to stop it."

"No," says Babette. "It's my fault. I thought she was ready. And she would have been, if not for that awful Margo Wiederman and her husband! That's who got her. Those two would step right over the Pope if he fell down on the sidewalk!"

"They were like maniacs," whispers Mom. "Raving maniacs."

"They're just old people dancing," points out Eric.

"Not the right time, man," says Graham, shaking his head. Then he turns around and starts speaking to the crowd. "Let's back it up a few feet. Give them some space. Emergency personnel are coming through."

He's right. Security guards, plus four EMT's, are making their way through the crowd with stretchers. I look at Graham in disbelief. I knew Mom and Dad's first night at Sunset Havens couldn't possibly go well. I just never imagined it ending like this. That'll teach me.

"Roger?" asks one of the EMT's. "Is that you down there?"

"Hey, Brian," says Roger. "Long time no see."

"You must be off the V?"

Roger points to his popped blue collar. "Back on it tonight. Good thing you guys picked me up."

Roger, noticing the look of confusion on my face, gives me a wink. "I call them whenever I have an erection lasting more than four hours."

And on that note, Mom and Roger are wheeled out of Rosa Lee's. Dad rides in the back of the ambulance, while Graham, Eric, and I follow behind in the Escalade. Tanya goes home with Graham's parents. As we follow the ambulance in its blaze of red and blue lights, I remind myself to ask John if he considers an ambulance ride to be part of the full Havens experience.

8

So, one might say that things did not get off to the greatest start.

The six of us are seated around the kitchen table the next morning, awkwardly chewing on McDonald's breakfast. Babette had planned on making us a healthy breakfast of turkey bacon, egg whites, and kale, but she felt so bad about last night that she wanted to do something extra special for Mom. In her mind, that was sending John out to surprise everyone with a boatload of greasy fast food. Apparently she can relate to my parents more than I thought.

Paper bags full of hash browns, Egg McMuffins, McGriddles, and several thousand ketchup packets, are scattered around the table. John didn't know what everybody wanted, so he just ordered a little of everything.

"Great meal, Babette," says Dad, as if she had cooked it herself. "Really. McDonald's in Florida is almost as good as McDonald's back home."

"It *is* good, isn't it?" says Babette, polishing off her second hash brown. "I've been trying to eat healthier since we moved here, but sometimes it's nice to indulge."

"What's unhealthy about this?" asks Mom.

"You just ate a sandwich made out of pancakes," I say, pointing to her McGriddles wrapper. "And they've been injected with syrup."

Graham picks up a bag of hash browns and shows Mom the grease stain slowly making its way across the bottom.

She shrugs. "It's not like we eat this way all the time."

"Only on the weekends," says Dad. "And every morning after I get the newspaper."

Babette chokes a bit on her coffee, but doesn't push the issue.

The men are leaving shortly to play golf—Dad included—while the rest of us head out to meet with the wedding planner. After a good night's sleep, Mom appears to be back to her normal self. Well, aside from the large bruise smack in the center of her forehead. After two hours in the emergency room, the doctor said she was fine and that the bruise should be a few shades lighter by the time we take our wedding photos.

If not, we can always Photoshop her out.

Just kidding.

Eric arrives at the house soon after we finish breakfast. He drops off Tanya and jumps into the passenger side of Graham's golf cart. I'm always surprised at just how subdued Graham's golf cart actually is. I mean, it's purple and has a horn that plays the *Beverly Hills Cop* theme. But that's the extent of it. He bought it last year, and his parents keep it for him in their garage.

Dad is riding with John, whose golf cart is, for lack of a better word, totally pimped out. Graham had it custom built for his dad's birthday and it cost a fortune. It looks like a yellow hot rod with red and orange flames painted on the front. Dad looks absolutely stunning in it, wearing his bright blue Hawaiian shirt and orange tennis visor that Mom, for reasons unknown, thought would make him blend in with the other golfers.

I lean in to kiss Graham goodbye. He's wearing red and white houndstooth golf pants that he purchased online, and a red polo shirt. Graham will never blend in, even if he wanted to. Which he doesn't.

"Have fun," I say. "And keep an eye on my father. He may need to be rescued at some point."

"It's kind of hard *not* to keep an eye on him," says Graham.

"Like you should talk," I laugh. "I'm serious though. Your dad doesn't always remember how to relate to outsiders."

"Don't worry," says Graham. "I'm on it."

"What about me?" asks Eric. "You don't trust me to take care of my own father?"

I look at the way that he's lounging back in his seat—one foot up on the dashboard, sunglasses upside down on the back of his neck—and I slowly shake my head. Eric sticks out his tongue and makes a rude gesture as they pull away from the curb.

"Have fun, Dad!" I call out. John beeps the horn and Dad grabs onto the front roof support.

Once they're out of sight, I walk back into the house to find Babette, Mom, and Tanya standing in a semi-circle around my wedding dress. They've taken it out from wherever Mom has been hiding it, and hung it from a hanger on the back of the hall closet. I smile at the sight of it. It looks just like I remembered.

Sort of.

As my eyes pan from the bottom of the dress to the top, I notice that there's something a bit off. I squint. Yes, there's definitely something off. Like, the sleeves.

Panic starts rising in my stomach. Did I just say *sleeves?* Oh my God. Why does my wedding dress contain sleeves? Where did *sleeves* come from?

I step forward, pushing everybody out of the way, and inspect the dress more closely. I swallow down the bile that has risen in my throat. Somebody has sewn sheer white *sleeves* onto my dress. Not only that, they've sewn an entire *panel* of sheer white fabric from what used to be a strapless neckline, all the way up to my throat, and then cinched it all together with a giant satin bow.

There is a *bow* around the neck of my wedding dress. It's like that horror story about the mysterious woman who always wears a bow around her neck until one day her husband unties it and her head falls off.

I can't breathe.

"Mom!" I scream. "What have you done to my dress!?"

"What?" she says. "It had so little coverage before. You'll be much more comfortable this way." She takes the dress down from the closet and holds it up in front of me, nodding with satisfaction.

She does all of this so earnestly that I find it hard to come to terms with the fact that she's playing a huge practical joke. It's like when she told me my dress was inside The Duffle, right? Haha. Nice gag. Mom made a funny. Time to take the real dress out now.

Except, she doesn't. She just looks at me, and I look back and forth between her and the dress, and no *other* dress is being produced from anywhere.

"You're…serious?" I ask. "You seriously thought it was okay

to add sleeves and a bow and a...a...a *dickey* to my wedding dress?"

"It is not a *dickey*. And really, you don't have to get an attitude about it," says Mom.

"An *attitude?*" How is she possibly making me into the bad guy? "Mom, I *liked* the dress the way it was. And, oh yeah, my wedding is in Florida! I don't want sleeves!"

"But they're sheer! You'll get a nice breeze right through them." She makes breeze-through-your-sleeves motions with her hands, which makes me even angrier than I already was.

"But I don't want a breeze through my sleeves!"

"Okay, fine." Mom rolls her eyes. "But the dress was *strapless!* How was it going to stay up?"

"What do you mean *how was it going to stay up?* Thousands of brides wear strapless gowns every day! Do you think they're all just dropping to the floor in the middle of the ceremony? No! They *stay up!*"

"Well, of course they do," says Mom. "Those girls have bosoms to hold them up with. They're not like *you*."

I gasp.

"I think Summer can hold her own in the bosom department," says Babette, coming to my defense. Tanya laughs. I feel my face turning red as I pray that nobody ever speaks of my bosom again. For once I wish Mom would just use the word *boobs*, like everybody else. *Bosom.* Who am I, Madam Bovary?

"Look, Mom. The dress fit fine. It fit, and it wasn't going to fall down, and now you've *ruined* it!"

"I'm having a nervous breakdown," says Mom, throwing her hands into the air and sinking down onto the couch.

"Why are *you* having a nervous breakdown?" I yell. "If anyone should be having one it's me! The one who's going to her wedding dressed like Little Miss Muffet!"

And on that note, I turn and stomp into my bedroom, slamming the door behind me.

My parents have been here less than a day and I'm already hiding in my bedroom and slamming doors. I sit down on the bed and stare at the wall, chewing on my bottom lip. After a few minutes, there's a quiet knock at the door.

"Summer?"

It's Tanya. I open the door.

"Hey," she says, slipping in through the crack. "I thought maybe you'd jumped out the window."

"No. Just contemplating how nice it must be to be Graham, out there golfing in his loud pants, nobody sewing anything into his tuxedo or talking about his bosom. Life is so unfair."

"True. But then again, he's *golfing* right now, in ninety-degree Florida sun. That *sucks.*"

I laugh. "Graham loves it here, whatever the temperature. The sun gives him energy. He's like a solar panel."

Tanya smiles and sits down on the edge of the bed.

"Look, I know you're upset about the dress," she says. "But Babette's going to call her seamstress and see if she can fit you in this afternoon, after we meet with the wedding planner."

"Oh, thank God," I say, flopping back against the pillows. "I can't believe my mother's only been here a day and she's already ruining my wedding."

Tanya frowns at me. "Go easy on her, Sum. I think she was just trying to be involved."

She puts quite a bit of emphasis on that word, *involved*.

"It's not my fault I won a free wedding," I say, defensively.

"Oh, please," she says. "Your fiancé is loaded. He would have been more than happy to pay for the wedding. You, missy, had some ulterior motive as to why you jumped at the chance to have your wedding at a *retirement community*. And I believe I know you well enough to say that you simply didn't want to plan a wedding with your mother."

I roll my eyes. Ulterior motive? I mean, obviously I took advantage of the free wedding in order to avoid planning a wedding with my mother. Anybody that has met my mother would agree that that was the only logical course of action. But it's not like I went out of my way to make it happen. It just kind of fell into my lap. Besides, Mom said she was totally fine with it.

"Look, maybe that was an added benefit of having the wedding here," I say. "But even if it was the main reason, why should I feel bad about it? Look what happened when my mother tried to get involved, Tanya. She sewed *sleeves* into my wedding dress. And a bow. Have you seen the bow?"

"True," says Tanya. "But she's still your mom. And you're her only daughter. Besides, who's the genius that left her wedding dress unsupervised at her parents' house? The same parents who, if I remember correctly, once sewed bicycle shorts into your prom dress? You really should have seen this one coming."

I sigh and sink back into the pillows. She's right, of course. But I don't exactly have an excellent track record of seeing things coming.

9

The four of us are driving two golf carts over to The Lakeview to meet with Nadine, the wedding planner. The Blendermans do own a car that we could use instead, but it wouldn't be the full Havens experience if we didn't spend an extra forty minutes getting there by golf cart.

The carts are two-seaters, so Babette will be driving Tanya, and I've volunteered to drive Mom. The Lakeview is at Duke's Landing, which is a four mile drive by cart path with lots of turns and tunnels. Whenever Graham and I go out there, I make him drive while I enjoy the scenery. So, to be honest, I don't exactly know the route by heart. But I'm going to follow Babette, so it will be fine.

Easy peasy.

"Um, Mom?" I'm already in the driver's seat, but Mom is still standing in the garage staring at the cart like I've asked her to board Mars One.

"*That's* what we're driving?" she asks.

"Yep. This is a golf cart, and we are in a golf cart community." I firmly pat the seat next to me. "Welcome to retirement."

Mom climbs in gingerly, hanging the garment bag containing my wedding dress from the roof behind us.

"Will that be okay there?" she asks.

I shrug. "Should be. We're not going very fast." Part of me almost hopes that it falls off, sleeves and all.

Mom fastens her seatbelt and stares stoically ahead as we back out of the driveway. I follow Babette to the end of our street, and then into the golf cart lane on the main road.

"What are you doing?" yells Mom.

I jump. "What?" God, a second ago she was like a statue.

"Why are we in the road? With the cars!"

"Oh. Well, sometimes there's no cart path so we have to go on the regular road." I glance over. Mom has gone completely white. "It's just for a short time though. I promise."

After what feels like forever, we turn off the main road and onto a cart path. Mom relaxes a bit as we drive along in silence, enjoying the warm breeze and the sunshine. It really is lovely down here. The weather is amazing, everybody is smiling and relaxed, and when I compare the lifestyle of John and Babette Blenderman, with the neurotic lifestyle of Richard and Joan Hartwell, I can't help but think that Sunset Havens is where all retirees should strive to spend their golden years.

"So, Mom," I say, glancing over at her. "What was up with that guy Roger last night?"

"What do you mean?"

"I mean, he was coming on a bit strong, don't you think? Especially in front of Dad. It was a little rude."

"He was a perfect gentleman in the ambulance," says Mom, defensively. "His back was in so much pain, but he still insisted on holding my hand the entire time. He even said that if he ended up paralyzed, he hoped it was from the waist up."

"He said that with *Dad* there?"

"What?"

"Duh, Mom. What exactly do you think he meant by that?"

"He meant that he wanted to be able to dance with me again!" says Mom.

I roll my eyes. "I'm sure that's one of the names he has for it."

"Summer!"

"It's true! And I can't believe you were letting him flirt with you, right in front of Dad!" I pause for a few seconds as I follow Babette through a golf cart tunnel. I'm not even sure if I should ask my next question, but I do anyway. "Mom...are you and Dad okay?"

She doesn't respond, and my stomach suddenly drops.

"*Mom?*" I look over at her and she shrugs.

"A shrug?" I say, starting to panic. "Why would you *shrug?* What does a shrug mean?"

"It's nothing for you to worry about," she says, meaning that it's definitely something for me to worry about. "It's just that once you moved out of the house, it got a little quiet. A little lonely."

"But you told Graham's parents that you were enjoying yourselves. What about the ballroom dancing and the day trips and the bicycle built for two?"

"Those things keep us busy, sure. But I'm talking about when the two of us sit down to dinner on a Tuesday night and your father wants to tell me about his hobbies. What do I care about silent film stars of the nineteen thirties? Or that he found some great deal on Betty Boop floor mats on eBay? Oy, please. The way he wastes his money."

"Well, can't you talk about stuff that you have in common? Talk about ballroom dancing or, or…"

I suddenly realize that I have no idea what my parents see in each other. Aside from a shared love of baked haddock and hand sanitizer, I'm at a complete loss.

"Did you know that the sound of your father scratching his big toe with his other big toe drives me *insane*," asks Mom.

Of *course* I know that. Hello. The sound of my father scratching his big toe with his other big toe was one of the main reasons I tried to find myself a husband on a cruise ship and get the hell out of that house. But I can't give her any ideas.

"So, what?" I ask. "They're just toes. Are you saying that Dad repulses you now?"

"You know I love your father, Summer."

"What does any of this have to do with Roger, anyway? Are you going to start looking for attention from other men? You would never consider chea—"

"Oy!"

Mom cuts me off mid-sentence and claps a hand over her mouth. With her other hand she points to an elderly couple in a golf cart, pulled over to the side of the road. I slow down for a closer look. Is that…Lorraine? And Gil?

"Oh my God!" I yell.

"What are they doing?" shouts Mom.

"What do you *think* they're doing!" I shout back, as I veer into the opposite lane.

"Stay on the road!" Mom grabs for the wheel.

"Let go!" I wrench the wheel from her hand, swerving us dangerously close to a tree. I come to a stop on the side of the cart path.

"What kind of a place is this?" shrieks Mom. Despite the horrified look on her face, she keeps turning around to sneak glances at Lorraine and Gil.

"A very friendly one," I laugh. "Stop staring!"

"Well, they're right out in the open! It's like they *want* people to watch."

She has a point. I put on my blinker and slowly pull back out onto the path. That's when I realize that in all of our excitement, I've completely lost Babette.

Shit.

I glance nervously over at Mom, trying not to panic. She probably assumes that I know my way around this place. Well, maybe I do. Graham and I have driven this route numerous times, so I probably have some sort of mental map ingrained in my subconscious. I just need to relax and open up my mind. I'll probably cruise right into the center of town. Easy peasy. Lemon squ—

Crap.

The path has come to an end and I'm forced to merge back into regular traffic. Now there's a rotary up ahead with about six different signs pointing in all different directions, and absolutely none of them look familiar. The cart in front of me turns right to get back onto a cart path, but I'm distracted by a sign with an arrow pointing straight ahead. Duke's Landing, it reads. The sign pointing toward the cart path reads Sunshine Recreational Trail.

I make the split second decision to continue straight.

"What did that sign mean?" asks Mom.

"Which one?"

"The one that said 'No carts beyond this point.'"

"Are you serious?"

"Of course I'm serious."

"We didn't drive past it, did we?"

"Yes."

"Oh, no."

"What?"

"Mom, please don't freak out."

A car blows past us on the left, laying on its horn.

"No carts allowed on this road!" shouts an old man.

"I know!" I shout back, throwing my hands in the air.

"Keep your hands on the wheel!" yells Mom.

Another car blasts past us. No, wait, it's a truck. An eighteen wheeler, actually. I nearly fall out of the cart when he lays on the horn. Then he flips us off. I don't know what to do. There's no exit anywhere in sight. To my right is a grassy area, but there's a high curb preventing me from driving onto it. Beyond the grass is nothing but a high stone wall, blocking people's backyards from the highway. Probably blocking homeowners from having to witness grisly golf cart/Mack truck collisions. On the other side of the highway I can see a cart path running along the side of the road. Over there is where all the friendly, smiling people are. Over here, is hell.

"What do we do?" shouts Mom. "How do we get out of here?"

"I don't know!" I shout. "There's no exit!"

"Stop the cart!"

"Are you crazy? We'll get creamed!"

"Maybe we can lift it up onto the grass!"

"Really, Mom? You and I are going to lift a golf cart? Who are we, female wrestlers?"

"I'm glad you find this so funny!"

Before I can reply that nothing in the world could be less funny than our current situation, another car pulls up next to us. It's an older woman and she keeps jerking her thumb behind us, probably telling us to take a hike.

"I know! I know! No carts on this road. Sorry!" I shrug.

She shakes her head and continues jerking her thumb behind us. Then she rolls down the window.

"You lost your bag!" she shouts.

My bag?

All of a sudden I'm seized with a terrible understanding. I slow down and bring the cart to a complete stop on the side of the road. The idea of not getting creamed doesn't seem quite so important right now. I whip my head around, and I see it.

My wedding dress.

In all of our bickering, neither of us noticed the garment bag blow off the back of the golf cart and into the middle of the highway.

"My dress!" I scream. "We have to go back for it!"

I slam the cart into reverse and back up down the side of the highway. I know that earlier I had almost wished my dress would blow off the back of the cart, but I didn't *mean* it. Wishes made in the heat of the moment aren't supposed to actually come true. What kind of a world would that be? I suppose it would be a world where I'm about to Frogger myself across a highway full of elderly drives.

My adrenaline pumping, I tell Mom to get out of the golf cart and stand away from the road where she'll be safe. As I wait for there to be a break in traffic, I hear her yelling to me that I'm going to get myself killed. Then something about how I should wait for her to call Dad. Yes, because Dad is who we want darting out into traffic right now. I ignore her and wait until I see no cars are on the road. Then I run into the middle of the highway and grab the garment bag. My heart sinks at the sight of it. It looks as if it's been run over by a thousand trucks. Which, it has. But at least the dress inside might still be protected. I run back to the grassy area where Mom is sitting, possibly having a nervous breakdown. I unzip the garment bag and, amazingly, the dress appears unharmed—just in need of some ironing. I zip it back up and lay it down on the ground. Then I walk over and flop down next to Mom, breathing hard, and looking up at the sky.

"That was insane," I say.

Mom doesn't respond. Maybe she's passed out. I close my eyes.

"Summer?" Mom finally whispers.

"What?"

Again, she doesn't respond. I raise my head slightly to look at her, but she's just staring at something in the grass, her eyes like saucers. Suddenly she grabs me by the hand, pulls me to my feet, and practically drags me back to the golf cart.

"What are you doing?" I hiss. "We left the dress!"

Instead of answering, she just shoves me into the golf cart and then points in the direction that we came from.

There's an alligator a couple of feet from where we'd been sitting. He's at least five feet long, chock full of teeth, and eating my garment bag.

Dress and all.

10

Clearly, Mom and I are not going to make our appointment with the wedding planner.

I call Babette from the side of the road—explaining how we witnessed her friends fornicating in a golf cart, how I then drove my own golf cart onto a highway, and how my dress was subsequently eaten by an alligator—and tell her and Tanya to go ahead without us. When she finally stops laughing, she gives me directions from the highway to a small shopping plaza where she and Tanya can meet up with us later and lead us back home. It turns out that the exit is only about a half mile up the road. The rest of the drive is relatively uneventful, with only one horn honk and no more middle fingers (that guy could easily have been scratching his nose).

I pull into a parking space at the shopping plaza and fist pump the air in relief. Then I reach over and squeeze Mom around the shoulders. She looks like she wants to get out and kiss the ground. She could, too. The streets down here are immaculate. We sit in silence for a few moments, just soaking up the relief that comes with the realization that your life is no longer in imminent danger. The fact that my wedding dress now resides in the digestive tract of a large reptile is momentarily forgotten. But all too soon, the memory returns.

"Mom," I say, tears prickling my eyes. "What am I going to do about my dress? I'm getting married in a few days!"

"That alligator didn't ruin your dress," she says, with a sigh. "I did. If it weren't for me, it wouldn't have even been in the cart with us at all. I'm sorry, Summer."

Wow. I don't know if Mom has ever apologized to me before. Or admitted that she may have been wrong. Not even the time she cut the label out of a vintage Chanel dress Graham bought for me because she thought it looked "scratchy."

"That is true," I say. "But you meant well, and I'm sorry that I yelled at you earlier. I guess we're even."

She takes a tissue out of her purse and dabs at her eyes.

"It's just that you bought that dress with Tanya," she says, looking at me with eyes full of hurt. "You went wedding gown shopping with your sister-in-law rather than your own *mother*."

I look shamefully down at my lap.

"It wasn't like that, though," I say. "We were out shopping— just for clothes, you know?—and we walked by this dress shop, and it was just *there*. I saw it in the window and we went in to try it on. It all happened so fast. It's not like I planned to go without you. It just sort of…happened."

Like the free wedding in Florida just sort of happened, I think. A fresh wave of guilt quickly washes away any trace of my previous high. What kind of a daughter am I? First, I don't let her plan her only daughter's wedding, and now I find out that she's been lonely and having problems with Dad ever since I moved out—a discussion that we never got to finish, thanks to Lorraine and Gil. But, now is not the time.

Mom snorts in a way that conveys the fact that she doesn't believe me at all.

"You know, I'm not the only one in the wrong here," I continue, my guilt making one last ditch effort to assuage itself. "When I told you that I wanted to have the wedding down here, you said that it was a *huge weight off your shoulders.* Why would you say that?"

"Oy, please," says Mom, waving her hand at me. "Of course I would say that. I wasn't going to force you to do something you didn't want to do."

I look at her with my eyebrows raised and a lifetime of sweaters, rain boots, and violin lessons flashing through my mind.

"It just would have been nice if you fought for it a little," I say. "You're not the only one who felt hurt."

Mom shrugs. "If you wanted the wedding in Florida, I didn't want to make you feel guilty about it."

"When in your life have you ever not wanted to make me feel guilty about something?"

"I've missed you since you've moved out," says Mom, quietly. "I guess I just didn't want to start a fight."

Tears well up again in my eyes, and I fiddle with the steering wheel.

"We just have this history that sometimes makes things difficult," I say. "Take my Bat Mitzvah, for example. Do you remember that you almost canceled it because Aunt Helen requested a vegetarian meal? How can you blame me for thinking something like that might happen again?"

"It was chicken or steak! Those were the options!"

I sigh.

"Okay, okay," she says. "I may have overreacted that one time. But I was planning everything on my own back then. You were only thirteen. You're a woman now, Summer. We could have planned this together. I wouldn't have done anything to stress you out."

Somehow I doubt that. But that's not the oddest part of what she just said. Mom just referred to me as a *woman*. It sounds so old and matronly. But I suppose that's what I will be—a married woman. A married woman with a bosom. I shake my head to clear my thoughts. Then I smile at my mother.

"You're here now though, right?" I say. "And there's still plenty of things left to do that I would *love* your help with."

Okay, I can't think of a single thing.

But then, like a gift from above, I see the words Martha's Bridal in tall red letters on the side of the shopping plaza in front of us. I blink a few times to make sure it isn't a mirage, but it's still there. A second chance at making this up to my mother is right there in front of us, sandwiched between a Subway and a Winn Dixie. I can see all kinds of dresses in the window and a big sign advertising fifty percent off.

I look over at Mom to find that she's also spotted the sign. She looks back at me. We give each other a series of affirmative shrugs and nods, and then we go inside.

***

It doesn't take long to discover that Martha's Bridal caters to the mature bride. Not surprising, considering we're in a retirement community where most people getting hitched are doing it for the second or third time. One wall of the store is covered with pictures of Elizabeth Taylor, celebrating all eight of her marriages.

My reject pile is soon filled with off-white suits and sheaths—absolutely nothing that I would be caught dead in, never mind wear to my wedding. I mean, they're all beautiful dresses, don't get me wrong. It's just that I'm not Rue McClanahan.

"No way," I say, staring in horror at my reflection.

"Why not?"

"Just, *no*."

I twirl around in front of the mirror, only the dress doesn't move. Actually, it's a two piece peplum skirt suit, with so much beadwork that I can barely bend at the waist. It's probably for the best though, since the Martha's Bridal consultant has also balanced a feathered pillbox hat on my head.

"I think it looks nice," says Mom, patting the shoulder pads and tugging on the sleeves. Always with the sleeves. I give her a look.

"I look like my husband is running for office."

She clears her throat. "Well, how about this one?" She points to a pale blue A-line dress covered in sequins.

"Blue? How did that even get in here?" I ask, rifling thru the rack. "No. Maybe we should just leave. We can take the car and go to a different store later."

"Oh," says Mom, stiffly. "You mean later with *Babette?*"

"And *you*."

Mom still looks disappointed. Martha's Bridal may suck, but I suppose here she feels that she has me all to herself.

"Okay, fine," I say, randomly grabbing another dress off the rack. "Give me some privacy." Mom smiles as I shove her out of the changing room. I step into the dress, and look at myself in the mirror. I gasp.

"Terrible?" asks Mom.

Hardly. I can't stop smiling at myself in the mirror. Where did this dress even *come* from? It's short, with a very gently pleated skirt and a sweetheart neckline. But it also has this gorgeous, deep V-neck lace overlay with, of all things, three-quarter length sleeves.

Sleeves!

The funny thing is that the sleeves totally make the dress. The sleeves are what give this dress its old Hollywood glamor. Or is it its Victorian elegance? I have no idea—I'm a librarian shopping in a retirement community, for Pete's sake. My point is that the dress is *amazing.*

I throw open the door and spin around.

"Oy, God!" yells Mom.

"What?" My stomach drops. She hates it. I feel a bit more devastated than I expected.

"It's beautiful!"

Oh, right. I forgot that 'Oy, God!' can occasionally be used to express great joy.

"It *is* beautiful, isn't it?" I gush. I turn around in the three-way mirror. The back is almost as lovely as the front.

Now we're both kind of jumping up and down and I'm actually glad that the alligator ate my other dress. *This* is the dress that I was meant to walk down the aisle in. This one, right here. The one that I picked out with my mom.

We beam at each other in the mirror, and a small piece of my wedding that I didn't even realize was missing, clinks into place.

GRAHAM

11

Summer's going to kill me. Much like everybody else on this golf course.

We've been letting people play through out of courtesy, but there's a limit. At some point we just have to play. We're on the fifth hole, and we've been out here for nearly two hours. Not to mention that polyester golf pants made in Taiwan—no matter how fantastically hideous the print—are never worth wearing in Florida heat. Lesson learned, though I'll never admit it to Summer. I pish-poshed her this morning when she told me I was going to die in these things.

Richard's connected with the ball a total of two times—first, sending it soaring into the back of a moving golf cart, and then launching it straight into the pond. Right now he looks like he's trying to hack something to death in the grass. I don't know what my dad was thinking dragging Richard out here. The guy is a nervous wreck. To help loosen him up, I suggested that we stop for cocktails on the way here—nine a.m. Manhattans never hurt anybody—but apparently even that wasn't enough to take the edge off. In regard to his golf game, I suspect it may have made things worse.

I rub the back of my neck and force a smile at the foursome waiting behind us. They're glaring at each of us in turn, and at Richard in particular. To a resident of Sunset Havens, there is only one thing worse than being stuck behind an inexperienced golfer, and that is being stuck behind an inexperienced golfer who isn't a permanent resident.

The old folks aren't exactly huge fans of outsiders. If you don't live here year round they call you names like Snowbird (someone who comes down for the winter) or Snowflake (someone who comes down randomly throughout the year), or worse. What's worse than Snowflake or Snowbird? Well, if you were to come down for the winter, get drunk, and drive your golf cart off a bridge, the permanent residents might take to Facebook and type such things as, "You can't fix stupid," or "Darwinism at work." Or even worse, they might just type a series of LOL's—blatantly rejoicing in the fact that you're dead.

Obviously, they don't say those things about *me*. They love me here. I light this place up, snowflake or not.

Usually.

At the moment, I'm finding it somewhat difficult to cope. There are no women in the group behind us. Nobody to appreciate the way my butt looks in these completely non-breathable pants. Nobody to chit-chat with about lemon squares or what happened on last night's episode of *The Bachelor*. There are just four crotchety old men, wearing—I'm not going to lie—some really nice argyle pants, who have nothing better to do except stand around a golf course giving my future father-in-law the stink eye.

I've got to do something.

"Rich," I say, stopping him before he can take another chunk out of the grass. "Why don't you take it easy for the rest of the round? Have a seat in the cart. Here, take my phone. You like Sudoku?" I gently pry the club out of his hands and lead him back to the golf cart. He looks at me, wild-eyed but grateful. I think he might be delirious. "Have some water, too. You've got to stay hydrated out here."

"I'm sorry I'm such a lousy golfer," he says, taking a drink. "I tried to tell your dad that I've never golfed before, except for the miniature kind. I'm an expert at the windmill." He mimes a golf swing with his open water bottle, spraying it all over me.

"Don't be sorry at all," I say, mopping my face with a towel. "It takes a lot of practice to keep up with my father. He's out here every single day." We both watch as my dad hits the ball almost onto the green. Richard lets out a whistle, then he sinks into the cart looking completely spent.

Eric saunters up to the tee and cracks his knuckles. He takes a few practice swings, then stops to watch a large bird flutter up into a tree. He smiles at the group behind us and points to the bird. Then he slowly takes his phone out of his back pocket and snaps a picture.

"Aw, come on!" yells one of the guys behind us. "We're not here to *bird watch*!"

I laugh. That's Eric, defending his father in his own special way.

"Is that a bald eagle?" I ask.

"I don't know, man. I think it might be your classic North American honey buzzard."

"Oh, for crying out loud!" shouts a second guy. "A North American *what*?!"

I nod at Eric—indicating mission accomplished—and then motion for him to hurry up and take his shot before somebody has a stroke. He does a series of leisurely warm-up stretches, then misses the ball four times in a row.

"Aw, Jesus!" The first guy throws his club on the ground and gets back into his golf cart.

"So, Rich," I say, clearing my throat. "Is there anything can we do today that you would actually enjoy?"

"Me?"

"Yes, you."

Richard glances around as if he's going to find a Sears or a Radio Shack out here on the links. Finding neither, he looks down at the steering wheel, and then over at the ignition.

"Well, if it wouldn't be too much trouble, I think I might like to try driving the golf cart."

"Oh," I say. "My dad's golf cart?"

A vision of Richard in Bermuda, crashing his scooter through a flock of chickens and a fire hydrant, passes through my mind. That was only two short years ago, and I don't believe he's had many opportunities for improvement.

"It's a real beauty."

"It is…it is," I say, slowly. My dad's golf cart is such a beauty because it cost me twenty grand to have it custom built for his birthday. It's been featured in front page news articles about life at Sunset Havens. It's my father's pride and joy. "I should probably just check with my dad first, you know?"

I look around, but don't see him anywhere. Then I spot him about two hundred yards away, already lining up his next shot. He didn't even bother waiting for any of us. He was the one who forced Richard out here in the first place, and now he doesn't even bother checking in to make sure everything's okay? An unfamiliar wave of annoyance at my father washes over me. I wonder if this is how Summer feels all the time.

"You know what?" I say. "It's fine. He won't mind. Why don't you wait for us to finish up, and then drive over and meet us at the next hole?"

I show him the gas, the brake, and the horn, and then I head over to take my shot. Richard waits until we finish putting, before slowly starting to make his way down the cart path. Dad's so busy telling Eric and I everything that's wrong with our golf swings—I've got a baseball swing that I've been hearing about since I was seven—that he doesn't even notice his cart driving away. Not until Richard toots the horn.

"What the—" asks Dad, looking up. "Why is he...who said he could..."

"I did," I say. "He wasn't having any fun golfing, so I told him he could drive the cart. Driving a golf cart is part of the full Havens experience, right?"

At the sound of his own words being parroted back at him, Dad's look of horror slowly morphs into a reluctant consent. We start walking toward the next hole, while Eric follows along behind Richard.

"He's really not having a good time?" asks Dad.

"Nope."

"But how can anyone not have a good time here? We're in paradise!"

"You're preaching to the choir, Dad," I say, clapping him on the shoulder. "I'm just the messenger, anyway. And the message says that golf is not even close to being Richard's idea of a good time."

Dad frowns. "I'll never understand those two. Richard and Joan. Nice enough people, don't get me wrong. Just so…*nervous.* I mean, what *do* they do for a good time?"

"I don't know," I laugh, rubbing my hands over my face. "I spent a week on a cruise ship with them, and I still don't have the answer. Summer's been a wreck these past few weeks, worrying about how they would fit in down here."

"Poor, girl," says Dad. "Okay, fine. Maybe golf isn't his thing, but we'll still show them a good time. Look, he's having fun right now. He's already there, he's—"

"Picking up speed," I say.

Dad stops walking and squints. "*Is* he?"

"Um, yeah. Quite a bit, too."

"Dear, God," says Dad, breaking into a jog. "You're right. Richard!" Dad starts waving his arms in the air. "Slow down!"

But he doesn't slow down. It's a downhill path, so he just keeps picking up speed and getting further and further away, winding off into the distance like a character in a Roadrunner cartoon. Eric's laying on the horn now—suddenly the *Beverly Hills Cop* theme song doesn't seem like such a good choice—but Richard doesn't seem to hear.

"I think something's wrong," I say, jogging alongside my father and starting to panic. "Like, with the brakes!"

"Shit!" Dad drops his clubs and takes off running toward his golf cart. I follow, trying to ignore the roar of laughter from the foursome behind us. We catch up in time to see Richard veer sharply to the left and drive up onto a hilly patch of grass. He must have assumed that the grass would slow him down. And it might have, if not for the fact that the other side slopes sharply downward into six large sand bunkers.

We watch, helpless, as Richard coasts full speed to the crest of the hill. He shoots off the other side, cutting through the air like a dune buggy, and lands in the sand pit with a sickening thud.

And then he keeps going.

Why the sand isn't slowing him down is beyond me. Apparently Dad's golf cart is more badass than we thought. He slams through pit after pit until finally reaching the green where a foursome, finishing up their putts, screams and jumps out of the way. And then Richard keeps right on going.

He's heading straight for the pond, actually.

Dad is manic. He runs after the cart, slipping and sliding down the sand traps. Eric's abandoned my golf cart and joined me at the top of the hill. We look at each other, then we follow. Not that there's anything we can do if we catch up. But, we can't just stand here.

"Get out of the cart!" I shout.

"Jump!" yells Eric.

"Abandon ship!" screams Dad.

But it's no use. There is no way Richard Hartwell is jumping out of a moving vehicle. My entire future flashes before my eyes. Worst case scenario, I've indirectly murdered my fiancée's father. Best case scenario, he survives and Summer calls off the wedding anyway. Because, sure, I can neutralize the situation whenever her mom is freaking out about something pointless, and I can rescue Richard whenever he's stuck in an awkward conversation.

But when it came down to life and death and she asked me to do one simple thing—to look out for her father—I completely failed her.

I let her father drive into a fucking lake.

The tires hit the water with a splash, and the painted yellow and orange flames quickly become submerged. In another instant I'm in the water, pulling Richard out of the cart and heaving the both of us up onto the grass. Panting, I look back at the cart, but it's already gone. Dad is on his knees at the edge of the water, swearing. Possibly crying.

I look down at Richard and notice that he's fumbling around trying to unzip his fanny pack. I help him to get it open, and he pulls out his waterproof cell phone case. He takes the phone out and holds it up for me to see.

"Still dry," he says, then collapses onto the grass.

12

"Bloody golf carts," mumbles Summer, taking a long sip of wine. "Bloody golf carts, bloody alligators, bloody old people." She ticks each one off on her fingers and then starts tearing a piece of bread into a zillion pieces.

She seems stressed.

We're out to dinner in Redwood Corral, just the two of us. Richard and Joan are back at the house, taking it easy tonight. Mom and Dad took off to Sunshine Springs with a couple of insulated mugs full of pre-made Margaritas. Dad needs to blow off some steam. He spent the rest of the afternoon on the phone with the insurance company, and taking photographs of a seemingly empty pond that, somewhere in its depths, contains one obscenely expensive golf cart.

"Come on. It's not so bad," I say, pouring myself another glass of wine and looking around. We're sitting on the outdoor patio, right next to the bar. I watch as a woman with long, blonde hair, well into her seventies, systematically makes her way down the line of male customers—laughing, flirting, checking for wedding rings. Her eyes latch onto mine. I quickly look away.

"Not so bad?" says Summer, dropping her bread and staring at me. Not in a good way, either. Not like the time I proposed and she stared at me with the love-light in her eyes and threw her arms around my neck. No, this look is pure Joan Hartwell death stare. "What did your dad have to go and force my dad onto a golf course for, anyway? He can be so condescending sometimes. *Big deal* if somebody doesn't know how to golf. We all used to live in the same neighborhood in Massachusetts, remember? Your father wasn't always Arnold flipping Palmer."

I laugh. "He just gets swept up in his Shangri-La life sometimes. But I talked to him earlier, and he understands that now. And you know what? Your dad is *fine*. His cell phone is dry as a bone. And my dad has insurance. It could have turned out much worse. And yes, an alligator ate your wedding dress. But then you found an even *better* one, *and* you had some bonding time with your mom. If you ask me, this wedding is right on track." I give her a wink and grab a handful of popcorn.

She's still staring at me, hunched expectantly over the table, as if waiting for me to say something worth listening to. I stare right back. She's got this kind of crazy Florida hair thing happening, and this great green dress on that I've never seen before. I don't know if it's the wine, or maybe just all of the adrenaline from the day, but I'm finding her irresistible. I can't imagine how far down her to-do list one would find the word *sex* right now. For Summer, I've learned that the stress of dealing with her parents is an anti-aphrodisiac.

Fortunately, my sense of humor is a total aphrodisiac. This bottle of wine here on the table helps, too. I pour her a refill.

Over the course of the meal, I watch Summer's mood steadily

improve. By the time the waiter clears our plates, she's laughing hysterically at my impression of the four crotchety golfers behind us this morning.

"And then he goes, *For crying out loud! We're not here to bird watch!*"

"Oh, geez," she laughs, wiping her eyes. "I know this is terrible, and I'm only saying it because it's over now and I know that he's fine. But I would give *anything* to be able to go back in time and see my father drive into a lake." She slaps the table with her palm. "A *lake!*"

In between laughs, I reach across the table and squeeze her hands between mine. "Sum," I say, trying to stay serious. "I know I said it before, but honestly, I'm so sorry about today. I told you I would look out for him, and I didn't. I sent him off in that golf cart because I was annoyed with my own father. I didn't even make sure Richard knew what he was doing."

"Oh, stop," she says, squeezing my hands back. "It wasn't your fault. Nobody could have known that the brakes were going to go. Besides, this is just what happens to my parents, no matter what. Even if you'd replaced the brakes and gone over the manual page by page, he would have managed to drive the cart up a tree or something. The fire department would have had to come get him down."

I laugh at the visual. "We're going to get through this week," I say, slowly stroking her hand with my thumb. "I promise. And then, we're off to Jamaica."

Her eyes light up at the mention of our honeymoon. Her faces flushes a bit.

"Come on," I say, after paying the check. "There's a Journey tribute band tearing it up out there. We're going dancing."

I lead her, giggling, out of the restaurant and onto the town common where the band is in the middle of "Anyway You Want It." Hundreds of eyes—male and female—swivel toward us.

Someone whistles, followed by, "Hey there, hot stuff!" I look left, and see Gloria of Dirty Uno fame. I wave.

"My night just got a *whole* lot better!" shouts another voice. It's Nadine from Tuesday night knitting circle, a/k/a our wedding planner. I blow her a kiss and she heads over to us.

"Hi, Nadine," says Summer. "I wanted to apologize again for missing my appointment this morning."

"Not a problem, dear," says Nadine. "Babette told you that we rescheduled for tomorrow morning, didn't she?"

She's talking to Summer, but her eyes are glued to me. She grabs both of my wrists and starts to dance in place.

"Um, yes," says Summer. "Thank you for doing that. We have quite a few things left to go over."

"Right, right," says Nadine, absently. "The wedding is only two weeks away!" She increases her grip on my wrists and begins pulling them roughly back and forth, attempting to make me dance like a marionette.

"Um, actually it's this coming weekend," says Summer, increasing the volume of her voice and glancing nervously at me. "You know that, right?"

"Of course," says Nadine, waving her hand dismissively. "This Sunday. One, two, cha-cha-cha!" She bumps me right in the crotch with her pelvis.

"Woah, hey there, Nadine," I say, backing up a step. "You'll have to excuse us. Tonight, I'm all hers." I gently pry Nadine's fingers from my wrists and motion toward Summer.

"And our wedding is on *Saturday*," says Summer. "Not Sunday."

"Saturday," says Nadine. "Of course. What did I say? Sunday? Ha! I'm sorry, dear. I was just a little distracted." She reaches over, cups my chin in her hand, and gives it a squeeze. "I'll see you later, Grahamy Cracker."

"Grahamy Cracker?" says Summer, as we watch Nadine retreat into the crowd. "That's sick."

"You should hear what the rest of them call me," I mumble, pulling Summer further onto the dance floor.

"I don't even want to know," she says. "I might have nightmares."

"Graham! Over here!"

It seems I'm being assaulted on all fronts. I turn to find Mom's friend Francine waving two glow sticks around like she's directing air traffic.

"Frannie!" I call out. "Work it, sweetheart!"

"Stop encouraging them!" Summer hisses. "Especially Francine. That one already hates my guts."

"Like you should talk. You're getting your own share of attention." I gesture toward the front row of elderly men with their eyes glued to Summer's legs. Several of them are wearing blue shirts with the collars popped. Even the Zumba God himself, Flavio, is here tonight. He's doing the Cabbage Patch and staring at us.

We've come to a stop in the middle of the dance floor and I pull Summer protectively toward me, running my hands up her back as the band transitions into the slow strains of "Faithfully."

Out of the corner of my eye I see Francine slowly waving her glow sticks back and forth over her head.

"Do you really not see the way they're looking at you?" asks Summer.

"Who?"

"All of them. Nadine, Francine. Your friend from Starbucks."

"Gloria."

"Right, Gloria. You realize that you're like a piece of meat thrown into the lion's den down here, right?"

"They're harmless, Sum."

"Well, don't look now, but one harmless old woman named Francine is giving me the evil eye. And her lips are moving a mile a minute. She looks like Snape that time everyone thought he was putting a curse on Harry."

"Who?"

Summer raises her eyebrows and gives me her *Don't-you-dare-pretend-not-to-get-a-Harry-Potter-reference* look.

"I'm just teasing," I say. "You know as well as I do that Snape was actually protecting Harry."

"Oh, so Francine is trying to protect me? From what, exactly?"

"Maybe from me." I lean down and nuzzle into her neck.

Summer laughs and puts her arms around my neck. She gently rakes her fingers through the back of my hair. Now we're talking.

"So, do you remember what we were talking about the other day?" she asks.

"Um, maybe?"

"About, you know, how it's been *kind of a long time.*"

I perk up and look down at her face, not at all expecting to have heard those words.

"Oh, right." I pull her in even closer. What we're doing is nothing compared to what I see Gloria doing over there with Burt from Twister Club. I mean, really. Wasn't she dating Lionel? A guy goes north for a few months and he misses everything around here. "What exactly are you suggesting?"

"I think I see a hotel over there," she whispers, pulling slightly away. She's pointing across the common to a building that clearly says "Hotel" at the top.

"Don't get excited. That's a facade."

"Really?"

"Yeah, there's a sales office on the first floor. The rest is empty. Same as how Starbucks used to be Ezekiel's Tavern. You don't think Duke's Mining Company is really located above that Dunkin Donuts over there, do you?"

"*No.*" She rolls her eyes. "Well, maybe we should just do it right here in the common. A lot of couples do that."

"*One* couple did that," I clarify. "And it was gross, and they got arrested."

It's true. They even had a drink named after them—*Copulation on the Common.*

Summer doesn't answer, she just pulls me into a long kiss. She still tastes like red wine, and her crazy Florida hair smells like coconuts.

"Okay," I say, catching my breath. "Time to go." I pull her by the hand, practically dragging her back to our golf cart.

"Where?"

"You'll see."

I'm dangerously close to just parking this thing behind a bush and having a drink named after us. But, being me, I've planned ahead.

13

I drive past my parents' house and pull up to another, almost identical house, a little bit further down the street. I press the garage door opener that I've been hiding in my pocket. The door goes up and Summer looks at me, confused.

"We're not breaking and entering, are we?"

I wave the garage door opener in front of her face, but she doesn't look convinced. Still, she follows me through the garage and into the house. I don't bother turning on the lights, as the house is awash in the glow of fifty flickering LED candles. I bought out all of Wal-Mart's home décor department earlier this afternoon. Two champagne glasses sit side-by-side on the coffee table.

Like I said, I planned ahead.

"Um, Graham?" says Summer.

"Yes?"

"Where the hell are we?"

"Where do you *think* we are?"

Her eyes widen in fear as she turns slowly toward me. "You didn't *buy* this place, did you?"

I can almost hear the gears in her mind turning—calculating how I could have managed to purchase a house in an age-restricted community. Sometimes she gives me more credit than I'm due. I let her freak out for a few seconds before breaking into a grin.

"Sorry, Sum. I can't make all of your dreams come true. At least not all at once. This is just where Aunt Jo-Ann and Uncle Chuck are staying after the wedding. Mom and Dad rented it for them. I swiped the keys."

As I dangle the keys in the air, her face melts with relief. Then she launches herself gleefully into my arms, wrapping her legs around my waist and kissing me.

I back blindly toward the couch, trying not to trip over anything, and lay her down against the pillows. I start at her neck and gently kiss my way down to her collarbone, sliding the strap of her dress off her right shoulder. Then I pause and pull away for a second.

"Would it really have been so bad if I'd bought this place?" I ask.

"Um, yes," she says, running her hand down the side of my face. "It would have been really, horribly bad. Really very horrible and bad."

"I'll ask you again in thirty years," I say, leaning back down and kissing along the other side of her neck. I slide off the other strap.

"Deal."

I sit up and pull my shirt over my head. Then I pause again before throwing it to the floor.

"But why would it have been so very horrible and bad?" I ask.

Summer raises herself onto her elbows and puts her straps back on her shoulders. "Are you serious?"

I shrug. "Just out of curiosity."

"Okay. Let me see. Number one, we're not a retired elderly couple. Number two, we're not yet ready to cut all ties with reality—although, you may have already done that years ago. Number three—"

"Okay, okay," I laugh. "I get it. I just think it's fun down here."

"I *know* you do," says Summer. "And that's what scares me. I have this nightmare that you're going to find some sort of loophole and move us here after the wedding."

"A loophole," I say, clicking my tongue. "Now *there's* an idea."

I dodge the punch Summer throws at my stomach and head to the fridge to grab a bottle of champagne. I pour us two glasses, place them on the coffee table, then pick up the remote control. I found one other little surprise for her this afternoon. Who knew a trip to Wal-Mart could be so lucrative? I turn on the TV and hit play.

"Sharknado!" Summer exclaims. "Oh my *God*. We haven't watched this since that night on the cruise."

"I'm a sentimental guy," I say, sinking down next to her on the couch. "And it was in the bargain bin."

She smiles and stretches her legs across my lap as the horrors of a swirling shark tornado begin to play out onscreen.

"You know I'm only joking around about moving here, right?" I ask.

"Nope," says Summer, not taking her eyes off the movie.

"I am. There are at least six other retirement communities around the United States that I would need to check out first. Never mind Mexico." I whistle.

Summer pinches me hard on the leg until I agree not to look at any real estate brochures until we're at least fifty. Luckily, she didn't mention websites. Come on, Sum. Who still uses brochures?

We drink champagne. We make sarcastic comments. And then history repeats itself, and we don't even come close to finishing the movie.

***

We're lying on the living room floor, wrapped in blankets, peacefully watching the shadows of candles flickering on the walls, when a brick sails through the front window.

"Shit!" I jump up and pull Summer into the corner of the living room, away from the debris field of shattered glass.

"What the hell?" she yells. "What the *hell?*"

"I don't know!" I scramble to find my clothes, succeeding in only finding my boxers. I pull them on, along with my shoes. Then I run to the front door, whip it open, and look out into the street. I see nothing but a set of golf cart taillights fading into the distance.

"Who's out there?" she shrieks. "Who would *do* that?"

"I don't know," I say again, stepping away from the door. My heart is pounding. I pick Summer's dress up off the floor and toss it to her. "Wait here. And lock the door behind me."

I run out into the street and head in the direction of the taillights. I go all the way to the end of the street, and then out to the main road. There are golf carts driving in every direction.

A few of them beep at me and whistle. It's no use. I run back to the house, grab a golf club out of the garage, and do a thorough search of the backyard and the shrubs. Nothing. I knock on the front door.

"Who is it?" Summer calls.

"Me."

"What's the secret code?"

I sigh. We once established a secret code to use in case either of us needed help. Like, if Summer ever texts me the secret word, I'll know that she's been kidnapped. We'd just watched an *America's Most Wanted* marathon and it seemed like the right thing to do. Having to use it while locked out of the house in my boxer shorts, however, wasn't exactly what I had in mind.

"Beef Stroganoff," I say.

She lets me in. She's holding a brick in one hand and a piece of paper in the other.

"I couldn't catch them," I say, walking over and surveying the damage to the window. "It must have just been random. I mean, nobody even knows that we're here. This is supposed to be a vacant rental house."

Summer looks at me, shaking her head and holding up the piece of paper. "No. It wasn't random. It was *her.*"

"What are you talking about," I ask. "Who?"

"*Francine,*" she says, exasperation in her voice. "Read this."

I take the paper out of her hand. Written in big block letters are the words *BACK OFF.*

"Back off?"

"Yeah, that's right. This was a message for me to back off of *you.*"

"Oh, come on."

"No *you* come on! She probably followed us here from Redwood!"

"You think Francine threw a *brick* through the window? I don't think she can even lift a brick."

"She's got you fooled," says Summer. "She smokes, she drinks, she did God knows what with some guy named Gil. I saw the way she was looking at me tonight. Francine is bad news."

"Who says that note was even for you?" I say. "Maybe it was meant for me. Maybe it was one of those blue shirt guys that were checking you out tonight. They're probably all amped up on Viagra and want me out of the picture."

"I've never seen any of those guys before," she says. "No. Francine was cursing me like Snape, and then she followed us here. And if it wasn't her, it was probably Nadine. Or maybe it was both of them together. The way you had to pry her hands off of you was totally brick-worthy."

"You think our *wedding planner* threw a brick through our window?"

"Um, maybe you didn't notice, but Nadine was so dazzled by your presence that she could barely even remember when our wedding *is*. She and Francine were probably hiding in the bushes this whole time, peeking in the windows." She shudders.

"They probably learned a few things, am I right?" I give her a wink.

"I can't believe you're making jokes right now. A crime has been committed, Graham. A *crime*."

"I know it, Sum. I just ran down the street in my underwear

and used the words *beef stroganoff.* It's just that all this speculation is pointless. It could have been some dumb kids for all we know."

"Kids? *Here?*"

Good point.

"Okay, fine," I say. "Whoever did it, we need to call the police. Agreed?"

"I don't think that'll be necessary," says Summer. "Listen."

Sirens. In the distance, but getting closer. I step back outside and confirm that there is in fact an ADT Security sign staked into the mulch in front of the house. I also confirm that there are two police cruisers turning onto the street with their lights flashing and their sirens wailing, while I stand on the front steps in my underwear. Now they're pulling up in front of the house.

Tonight on Cops…

I've seen enough episodes to know that now is not the time to dart back into the house looking for pants. I put both hands in the air and wait for them to approach me—which they do—quickly, and with guns drawn. And then—

"Graham?"

I squint into the bright lights. "Daryl?"

"What are you *doing* here, man?" Daryl lowers his gun and instructs his partner to do the same. Daryl is Edna Spurlock's son. He took Summer and I out for drinks a few weeks back after I taught his mother how to use Twitter. Nice guy.

"Long story," I say, shaking his hand. "All I know is that someone just chucked a brick through the window and took off in a golf cart." I motion to the broken front window.

"Oh, wow," says Daryl. "Would you look at that. Oh, hey

Summer, nice to see you again." He waves through the screen door.

"Hey, Daryl," says Summer.

"By the way, Graham, you know you're in your skivvies, right? And what are those? Pink Sperry's? I didn't even know men's shoes came in that color."

"It's been a long night, Daryl. You think we could—" I motion toward the front door.

"Oh, yeah! Listen to me going on and on. Let's get you inside and we'll fill out a report." Daryl steps into the house. "Oh, wow! Look at all those candles. Okay, now I see why you're in your skivvies." He steps back outside to give me a wink and a fist bump. Summer rolls her eyes.

A crowd of gray-hairs is beginning to gather on the street, watching as the other officer takes a roll of yellow caution tape out of his trunk and starts winding it around the perimeter of the house.

"Is that necessary?" I ask.

Daryl shrugs. "Retirement community. People feel safer if we use the tape."

That's when I see them.

"Oh, no," whispers Summer. She sees them too.

Mom and Dad may not be home yet, but Richard and Joan were in for the night—in for the night about four houses down. And now they're standing there in the street, watching me talk to a police officer, in my underwear, in front of a house that's slowly being wrapped in caution tape.

I could almost laugh at the looks of horror on their faces, as they turn from red to blue to red again in the flashing lights of the police cruisers. I could laugh if only I weren't marrying their daughter in a few short days.

I give them a little wave before following Daryl into the house.

They don't wave back.

SUMMER

14

Graham's parents weren't exactly thrilled when they arrived home to police cruisers and rubberneckers all over the street. They were actually less upset about the fact that we had snuck into the rental house to do the deed—completely mortifying, by the way—than they were about the fact that Graham's aunt and uncle are flying down for the wedding in a few short days. John's been talking up Sunset Havens as some sort of crime-free paradise for years, trying to convince them to move down here. If they think that the place is overrun with window-smashing hoodlums, it's not going to help his case. I tried to help by saying that the *Back Off* note pointed more toward one of the elderly residents, rather than a random hoodlum. But John just gave me a look that said *You're making things much, much worse*, so I shut my mouth.

I told my own parents that Graham and I had gone into the house to practice our wedding vows in private, and that Graham was just about to try on his tuxedo when the brick came through the window—hence the reason that he was in his boxers. I think that they bought it. Graham is still embarrassed. He's afraid that

Mom and Dad think he's some sort of criminal domestic abuser. I have to admit, it's kind of refreshing seeing this new, neurotic side of him. Maybe that thing about girls marrying men like their father is true after all.

Anyway, Graham knows a lady who knows a lady who has a son in the glass repair business, and she's sending him over this afternoon. John can continue to promote Sunset Havens as a crime-free paradise, and Aunt Jo-Ann and Uncle Chuck will be none the wiser. I suppose there are some benefits to Graham being a ladies' man. Of course, those benefits come with the chance that a brick might sail through your window and you will have to admit horribly embarrassing things to your in-laws.

This morning, Mom, Babette, Graham, and I have arrived at The Lakeview for our rescheduled appointment with Nadine. I plan to watch her like a hawk for overt signs of guilt. Chipped nail polish? Bags under the eyes like she's been up past nine o'clock? Unusually large biceps? I'm on it. We've only just entered the lobby when she comes hurtling toward us, full speed, and straight into the arms of my fiancé.

"Graham!" she cries. "Are you ready for the big day?"

Honestly, you would think that he's the bride. She pumps his hand up and down, her curly, rust-colored hair bobbing enthusiastically along. She doesn't seem the least bit tired, or guilty. And her arms, poking out of her pastel pink, short-sleeved suit jacket, look disappointingly scrawny. I suppose that narrows it down to Francine.

I stand patiently by while she continues to fawn over Graham, asking him—I kid you not—if he's had his hair and nails done yet. Finally, she glances fleetingly in my direction.

"Oh, hello again, Summer."

"Hi, Nadine," I say. "I'd like you to meet my mother, Joan Hartwell."

"The *mother of the bride*!" she exclaims, snapping out of her Graham-trance and turning to look at Mom. She blinks rapidly, her thick, clumpy mascara looking like two large, squashed spiders. "How *unusual* to meet the *mother of the bride* so late in the planning! Usually the *mother of the bride* is very involved. Unless, of course, she's deceased!" Nadine lets out a burst of laughter, as if she finds deceased mothers to be just hilarious.

And the way she keeps putting emphasis on *mother of the bride* is making me cringe. Or maybe that's just my guilty conscience.

"My mother lives very far away," I explain. "It was just easier if Babette handled things, since she lives here in Sunset Havens." I glance nervously at Mom who forces an understanding smile and nod in my direction. Still, I can sense that she's hurt. We may have cleared the air in the golf cart yesterday, but I still have to live with the consequences of my decision.

"Say no more," says Nadine looking back and forth between the two of us. "I try to stay out of personal family matters, if I can help it. You two sort this out on your own!" She lets out another shriek of laughter, and starts dragging Graham toward a table in the corner of the room.

"But there are no *personal family matters*," I say, air-quoting the words as I jog along, trying to keep up. "It was just a matter of logistics. Seriously."

Nadine waves her hand in the air. "Logistics, family feuds, strained mother-daughter relationships, call it what you want! All

I know is that none of it is any of my business." She puts her fingers in her ears and says *la-la-la-la* a bunch of times.

God, I hate this woman.

"The place looks great," says Graham, attempting to change the subject. "It looks like they do really nice weddings here."

"Oh, they *do*," says Nadine. "At least that's what it says in the brochure."

"What brochure?" asks Mom.

"From The Lakeview."

"You mean you haven't actually planned a wedding here before?" asks Mom, turning to me and putting a hand on her chest. She staggers backward a few steps.

"Well, not exactly," says Nadine. "I was a wedding planner in New York City for *many* years before I moved to Sunset Havens. The Lakeview hired me special to assist the lucky contest winner!"

I knew it! I knew Nadine wasn't a full-time wedding consultant for this place. She probably hasn't planned a wedding in forty years. A sick feeling starts bubbling up in my stomach as I take a seat at the table. I could have been having an awesome wedding back home in Boston, with all of our friends and family and a youthful wedding planner who doesn't ask if you'd prefer the band play the Hokie Pokie before or after the Chicken Dance.

What have I done? Would planning a wedding with my mother really have been *that* bad?

I mean, yes, of course it would have been that bad. But would it have been worse than Nadine? Why did I put so much blind trust in Babette? Babette's no spring chicken herself. Maybe she doesn't even realize how outdated and weird Nadine is. I'm going to have to go over every single detail, like, right now. I need to—

"Oh my God," I say, picking up a piece of hideous, shiny pink satin from the table. "What is this?"

"That's a sample of your table linens," says Nadine.

I raise my eyebrows. "But my wedding colors are white and *peach*."

Nadine looks at me as if I've completely lost it. She turns to Graham for confirmation that he actually wants to marry such an airhead, before reaching for her binder.

"That's not what you said when you called me last week." She opens the binder and flips to a page. "Right here. You called and changed your colors to, let me see...oh yes, bubblegum."

"*Bubblegum?*"

"That's what it says."

"I don't care what it *says,* Nadine. I most certainly didn't change my wedding color to bubblegum! Babette, did you change my wedding color to *bubblegum?*"

"Of course not!" says Babette. "That thing is repulsive!"

I give Nadine a triumphant look, and silently apologize to Babette for having doubted her good taste.

"I see," says Nadine, with a sigh. She gives me a placating smile and scribbles a few notes into her binder. Then she picks up the pink fabric sample and drops it dramatically onto the floor beside her chair.

"So, it's fixed then?" I ask. "I'm not going to walk in here on my wedding day and be blasted in the face by a sea of Pepto-pink napkins, am I?" I sound a bit rude, I know. But for heaven's sake, those napkins have Bonita's Bridal Bonanza written all over them. Like, they might literally have the words Bonita's Bridal Bonanza embroidered somewhere on the back.

"No, no. We're back to peach," she sighs. "Now, Summer. Just remember that the wedding is *very* close. You can't keep changing your mind like this."

"I didn't change my mind!" I shriek. "Are there any other changes that I supposedly made? We still have a band, don't we?"

Nadine looks up at me, one eyebrow raised, an expression of concern surfacing from beneath all the layers of makeup. She starts flipping through the binder again.

Oh, no. Oh, God. Not the binder.

"Nadine?"

"Right here." She points to a page. "When you called me last week to change the colors, you also asked that I cancel the band. You said something about replacing them with a bassoon trio."

"Ba-bassoon trio?" I stammer. "I…I never called you about any bassoon trio, Nadine. There must be some mistake. You didn't actually *cancel* the band, did you?"

Nadine looks around at all of us, her face frozen into a maniacal smile. "Well, of *course* I did. *You're* the bride, not me. I simply do as I'm told!" She waves her hand in the air with a flourish. "I must say, I've never heard of such a thing as a bassoon trio at a wedding. But I have been out of the scene for quite some time. If you say bassoon trios are in right now, who am I to argue! I'm just not sure you're going to *find* one on such short notice. You won't give a rats behind what color the table linens are when everybody's standing around the dance floor in total silence!" She lets out a loud cackle of laughter.

"I did no such thing!" I say, my voice reaching boiling-tea-kettle range. "I don't know who you talked to, but it wasn't me!"

"A bassoon trio? Honestly, Nadine." Babette throws her hands into the air.

"So, we have no band?" I ask, looking frantically around the room, as if I'm going to find an unemployed, ten-piece orchestra just hanging out in the corner. "Graham! We have no band!"

And then, at the sound of his name, it hits me. Nadine, who can't keep her paws off of my fiancé, has all the power over the details of my wedding. She can do whatever she wants and then pretend that it was all my idea—the flaky bride, always changing her mind. The brick through-the-window, that wasn't her, that was Francine. But destroying my wedding from the inside out—the psychological games—that's all Nadine. This is a team effort.

Oh, they're good.

15

Am I allowed to fire her? I mean, it's my wedding, I should be able to do what I want. Then again, she did come with the venue as part of the deal. And she has all the details in that damn binder. Firing her five days before the wedding might be more disastrous than having to undo all of her nasty little changes. I just need to stay one step ahead. I need to subtly let her know that I'm on to her games, and that I'll be watching.

"So," I say, giving her my best bad-cop stare across the table, "we're playing dirty now, is that it?"

"Excuse me?" asks Nadine.

"What are you talking about?" asks Mom. "Who's dirty?"

"Mom, please," I say. "Let me handle this."

"Handle what?" asks Nadine, peering at me over the top of her glasses.

"Oh, *you know*," I say, loading up the words with as much meaning as possible. "*This* and *that*."

Nadine raises her eyebrows and looks from me to Babette, then back to me. Now Babette and Mom are staring at me too. I just keep nodding slowly because I'm at a total loss as to what to say next. I would make a horrible cop.

"Oy, please," says Mom, waving her hand at me. "What we need to know is, did Summer make any other changes that we should know about?"

I whip around in my chair. "I didn't *make* any changes!"

Ignoring me, Nadine flips through the binder. "Let me see. I think there was one more tiny thing. Oh, yes. Here." She jabs a long fingernail into the page. "You asked that the cake be changed to carrot."

Oh, for Pete's sake.

"No. No carrot cake," I say. "Change that back to red velvet. Now get the band on the phone and tell them that their gig is back on. *Now.*" That's more like it. No more subtle hints. What I need to do is take charge and let her see that I'm not going to take any more of her crap.

Nadine takes out her cell phone, flips through the binder, and dials the number. While she's speaking, I turn to my mother.

"This is a complete nightmare," I whisper. "I didn't make *any* of these changes!"

Mom reaches over and squeezes my hand. "Everything's going to work out just fine." *Everything's going to work out just fine?* My mother has never uttered those words in her life.

Nadine hangs up the phone and clears her throat. "Well, that was a bust."

"What do you mean? What's a bust?"

"The band. They've already been re-booked."

"Oh, no!" groans Babette.

I clamp a hand over my mouth. I'll bet you anything that Nadine booked the band herself. She probably put down a deposit and everything. The colors and the cake, those were just extra touches. Stealing my band, however, that was the big guns. That might be enough to make me call off the wedding. I wonder if she even really called the band just now. She probably called Francine and used a bunch of code words. *I'd like to re-book the band for Saturday* probably meant *We've successfully given Summer Hartwell a bleeding ulcer, martinis at five?*

I look desperately at Graham. "Don't you know any bands? Didn't you once go to an album launch party for Maroon 5?"

"Yeah, five years ago," he says. "And even if I did know them personally, which I don't, I doubt they're available this coming weekend."

I slump back in my seat. Does he always have to be so difficult?

"Okay, fine," I say. "Babette, what about the bands that play on the common? Who was that guy from the other night? Squirrelly Dan?"

"Squirrelly Dan and The Nuts!" says Babette, perking up.

"You want Squirrelly Dan and The Nuts to play our wedding?" asks Graham, raising an eyebrow.

"Well it doesn't look like we're getting Maroon 5!"

"Summer," says Mom. "Relax."

"*Relax?*"

"Yes. Relax. I'm not about to let my only daughter's wedding turn into a disaster."

What planet am I on? Why is she suddenly so calm? Normally, Mom would have been the first one to call off the wedding.

"So, what then? You're going to find me a band?"

Mom runs a hand smugly through her curls, fluffing them up a bit.

"I might know a guy," she says.

"You know a guy with a band?" I ask. "Not a marching band or an oompah band, but a real band?"

Mom nods slowly. And then it hits me. This bizarre calmness about her is actually confidence. My wedding—the one that I went ahead and planned without her—is in shambles. Yesterday my dress was eaten by an alligator, and she was there to help me find an even better one. Today my band got canceled, and she thinks she's going to swoop in and find me a better one of those, too.

Well, we'll see about that.

***

As soon as we return to the Blenderman house, Mom locks herself in the guest bedroom with her cell phone. I can hear her yelling something at directory assistance, but can't quite make out the name. A couple of times I think I hear 'Springsteen,' and then later, 'Jovi,' but that may just be wishful thinking. Although, it's not totally out of the question for Mom to have dated Jon or Bruce way back when. We don't know everything about our parents.

She comes out of the room ten minutes later with a smile on her face, but still refuses to offer any word of explanation. This sort of strangeness continues for the next half hour, with Mom's cell phone randomly blaring "Glory Days" (I *told* you!), and her scurrying back into the bedroom for another hushed conversation. The rest of us are sitting in the living room eating

Cheez-Its and watching the news—three car accidents, two convenience store robberies, one homicide, and a disturbing amount of close calls with alligators. Dad's dozing in the recliner.

"We should go somewhere," I say, after watching the weatherman's face light up at the possibility of a hurricane. "Before I become seriously depressed."

"You could change the channel," suggests Graham.

"It's Monday," I point out. "All that's on during the week are paternity tests and women screaming about cellulite cream. Or that show with the doctors. Did I tell you about this new obesity device you can have inserted into your stomach? It's like a little trapdoor above the hip that drains the food directly into the toilet." I tilt my head back and shake the last of the Cheez-Its directly into my mouth. Then I toss the empty box into his lap. Graham looks at me, his face contorted with horror.

"What?" I ask, crunching loudly.

He doesn't answer. He just keeps making his funny, horrified face at me until I laugh. Then he smiles and looks over the back of the couch. "So, Mom. What else did you want to do today?"

"I was thinking maybe we could do the boat tour," says Babette. She's been sitting at the kitchen table flipping through a copy of the Sunset Havens Recreation Guide, which is roughly the size of a telephone book. "Remember that, John?"

Yesterday was John's last day to play golf. Babette made him promise to take the rest of the week off to spend more time with the family, and also because his golf cart is now at the bottom of a lake. John looks like he doesn't know what to do with himself.

"Boat tour?" he asks. "What boat tour?"

"The one on Lake Fillmore. We did it the first time we came

down here. I believed *everything* the captain said. Even the part about the lighthouse being used to protect against pirate attacks during the Civil War." Babette laughs. "I only found out a few years ago that Lake Fillmore was man-made in the year two thousand!"

I clear my throat and shoot Graham a look. I *knew* these people would fall for all that fake history. And my own mother-in-law, of all people. I sigh.

John sighs too. "If we must."

"Are you up for a boat ride, Dad?" I ask. I'm not exactly enthralled by the idea. It seems like my parents and I end up on an awful lot of boats together. But it's something to kill a couple of hours.

"I should check with your mother," he says, getting out of the recliner and looking nervously down the hallway. "I should see what she wants to do."

Dad really is a sweetheart, always full of concern for Mom. I think back to our conversation in the golf cart. Poor Dad. I can't believe she finds him so irritating lately. Boring, even. Sure, he's not as exciting as Springsteen or Bon Jovi, but you know what? I bet even Bruce bores his wife once in a while with what he found on eBay.

"I'll go check on her," I say. I've been dying for a reason to go down the hall and eavesdrop, but there's only so many times a girl can pretend to go to the bathroom. I walk down the hall and knock on her door. I can't hear a thing. I don't even think she's on the phone. After a few seconds, she flings the door open.

"I was just speaking with Nadine," she says in a loud, weird robot voice. "We're meeting at The Lakeview tomorrow morning. Everything has been settled."

And with that, she pushes past me and marches into the living room. I stand there for a few seconds, staring at the wall, wondering what on Earth she's up to. She was most definitely *not* just speaking with Nadine. That's when I notice her cell phone on the bed. I pick it up, intending to bring it out to her— only, a text message has just come in. Since when does Mom know how to text? I don't *try* to read the message, I swear. It's just there, already open on the main screen because Mom doesn't know how to change the settings on her smartphone. Also, it says *Roger*, so how can I possibly not read it?

LOL. Me 2. CU 2-nite. 5632 Orange Court. Bring hubs and an open mind ;)

CU 2-nite? Hubs? Open mind?

Wink?

Oh, dear lord. It's really happening. Mom and Dad are going to an orgy.

16

"It's probably just a dinner party," says Graham.

"What would they need open minds for at a dinner party?" I ask. "Huh?"

Graham shrugs. "Maybe Roger's a terrible cook."

We're all standing around the pier at Lake Fillmore, waiting for the tour boat to arrive. Graham and I have wandered off a little ways in order to have a hushed discussion about why my skin is crawling with willies. The reasons are as follows:

1. Mom
2. Dad
3. Roger
4. An open mind
5. Wink

"It's a swingers party," I say, with a shudder. "I know it is."

"But Roger isn't even married," says Graham. "Who's he going to swap?"

"Do you have to be married to be a swinger?"

"I think so."

We contemplate this in silence for a few seconds, while we

watch a bird nipping at a French fry. Then I pull out my phone and Google *What is a swinger?* My Google search history since arriving at Sunset Havens is disturbing to say the least.

"Look, right here," I say, shoving my phone into Graham's face. "Couples or *singles* who choose to have an open relationship. Roger can just bring Barbara. Oh my God. Dad's going to have sex with Barbara."

"Will you stop," Graham laughs. "Nobody is having sex with anybody."

"We're at Sunset Havens, Graham. *Everybody is having sex with everybody!*"

Okay, I may have shouted that last part and now everybody in the vicinity is staring at me—including the ten year old boy who's been feeding his French fries to the birds. I smile apologetically at his grandmother.

"I didn't mean *you*," I explain to her, which doesn't seem to help at all.

"Didn't we already talk about this?" asks Graham. "Why would my dad want to swap my mom? She's younger and hotter than any of the women here." He waves his arm around, inadvertently motioning to the grandmother. She shoots us a dirty look before grabbing her grandson and vacating the area.

"Maybe your mom wants to swap your dad," I whisper. "Did you ever think about that?"

"*No*," says Graham, crinkling up his nose. "Who would think about that?"

"Boat's here!" calls out Babette.

"You are so naive," I mutter, shaking my head as we walk down the pier.

It's a pretty relaxing little boat ride, I'll admit that much. Mom and Dad are the only people over the age of eight wearing life jackets—which is good, because Mom almost fell overboard when the captain threw a rubber alligator into the center of the boat—but other than that, it's been going well.

"And on the right," says the captain, "if you look closely, you will see a rare animal that inhabits the shoreline of Lake Fillmore. It's called the Workus-no-morus." He points to the happy retirees sitting at the outdoor bar overlooking the water. Everybody on the boat waves. One of them actually snaps a picture.

"And on the left, you will see the remains of a pirate ship sunk back in eighteen seventy-six by Sunset Haven's own, Benjamin Crawford. Benjamin wasn't about to let his hometown— Florida's *friendliest* hometown," he gives us all a wink, "—be pillaged and burned by some mean old pirates. No, sir. All by himself, he rolled the Sunset Havens town cannon down to the edge of the water—you can still see that cannon today, inside the T.G.I. Fridays on four forty-one—and he pumped that pirate ship full of iron."

I roll my eyes.

"A few of those pirates did make it to shore," he continues, "only to be taken care of by Sunset Haven's resident alligator…Big Al." On that note, he once again tosses the rubber alligator into the center of the boat. Mom holds it together this time, giving the captain a smug, *fool me once,* sort of a look. That's when he reaches behind his back and flings a rubber octopus onto her lap. Mom screams at the top of her lungs.

I wait until Mom has composed herself, and the captain has

taken a break from revising history, to broach the subject that's still freaking me out.

"So, Babette," I say, leaning over all casual-like and tapping her on the leg. "What are you up to tonight?"

She glances at John. I glance at Graham. Graham looks at his watch.

"Roger invited us to his house tonight," she says. "For a swap. I hope you don't mind. It's um, grown-ups only!" She giggles and looks at John again.

A swap! It's really happening. And she's so open about it!

"Graham and I are adults," I say. "How come we didn't get invited to this swap?"

"Oh, you don't want to spend the night swapping with a bunch of boring old fogies," she says. "All of our clothes will be thrown around everywhere. It's nothing you'd be interested in seeing."

My jaw hits the bottom of the boat.

"And what about you?" I ask Mom. "Are you guys going to this grown-ups only *swap*?" I air quote the word.

"We were invited." Mom shrugs. "It would be rude not to."

"You're kidding?"

"What? It sounds like fun. I'll probably just watch anyway. I didn't bring anything to swap except your father." She laughs and bats a hand at Dad, as if nobody on Earth would ever be interested in him. She's got some nerve.

"Dad, you're okay with this?" I ask, feeling sick to my stomach.

"I have to admit I'm curious about it," he says. "I've seen them do it on TV a few times."

Oh.

My.

God.

Life as I know it is over. I look over at Graham, satisfied to see that he too looks sufficiently horrified. John seems pretty nonchalant about the whole thing, which is even worse. I mean, is that how he reacts when his wife is...is...ugh, I can't even say it...being *intimate*, with another man?

"Excuse me," I say, standing up and diving off the side of the boat, where I drown, mercifully, in the depths of Lake Fillmore.

Just kidding.

In my mind, I totally jumped. In reality, I dug my nails into Graham's upper thigh until he pried them out, and then we finished the boat tour in silence.

***

"You know we have to follow them, right?" I ask Graham. I'm lying in bed watching him spike up his hair for the evening. He has this obsessive compulsive kind of ritual. It's like watching Nomar Garciaparra getting ready to bat. First, he squirts gel into each hand, then he rubs them together—left over right, flip, right over left, flip—then he moves his fingers around his head with an impossible to follow series of twists and yanks and scrunches. Impossible to follow, yet always the same. Then he repeats. By the time he's done, he looks like a totally hot mad scientist who just rolled out of bed. It helps that I'm sympathetic to neurotic behavior—once again, I appear to be marrying my father—and also a huge fan of *Doctor Who*. I really should get him a trench coat. And a big blue spaceship.

"Of course we're following them," says Graham, putting his bottle of gel down and turning to look at me. "What else would we be doing tonight?"

I smile. "You know, you can't wear that shirt though, right?"

He glances down at his orange button-up with the neon, pink fish all over it. "What's wrong with my shirt?"

"It glows in the dark, dummy. You bought it at a glow-in-the-dark gift shop at the airport. We're going to be hiding in the bushes under the cover of darkness, we can't have you lit up like a Christmas tree. We need to wear black. And maybe ski masks."

He raises his eyebrows. "My ski mask is red, and it only covers the lower half of my face because I'm not a cartoon bank robber. Also, I left it back in Massachusetts along with the rest of my ski clothes. Because, you know, *Florida.*" He motions all around us.

"Okay, smarty, what do you suggest we do?"

"Roger's house is two streets over," he says. "I thought we'd just walk there, ring the doorbell, and see what's up."

"Oh."

I suppose that's one way to do it. One *boring* way to do it. What happened to the crazy guy I fell in love with? I finally come around to wanting to dress in disguise and hide in the shrubs outside swingers parties, and he shoots me down.

"But what if we walk in on some sort of *Eyes Wide Shut* situation?" I ask. "I'd rather peek in through the blinds than face it head on."

"Do you want to be the kind of person who goes through life peeking through blinds?" he asks. "No. If we're going to spend the next twenty years in therapy, we're going to do it as a result of something we faced head on. Be brave, Sum."

"Can't we be brave tomorrow? We can go BASE jumping or something."

Graham gives me that *look,* the one that says *At this time tomorrow we can free-fall off a sixteen hundred foot antenna tower if that's what you would really prefer to do.*

"Okay, okay," I say, quickly. "We walk right in. Then what? Are we going to physically pull them out of there? Like, you'll grab my parents and throw them over your shoulders? Maybe we should bring tear gas. You know, smoke them out?"

Graham laughs. "You've got tear gas?"

"Well, no. But we could buy some. You think they sell it at Publix? On the aisle with the bug spray and the lighter fluid?"

Now he's giving me another look. He's really got quite the arsenal. This one is more of a *How can I marry someone who comes up with such terrible ideas?* sort of a thing.

"What about *my* parents?" he asks. "You can't expect me to throw all four of them over my shoulders."

"Who cares about *them*? This whole thing is their fault. *My* parents are the innocent ones."

"Actually, it was *your* father that said he was excited to go because he'd seen something like it on TV. What do you think he was watching, anyway?"

"*Eyes Wide Shut,*" I repeat. "I told you. There was probably some mix-up with their Netflix and they got the wrong disc in the mail."

Graham sits down next to me on the bed and pats me on the thigh.

"Well, Sum. This is what happens when you choose to have your wedding at a retirement community. You don't have to pick out table linens with your parents, but you do have to consider gassing them out of an over sixty-five orgy. Would you say that it was a fair, um, swap?" He gives me a wink.

I give him a Joan Hartwell look of death, then I reach over and mess up his hair.

17

Roger answers the door shirtless.

I repeat, Roger has answered the door shirtless. I look wide-eyed up at Graham, but he seems relatively unfazed by the sight of Roger's nipples. Okay, breathe Summer. Men go shirtless all the time. It doesn't mean anything. Maybe Roger doesn't have air conditioning, and if he walks around his house in a shirt, he'll die of heat stroke. Is that what I want? For Roger to die?

Rhetorical question, obviously.

As I try to avoid looking at Roger's chest, I see Janice walk across the living room in nothing but a bra.

I repeat, Janice is walking around in nothing but a bra.

Well, she does have pants on. And shoes. But on top she's wearing nothing but a black lacy thing, which is enough for me to begin sounding the alarm.

"Mom? Dad?" I yell, pushing my way into the house. "Are you guys here? Are you okay?"

Oh, dear God, there are clothes everywhere. We're too late. Pants and skirts are strewn about—some hanging from lamps, others in messy piles on the floor. How many people are *at* this thing? I see six or seven bras hanging over the back of the couch, and…I can barely say it…an equal number of men's white briefs, stacked up in the middle of the coffee table. Did they all strip buck naked in the living room and then pile their underwear on the table? Why would they *do* that? Also, where are they all now? Roger can't possibly have enough bedrooms for something of this scale.

I take a few staggering steps backward, only to bump into the open door of Roger's entertainment center. I grab onto it to steady myself, and come face to face with a cardigan sweater that's been draped over the top. Oh no. Oh no oh no oh no.

I'd know that cardigan anywhere.

"Graham!" I shout, but he doesn't respond. I look around, but he's nowhere in sight. Even in a glow-in-the-dark shirt, I can't manage to find him. I yank the cardigan off the door and start making my way toward the kitchen. With or without Graham, I'm in this now. There's no turning back. Even if Mom and Dad are in their birthday suits, I still might be able to stop them before they do anything they're going to regret.

As I continue to look around, I recognize Gil by the sliding glass door, taking off his pants. I see a woman lounging on the couch, dangling a clear, plastic, high-heeled shoe off of one foot. And over there by the bookcase is Gloria, pulling a sweater over her head. They're all giving me strange looks, too. Like I'm some sort of narc. Which I am. But it's not like I'm going to call the cops. I just want to grab my parents and go.

"Mom? Dad?" I say again, walking into the kitchen. It looks fairly normal in here. Everybody's dressed, and there's a buffet set out on the table. I scan it for suspiciously large amounts of whipped cream or chocolate sauce, but nothing seems out of the ordinary. I suppose they've already moved that stuff into the bedrooms, along with the raw oysters. I gag a little.

"Has anybody seen my parents?" I ask random people milling around the kitchen. "One's got short, black, curly hair, and kind of a grouch face, and the other one looks like he was beamed in from outer space?"

"Summer?" says Mom.

I spin around to find her and Dad standing side by side, holding paper plates full of food.

"Oh, thank goodness," I say, grabbing the plates out of their hands and dumping them into the trash. "We need to get you out of here."

"What are you doing?" shrieks Mom. "That was perfectly good potato salad!"

"The potato salad doesn't matter, Mom. What matters is getting you guys out of here while you're still dressed!" I start pulling them toward the living room.

"Of course we're dressed!" says Mom. "We're not supposed to try anything on while we're eating."

I stop in my tracks. *Try anything on?* I slowly turn around and look at them.

"Try anything on?" I ask.

"Like this," says Dad, smiling and unzipping his fanny pack. "I swapped one of my own neckties for this one. It's a Donald Trump!" He proudly unrolls the tackiest necktie I've ever seen.

I stare at him, uncomprehending, for several moments. Then I turn and walk back into the living room to take another look at the other guests.

Suddenly everything appears slightly less sinister.

Gil, over there by the sliding glass door, wasn't taking his pants off—he was trying a pair *on*. His girlfriend, Lorraine, is standing next to him with her hand on his shoulder, making sure he doesn't fall over. I look at the woman on the couch. She's removed the clear plastic stripper shoes, and is trying on a pair of sensible brown Birkenstocks. Gloria, by the bookcase, has a long-sleeved shirt on underneath the sweater that she pulled over her head. And Janice isn't wearing a bra, she's wearing a black bikini top (although, there really isn't enough of a difference between a bra and a bikini top to make me completely comfortable). But at least she's stepped behind a privacy screen before taking it off.

"You guys have been swapping…clothes?" I ask, walking back into the kitchen.

"There you are, Sum," says Graham, coming up next to me and putting an arm around my shoulders. "Look what I got." He's wearing a yellow, argyle sweater vest.

"They're swapping *clothes*, Graham," I say, shaking Mom's cardigan that's still in my hand. "*Clothes.*"

"I know. I realized it the second we walked in. If you hadn't taken off like that, I would have told you. I traded my shirt for this cool sweater vest."

"How?" I ask. "We've been here for five minutes!"

Graham shrugs.

"Graham? Summer?" Babette and John walk into the kitchen, drinks in hand, looking at us quizzically. "What are you two doing here? This is a private event for Sunset Swishers!"

"Sunset Swishers?" I ask.

Okay, maybe I did have it right the first time. Don't they always tell you to trust your instincts? Swingers, swishers, there can't be much difference. Maybe the clothing swap is just the beginning of it. Maybe Dad has to sleep with the wife of whoever used to own that ugly Donald Trump necktie.

"Haven't you ever heard of swishing?" asks Babette.

"God, no," I say. "What kind of websites do you think I visit?"

"It's all the rage," she says. "Swishing is when you get together with a group of friends, have a few drinks, some food, and then you—"

I clamp my hands over my ears. Graham pulls them away.

"—swap clothes and assorted household items."

Oh.

"Nadine told us about it because she used to live in New York," she continues. "That's where it originated. It's very economical for those of us on a fixed income. It's become so popular that Sunset Swisher events are by invitation only!"

"Roger and I have been trading golf shirts for years," says John.

Golf shirts. They've been trading golf shirts. No wonder John looked so blasé about the whole thing.

"So, you guys swap clothes?" I ask. "That's it? Just clothes?"

"Well, like I said, sometimes we swap household items. But that's really up to the host. What on earth did you *think* we were doing?" Babette laughs and takes a sip from her cocktail.

I look at Graham who's giving me another one of his looks. I'm not sure I've seen this one before—both of his eyebrows are raised and his cheeks are kind of puffed out. I'll take it to mean *You're on your own, sweetheart.*

"We, um, we thought you guys were swingers." I say, simply. "You kept making vague references to swapping things. So, we um, we thought you took my parents to a swingers party."

"Oy, Richard!" says Mom. "We're at a swingers party!"

"Did somebody say swingers party?" Roger comes up behind Mom, makes an obscene motion with his hips, and plucks a chicken wing off the buffet table. "Because that's not until Thursday." A glob of barbeque sauce drips off the chicken wing and catches in his chest hair.

"Where's your shirt?" I ask. "Why are you the only one strutting around here like David Hasselhoff?"

Roger clamps the chicken wing between his teeth, holds both hands in the air in a *sue me* gesture, and walks back into the living room. He returns a moment later wearing Graham's glow-in-the-dark shirt. Figures.

"Look, Summer," says Babette. "I'm sorry if you misunderstood me. But, my goodness! John and I would never go to a swingers party, let alone take your parents! Why would you even think that of us?"

Several reasons float through my mind—the excessive drinking, the live-like-there's-no-tomorrow philosophy embraced by all residents of Sunset Havens, the twinkle in her eye every time she jokes about swingers parties—but I can't actually say any of those things to my future mother-in-law.

"I'm sorry," I say. "I guess I just let my imagination run away with me."

"So, we're good then?" asks Graham, clapping his hands together. "Mystery solved? We should probably get going. Let these good folks get back to their swooshing."

"Swishing," says Babette.

"No, wait," I say, suddenly remembering one more thing. "How come Roger told Mom that she should *bring an open mind*? What would she need an open mind for at a clothing swap?"

Babette and John just look at each other and shrug. Roger can't answer the question because he's conveniently disappeared back into the living room.

"Maybe he thought I couldn't wear polyester," says Mom.

"What?"

"Some people are only able to wear cotton. Maybe he thought I needed an open mind in order to try synthetics."

"Geez, Mom. Do you seriously believe that? Roger only has one thing on his mind, and it's got nothing to do with what your clothes are made from."

Yes, I realize that I just spoke the same words my mother spoke to me on the cruise—*men only have one thing on their minds, Summer. S-E-X*. I suppose if Graham is starting to remind me of my father, it's only natural that I should turn into my mother.

"Oy, please," says Mom, without nearly enough conviction to satisfy me.

"Just don't swish anything you're going to regret, okay?" I give her a meaningful look. "Some things, once swished, can never be un-swished. Do you get what I'm saying?"

"Do you know what she's talking about?" Mom asks Dad.

"Babette," says Dad. "Is there any sort of return policy on swished items?"

"Oh, for Pete's sake," I mutter, grabbing Graham by the

elbow and hustling him toward the front door. "Let's just get out of here."

He has the decency to wait until we reach the street, before laughing at me for the entire rest of the night.

18

Just as Mom promised, all eight of us are back in the function room of The Lakeview this morning, drinking Bloody Mary's and eating brunch, while watching a band audition for us on-stage. It's not really an audition, though. I mean, we have no choice, these are the guys we have to use. Luckily for us, they're *fantastic*.

Mom totally saved the wedding.

It turns out that her mysterious phone calls yesterday were to her childhood friend, Eileen Maxwell—which explains why she was yelling at directory assistance, as she and Eileen lost touch years ago. Eileen is the mother of Tyler Maxwell, who happens to have been a runner-up on one of the early seasons of *American Idol*. I don't know how I could have forgotten about this. For weeks, Mom talked about nothing but Tyler's beautiful voice and how she and his mother used to have tea parties with their Nancy Ann Storybook Dolls (I don't know, Mom's pretty old). Anyway, for weeks she had me on the phone until eleven o'clock at night, dialing in my votes. At least she thought I was on the phone until eleven o'clock dialing in my votes. In reality I dialed in twice and went to bed.

Now Tyler Maxwell performs on cruise ships and lives nearby in Orlando.

He's just finished singing "Fly Me To The Moon," in a voice that sounds exactly like Sinatra. On short notice, he was only able to bring along a drummer and a trombone player, but he says that he can get the whole band together for Saturday night. It's unbelievable. I mean, the band I originally had was crap compared to this guy. Total crap.

"You really came through, Mom," I say. "This guy is amazing. I don't know how to thank you."

"Being allowed to help with the wedding is thanks enough," she says.

"Of course you're *allowed* to help," I say. "Why do you have to word it that way?"

"Maybe because you planned the whole thing without me."

Touché.

"I know," I sigh. "And I already apologized for it. Are you going to hold it over me forever?"

Of *course* she is. Who am I kidding?

"All I'm saying," says Mom, "is that I could have hired Tyler a long time ago. I told you he was talented. It's a shame he didn't win that *American Idol.* We certainly voted for him enough times."

"Right." I clear my throat. I'm sure he would have lost even if I had actually voted for him. I mean, it's not like he lost by four votes or anything.

"Eileen said it was *such* a close vote," says Mom. "Not winning really changed the entire course of his life. He fell into a deep depression after the show ended and didn't leave the house for *months.*"

Oh, geez.

"Well he looks great now," I say. "And if he'd won, he might not have been living here in Orlando, right? So, it was all for the best. For us, at least. Anyway, it was really cool that you were able to get him."

"You've never given me credit for being cool before," says Mom.

"That's because you're always afraid of being cool," chimes in Eric. "That's why you own so many sweaters."

"*See?*" says Mom. "I'm nothing but a joke to the two of you."

"What are you talking about?" he asks.

"I see the things you say about me on Twitter."

Eric's eyes widen. "You're on Twitter?"

"I told you I was cool. Your father and I set up accounts last year. We follow you, Dr. Oz, and the Center for Disease Control."

"I've sent six tweets!" says Dad.

"Oy, please." Mom bats her hand. "He makes me tell him what to type."

"What are your Twitter names?" asks Eric. He looks completely engrossed.

"MrBoopster," says Dad. "Because I like Betty Boop."

"Clearly," says Eric. "Mom, what's yours?"

She hesitates for a moment, glancing quickly at me and then back at Eric.

"EmptyNester123," she says.

Oh, man. That is *such* a Mom thing to do. She probably signed up for that name as soon as I told her I was planning the wedding with Babette. She knew that someday, somehow, I would find out about it, and I would feel guilty. Which I did, and I do. Mission complete.

"But what do you guys tweet about?" asks Eric, the sadness of Mom's screen name going right over his head.

"Is this really important right now?" I interrupt. "Look, Mom. I was wrong to have not included you and I'm sorry. But you're here now, and you've proven yourself cool...well, maybe not the part about following the Center for Disease Control on Twitter...but you get an A plus for Tyler Maxwell."

Mom smiles. "Thank you."

"You're welcome. Now, have a muffin." I push the basket across the table, along with the little bowl of butter packets. Mom's smile drops from her face like a ton of bricks.

"What? What's wrong?"

She unwraps a packet of butter and holds it up for Dad to see, squishing it out in front of his face. "Look, Richard. It's softened!"

"So, what?" I ask.

"That means it hasn't been refrigerated properly. Or maybe they gave it to us from *somebody else's table*."

One of Mom and Dad's greatest fears in life is of being given butter that once sat on somebody else's table. Mom likes her butter straight out of the fridge, rock hard, and totally unspreadable. She peers at it quizzically through her bifocals, as if the face of its previous owner is going to materialize on the golden foil.

"Did you know, Joan, that butter can actually go without refrigeration for several days?" asks Graham.

"Really?" asks Eric.

"Yep. Its fat to water ratio discourages bacterial growth."

"Interesting," says Eric.

"I thought so," says Graham.

"I hope this isn't how they handle the wedding food!" says Mom, ignoring the both of them. "Babette, did you tell the kitchen to make sure the steaks are well done?"

Babette looks like a deer caught in the headlights. "Oh. I, um, I believe Nadine said that they cook all the steaks medium."

Wrong answer.

"Oy! You need to specify well done or everybody will come down with food poisoning!" Mom marches off in the direction of the kitchen armed with the bowl of softened butters, and Babette hot on her heels.

She has a point. After Nadine switched my wedding cake to carrot, she probably requested that the steaks come out so rare they're grazing on the salad.

Ba-dum-ching!

"I like a good medium rare," says Graham.

"Too bad," I say. "You're getting it well done. Everybody is. Even if they ordered the vegetarian meal."

I'm slightly disenchanted with Graham at the moment. I talked to him this morning about my theory of Nadine being in cahoots with Francine to ruin the wedding. He looked at me like I was completely mental, and then actually had the nerve to defend her. He said that Nadine is working very hard on our *free* wedding—he always has to emphasize how free it is, as if this whole thing were my fault—and that he'd like to see *me* organize an entire wedding without making a few mistakes.

A few mistakes?

Sure, I might goof up the seating chart a bit—seat Aunt Esther next to her verbally abusive ex-husband or something—

but it would be a cold day in hell before I accidentally switched anybody's wedding colors to *bubblegum pink*. I'm sorry, Graham, but there is simply no excuse. The conversation ended with me storming out of the room, blathering something along the lines of *The truth shall set you free*! How that even relates to this situation, I have no idea. But when I start throwing bible quotes around, you know we're in a bad way. I was also still on edge over last night's Sunset Swishers party—still am, to be honest—and may have overreacted.

Anyway, here we are.

I head up to the stage and thank Tyler Maxwell for coming. Then I bring him over to Nadine who has a vendor contract waiting to be signed. I read it through to make sure she didn't slip in any funny business, such as a clause about every third song being "Who Let The Dogs Out," but everything looks good. Apparently legal jargon isn't in Nadine's bag of tricks.

"We'll see you on Saturday then," I say, smiling and shaking his hand. I give Nadine a stern look before heading back to our table. Mom and Babette still haven't returned. John looks totally bored. Dad's staring up at the light fixtures.

"So, what's on the agenda for the rest of the day?" asks Eric. "Cake testing? Open bar sampling?"

I snort. "If you think they threw open bar in with the free wedding package, you're nuts."

Eric freezes with a piece of muffin halfway into his mouth. "Are you serious?"

"Um, yeah."

He and Graham look at each other, then Graham looks at me.

"How come you didn't tell me this before?"

"I don't know," I shrug. "How come you didn't ask about it before?"

"I don't know," says Graham. "I just assumed a Blenderman wedding would have an open bar. I didn't think it needed asking about."

"I think a little chat with the wedding planner is in order," says Eric, pushing his chair back and standing up. "Shall we?"

"We shall," says Graham, and they head off to look for Nadine.

"I can't believe Babette didn't request an open bar," says Tanya. "I figured that would have been her number one priority."

"Oh, it was," I say. "She offered to pay for it too. But the thought of her and John's friends getting hammered on my wedding day grossed me out. Can you picture Roger on the dance floor with access to unlimited quantities of alcohol?"

"Nice try," laughs Tanya. "But it's happening now, missy. Whether you like it or not."

She motions toward Graham and Eric, standing in front of Nadine putting on some sort of pantomime performance. Graham is pretending to pour shots, while Eric pretends to throw them back. Then Graham does a little spin and pretends like he's juggling liquor bottles. He did that once with real bottles, back when we first started dating. We were hanging out at his condo one night when he came bounding into the room dressed in this purple sequined shirt, and referring to himself as The Amazing Blenderman. He put "It's Raining Men" on the stereo, grabbed a few bottles, and had me in hysterics right up until he dropped and broke a three hundred dollar bottle of Cristal. Still, it was a good night.

I smile at the memory, my annoyance at Graham quickly starting to dissipate.

"At least I can say that I tried," I say.

"You know," says Tanya, gently pounding her fist on the table. "If you'd only had the wedding back home—"

"Do not finish that sentence."

"Sorry," she says, smiling. "I'll change the subject. You know, you never did answer your brother's question. What *is* on the agenda for today?"

19

I bring Tanya with me for back up.

We told the rest of the family that we were going shopping for wedding night lingerie, which took care of the chance that anybody else would want to come along. Well, Graham still wanted to come, but I told him that it was bad luck for the groom to see the bride's underwear before the wedding. Now we have to swing by a Victoria's Secret on the way home, or whatever the equivalent is down here at Sunset Havens. Margaret's Unmentionables would be my guess.

Where we're really going is to Francine's house. I need to have a little chat.

We pull up out in front of the house and turn off the golf cart. A sign hanging from the lamppost reads *Francine & Frederick,* confirming that we're in the right place. All of the houses around here have them—*Francine & Frederick, Babette & John, Roger & Whoever's Drunkest.*

"Francine's a widow, right?" asks Tanya, looking at the sign.

"Yeah," I say. "But I don't know the etiquette for erasing your spouse's name from your lawn ornament."

"I can't believe you think this poor woman is out to get you," says Tanya. "She's probably just lonely."

I filled Tanya in earlier on my suspicions regarding Nadine and Francine, and I can tell that she thinks I'm a paranoid lunatic. Just like everybody else. That's okay, though. I don't need her to believe me. I just need a witness.

"Just because she's old, doesn't mean she's nice," I say. "It's a common misconception. Hansel and Gretel fell for it too, so don't feel bad."

"You're not going to *hurt* her, are you?" asks Tanya, furrowing her eyebrows and, if I had to guess, picturing the outcome of Hansel and Gretel (evil witch shoved into oven).

I hold my hands up in the air. "Do you see any weapons on me? No, I'm just going to ask her some questions and make a few things clear. I need her to understand that this behavior is unacceptable. I can't have these women ruining anything else. Mom only knows so many *American Idol* contestants."

"But you can't just go in there and start accusing her of things!" says Tanya, looking more horrified than when she thought I was going to cook her.

"Says who?"

"Says the rules of living in a civilized society!"

"Those rules don't apply to wedding planning."

"What if you're *wrong*, Summer? These are Babette's friends. Maybe you're skipping town after this weekend, but Babette has to live here with these people."

"That's her fault, not mine."

"That's it, I'm leaving." Tanya jumps out of the cart and starts walking briskly back up the street.

"Okay, okay!" I shout. "I'll be subtle! Geez."

Tanya stops walking, turns around, and reluctantly gets back in the cart.

"If we're going to do this, we can't just barge in there and start questioning her," she says, firmly. "We need some sort of excuse for being here. Any ideas?"

I shrug. "We could invite her to the bachelorette party."

"Seriously?" Tanya laughs. "You think this woman is sabotaging your wedding, and now you're going to invite her to your bachelorette party?"

"Well, it's the same night as Graham's bachelor party. At least if she's with us I'll know she's not out, hiding in the bushes, taking incriminating photos to send me in the mail."

"She could hire a photographer to do that. And if Graham's actually doing something incriminating, wouldn't you want to know?"

I narrow my eyes, the wheels in my head spinning. God, there are so many levels of craziness involved with planning a wedding. And being in a relationship.

"I was *kidding*!" says Tanya, seeing the look on my face. "Man, you really have lost it. Look, I know you don't want to hear it, but if you'd just had the wedding back home—"

"I *know*," I say. "I know it and I'm being duly punished for it. My mother hates me, and I'm about to interrogate an old woman. I've come to terms with the fact that Martha Stewart Weddings isn't going to be contacting me any time soon." I jump out of the golf cart. "Coming?"

Tanya rolls her eyes and follows me grudgingly up the walk to Francine's front door. I ring the bell. I'm not even sure she's home right now, but it's four o'clock so there's a good chance that she's primping herself for the early bird dinner. After a few seconds, we hear somebody fiddling with the bolt and the door swings open. Francine is standing there, wrapped in a pink bathrobe, her hair in curlers.

"Girls!" says Francine, looking from Tanya to me. "What a nice surprise."

"Hi, Francine," says Tanya. "I hope we didn't disturb you."

"Not at all. I was just putting on my face for dinner. Come on in."

We follow her into the house, where it smells like the Marlboro Man was holding a bake sale. On the table is a plate of freshly baked chocolate chip cookies.

"Would you girls like a cookie?" asks Francine.

"Yummy," says Tanya.

"No, thanks," I say, shooting Tanya a look. No way was Francine in here innocently baking cookies. I don't think that she'd go as far as poisoning me, but I'm not convinced she wouldn't toss in a box of laxatives. Not that she knew we were coming. Still, a girl can't be too careful behind enemy lines.

"Suit yourself," says Francine, picking a cookie up off the plate and taking a bite. Okay, fine. Maybe they're not laced with laxatives. *Or,* maybe Francine is constipated. Just call me Sherlock.

"So, what brings you girls by?" she asks, finishing her cookie and lighting up a cigarette.

"We, um, we wanted to invite you to my bachelorette party," I say, trying my best to sound genuine. "It's this Thursday."

"This Thursday?" says Francine. "Isn't that the same night as Graham's bachelor party?"

I shoot Tanya a triumphant look. Why would she know the date of Graham's bachelor party if she wasn't planning on causing trouble?

"Yes, that *is* the same night," I say, taking a step forward and looking her straight in the eye. "How did you know?"

Francine shrugs. "Babette may have mentioned it."

"Is that so?" I take another step closer, searching her face for signs of guilt.

Francine takes a long drag from her cigarette and takes a step forward. We're standing about a foot apart. Then she blows a cloud of smoke into my face.

"Take a picture," she snaps. "It lasts longer." She bursts into laughter and grabs her pack of cigarettes off the kitchen counter. "You gals want a smoke?"

"No!" I say, waving my hand in front of my face and backing into the living room. "Gross."

"Your loss," says Francine. "Anyway, count us in."

"Us?"

"Can't Janice come too?"

"Oh, right. Sure, Janice can come too."

"Great," says Francine. "I know she'd hate to miss a strip show."

"Excuse me?"

"We're going to a strip show, aren't we?"

Leave it to Francine. Babette won't tell me what she has planned for my bachelorette party, but I told her specifically that I don't want any male strippers. I should mention that this will be my second bachelorette party. I already had my real one a month ago when Tanya and a few of my girlfriends flew down to Miami, while Graham and his friends took off to Vegas. Graham being Graham, however, thought that we should each have a second party in order to include our parents. Maybe it's just me, but the words *parents* and *bachelor party* don't ever need to go together.

But, I went along with it because we'll probably just end up dancing in one of the town commons, wrapped in feather boas. Pretty much a typical night for Francine and Janice.

"No," I say, shaking my head. "No strippers." I wander further into the living room, looking at all the photographs on the mantel above the fireplace. There are several photos of a young man—high school senior picture, wedding photo, several smaller framed photos of young children. Tanya joins me, looking at each one.

"Is this your son?" she asks.

"Yes, that's my Joseph. He's the spitting image of his father, God rest his soul." Francine lets out a long, hacking cough. "I haven't seen him or my grandchildren in over a year, though."

"A *year*?" says Tanya. "That's awful. Why don't they visit?"

"Joey is very busy," says Francine, waving her hand in the air. "He owns a hotel up in Connecticut that's not doing so well. One terrorist cell sets up shop in your penthouse, and suddenly nobody wants to stay there anymore. It's not like they didn't find the explosives in time." Francine shrugs and sits down at the kitchen table.

Tanya and I just stare at her, wide-eyed.

"The last time I saw him, I told him he should just set the place on fire for the insurance money." She jabs her cigarette toward us. "Now there's a scam that never gets old."

"Anyway," she continues, "He can't just drop everything to bring the kids down to visit their boring, old grandmother, can he?"

"Boring old grandmother?" I say, raising an eyebrow. "Do they know what their boring, old grandmother's been up to with boring, old Gil in his golf cart?"

"Summer!" hisses Tanya.

Francine just laughs. "They most certainly do not. But they can't expect me to just sit around waiting to *die* now, can they? No, I've done enough of that. I've got to do something else to pass the time." She takes another drag from her cigarette. "May as well be Gil."

"So, Francine," I say, leaning my elbow on the table and propping my chin up with my hand, all casual-like. "Speaking of things you've done to pass the time. When Graham and I were picking out his wedding tuxedo, he mentioned that he hadn't worn a tux since the time he took you to something called the *Senior Prom*. What was *that* all about?"

Francine stares into the distance for a few seconds—probably picturing Graham, all handsome in his tuxedo, fastening a corsage onto her bony wrist—and then she starts to speak.

20

"It was about six months after my Frederick passed away, and I'd been having a real tough time adjusting to life on my own. Freddie may not have been the smartest guy in the world, or the best looking, or the wealthiest—"

Geez. The woman can't even give her dead husband a compliment.

"—but he was always *there*. Do you girls know what I mean?"

Tanya and I nod in agreement. At least Freddie had one thing going for him.

"After he passed on," she continues, "Babette was great, always bringing me food and taking me out to dinner, trying to introduce me to new people. But it was hard being alone. Even in The Havens, when you're surrounded by people, you can still feel very alone." She looks up at the ceiling and blows a long, disgusting stream of smoke into the air, tears welling up in her eyes. Tanya reaches across the table and takes Francine's hands in hers.

Oh, God. Did I just make an old woman cry? That wasn't my intention. I mean, Francine isn't supposed to have *feelings*.

To be honest, I've sort of started viewing her as one of those Ringwraiths from *The Lord of the Rings*—draped in cloaks, made of nothing but smoke and shadows and evil. I clear my throat to help move things along. Maybe we just need to get past the weepy part. Francine looks up at me, sniffles, and continues.

"One day everybody started talking about this Senior Prom that was going to be held in the rec center. You could wear fancy gowns and tuxedoes and corsages, and there was going to be a live band. A real to-do. Well, obviously *I* had nobody to go with. The last time I went to a prom was back in fifty-seven with my Frederick. I certainly wasn't ready to starting dating again. But still, a small part of me couldn't help wanting to go. Everyone was talking about it, on and on, and Roger made such a scene asking—oh, who was it? Lillian? No. Maybe Carol—anyway, he got up in front of everybody at Bingo and asked whoever it was if she would do the honor of accompanying him to the Senior Prom."

I cough. "Roger did a prom-posal?"

"A what?"

"Never mind."

"So, what happened?" asks Tanya. She looks completely riveted.

"Well, one day Babette came over to my house, and she brought her son, Graham, along with her. I'd never met him before, but he was visiting for a few weeks and Babette was showing him off to all of her friends. Well, I *never*." Francine leans back in her chair and waves her hand in front of her face—not to fan away the cigarette smoke, but to cool herself from the hotness of my fiancé. I crinkle my nose.

"Love at first sight, eh?" says Tanya. I kick her under the table.

"He was quite the tall drink of water," she says. "And the *colors* he had on. I'll never forget. It was a Hawaiian shirt, but instead of flowers, the pattern was made up of *lizards*."

I stifle a laugh. I know that shirt.

"My goodness," she continues. "He lit up my front steps like an angel. And then he started showing up at all the different activities—shuffleboard, pickleball, water aerobics. He said he couldn't just hang around being lazy when people three times his age was being so active. Besides, he loved talking to the residents and hearing their stories. One day he said to me, 'Frannie, I would like to take you to that Senior Prom.' And I said 'Oh, please. What's a young man like you want to go to a boring old thing like that for?' And he said, 'I'm on vacation at a retirement community, what the hell else am I going to do on Saturday night?'"

Francine laughs and rocks back in her chair. "He saw how much I wanted to go—even though I wouldn't admit it—and he wouldn't take no for an answer. Oh, the time we had. Babette took me out shopping for a dress, and Graham bought me a corsage and decorated his golf cart with streamers. We danced the night away. I don't think I need to tell you ladies that every other woman at that prom was green with envy."

"Graham's a special guy," says Tanya, smiling.

Francine nods. "It was after that night that I started taking an interest in other men again, without feeling guilty about Freddie. I started participating in more activities and spending more time next door with Janice. Pretty soon we were dying our hair and joining the Twister Club. Graham helped me see that I have a lot of life left to live, and that there are a lot of new things still out there waiting for me to try."

Francine shrugs and stubs out her cigarette. "That's all I've got."

I just stare silently at her, feeling like a total ass. Graham taught me a similar lesson one time on a cruise ship. Not about dying my hair or joining the Twister Club, but about living my life and not being afraid to leave my comfort zone. And what happened to me? I fell in love with the guy. How can I blame Francine if she developed a little crush on him, too?

I sigh and sit back in my chair. Maybe I was wrong about her. Maybe everybody has been right all along and I'm overreacting. Maybe—

That's when I see it.

Through the sliding glass door, I have a clear view into Francine's tiny back yard. Not far from the door is a small flower garden surrounded by bricks. And right there in the front, one of the bricks is missing.

"Oh. My. God," I say, standing up and walking slowly toward the door.

"What?" asks Tanya, sounding nervous.

"Out there," I say. "The brick. There's a brick missing. Look! There's a space where there used to be a brick! Where's the brick, Francine? Huh? Where's the brick?"

I don't care if I promised Tanya I'd be subtle. I mean, there's a brick missing from Francine's garden. I pull out my cell phone and snap a photo. Take that, Graham! Take that, kid at Ben & Jerry's! Proof! I never should have doubted myself. I have the urge to shake the photo around triumphantly, like a Polaroid, but all I have is my phone. I shake it anyway.

Francine walks calmly over beside me, and peers out the door.

"You're right," she says. "Shame. The landscapers must have kicked it out by accident."

"Landscapers?" I say. "Good one. Tell me, Francine. Where were you two nights ago?"

"I believe I was at Redwood Corral," she says. "Just like you. You *saw* me, remember?"

"Oh, I remember," I say. "I did see you. I see *everything*, Francine. And I *know* everything." I sound like a total madman. I know I do. But I don't care. She did it. She *did it*!

Francine just shrugs and lights up another cigarette. "Are you finished? Or do you want to go into my bedroom and take some photos of my bloomers? Maybe there's proof of something else that you think I did." She glances at Tanya and breaks into a cackle of laughter.

"Gross," I say. "No. I would, however, like to know what you and your pal Nadine plan on doing with my band this Saturday night. You know, the one you guys canceled, then booked, so I couldn't hire them back? Will they be coming by the house? Playing romantic songs for the two of you?" I'm speaking in this mocking tone that I've never heard come out of my mouth before. I might be possessed.

"Summer!" says Tanya. "Stop it!"

"I've got news for you, *Frannie*," I continue. "The wedding is still on. Oh, that's right. Graham and I are getting married this weekend. Not *you* and Graham. *Me* and Graham. We're getting married, and then we're going on our honeymoon, and then it's happily ever after to us!"

"Summer!" Tanya grabs me roughly by the hand and pulls me towards the front door. "I am so sorry, Francine. Forgive us. Summer is just a little stressed over the wedding. Delirious, actually. Yesterday she asked me if I'd seen the kangaroos on the golf course! Anyway, enjoy your evening. See you Thursday!"

Tanya slams the door behind us and practically throws me into the golf cart. She demands the keys and starts up the engine in as angry a manner as one can start up the engine of a golf cart.

"What is *wrong* with you?" she asks once we've started driving.

"Me?" I ask, offended. "What about her?"

"Oh, come on! She's a lonely old woman who owes a great deal to Graham. That's it. Same as you, in case you've forgotten. And you do realize it's not just *your* wedding she'd be ruining, but Graham's too? Why would she do that to him?"

"Because she's thinking long-term, Tanya. She doesn't care if she hurts him a little now. Once the smoke clears, she thinks he'll realize that she's the one he wants to be with."

Tanya laughs. "Don't tell me that you're *threatened* by a seventy-five year old woman?"

When I don't answer, she stops laughing and looks at me incredulously. "I'll tell you what, Summer, Graham's a good looking guy. If you can't handle him getting attention from women old enough to be his grandmother, then I don't know how long the two of you are going to last."

I sit back huffily in my seat and roll my eyes. Of course I'm not *threatened* by Francine. I don't think Graham's actually going to dump me for her. That's not the point, why can't anybody see that? The point is that Francine is a total sociopath.

But there's no use in arguing. Nobody is going to believe me—not Tanya, not Graham, not Babette, not the kid at Ben & Jerry's. Nobody. My only hope is to make it to Saturday without anything else going majorly wrong. What more could she do, anyway? Maybe now that Francine knows I'm on to her, she'll knock it off.

Five more days. That's it. Five more days, and then we're off to Jamaica, and out of this God forsaken retirement community.

Well, at least until Christmas.

21

It's early evening when Tanya drops me off at the Blenderman house, and I find Graham sitting quietly in the living room, drinking a beer. He doesn't have the television on or anything. He's just sitting there drinking, and I can't shake the feeling that Francine called and tattled on me the second that I left her house.

"Hey," I say, dropping my purse on the floor and joining him on the couch. "Whatcha doing?"

"Just waiting for you," he replies, taking a sip of beer and glancing at my purse. "Shopping not go so well?"

Crap. I totally forgot we were supposed to have been going shopping. I could have at least brought in a bag stuffed with tissues or something.

"Um, yeah," I say, laughing nervously. "Who knew it would be so hard to find youthful underwear in a retirement community?"

Graham nods slowly. "It's okay. You still have some time."

"Right. Of course." I nod along with him. "I'll find something. Definitely."

"Perfect."

We sit in awkward silence for a few seconds. I clear my throat.

"So, um, where is everybody?"

"Out to dinner," says Graham.

"All of them? Without us?"

"I told them we'd meet up with them later."

"Oh."

Yep. Francine definitely called and tattled on me. Graham's acting way stranger than normal, and his phone is on the coffee table instead of in his pocket, which is highly suggestive of the possibility that he just took a call. If I checked his recent call list I would probably see her name in there. Maybe if he goes to the bathroom I can—

No!

Did I seriously just consider snooping on Graham's phone—a few days before our wedding—to see if a seventy-five year old woman called him? What kind of a monster am I turning into? Tanya was right—Graham and I aren't going to last very long if I don't trust him. But the thing is, I *do* trust him. I fully trust that if Francine called and tattled on me, Graham would come right out and tell me. Just as Graham should trust that if I ever did anything crazy—say, flip out on an old woman whom he thinks of as a grandmother—that I would come right out and tell *him*. And I will. We just need to get the conversation started, instead of wasting time with all of this awkward small talk. Once we clear the air, we can go on our merry way as a united front, together forever in holy matrimony.

I hope.

"So, Graham," I say, twisting the end of a blanket around in my hand. "Have you, um, have you talked to Francine lately?"

"Francine?"

"Yeah, Francine." I tilt my head to the side and flip my hair behind my shoulder. "You know, older gal, black hair, smoker's cough?"

Graham puts his beer down on the coffee table and turns to look at me, the corner of his mouth pulling up into a half smile. "Do *you* think I've talked to Francine lately?"

I look him straight in the eye. Just be honest, Sum.

"Maybe?"

Baby steps. Sue me.

Graham stares back at me, then puts his arm around my shoulder and pulls me close so that his lips are right up against my ear. Normally this type of thing would be kind of hot. But at the moment, he's giving off more of a Hannibal Lecter vibe, which isn't really my thing.

"You know, Sum," he whispers. "It's perfectly normal to be overwhelmed and stressed out before a wedding. What's not okay is accusing senior citizens of committing acts of vandalism."

I stop breathing and feel the color drain from my face (which, up until this moment, I thought was only a figure of speech). I don't know why I feel so stunned. I mean, I know what I did. And I pretty much already knew that Graham knew what I did. But, hearing it straight from his mouth is just *so* embarrassing. I pull away and look down at the floor, still twisting the corner of the blanket around in my hand.

"I've been researching those loopholes that you mentioned the other night," he continues. "And it looks like maybe we *can* move back down here after the honeymoon. That way you'll have a nice, quiet place to relax and recuperate."

Hold on a minute, is he *threatening* me?

I look over at him, trying to determine if he's joking. He's looking at me with the Blenderman twinkle in his eye, but there's something else in there too. Maybe it wasn't exactly a threat. It was more of a plea. A plea for me to return to the land of the sane before I cause any serious damage.

I know he's right. I really do. I flipped out when I should have behaved more like the mature adult that I am, and I regret that. But *come on*. I'm the one receiving threats and pleas, while Francine gets to go around wreaking havoc without a single repercussion? Old people can get away with anything, I swear. Without another word, I pick my purse up off the floor and whip out my phone.

"I may have flipped out," I say. "And I'm sorry about that. But you know what? I got proof. *Look.*"

I shove the phone triumphantly into his hand. He studies the photo of Francine's garden for a few seconds, and then puts my phone down on the coffee table.

"What are you doing?" I ask. "Did you even look? There was a missing brick! I may have acted like a lunatic, but it was *justified.*"

Graham sighs. "Look, Sum. Francine did call me tonight. And she told me that you and Tanya showed up at her house, and that you invited her to your bachelorette party—which was very nice, by the way—and then she told me what else you said."

"And?"

"And I apologized for your behavior. These women are my mother's friends. You can't just go around pointing fingers."

"But I—"

"*But,*" Graham cuts me off, "I also told her that I didn't

believe my fiancée would act that way unless she had good reason."

I whack him in the chest. "So you *do* believe me!"

"I *would* have believed you, if the police hadn't stopped by the house right before Francine called."

If I thought all of the color had drained out of my face a minute ago, I was wrong. I feel the last few ounces of blood drain all the way down to my flip-flops.

"The police?"

Did Francine seriously call the police on me? I mean, all I did was yell at her a little. I didn't even touch her. At least I don't remember touching her. Does it even matter? It's not like she has security cameras around the house. Still, I start frantically replaying the whole scene in my mind.

"They were following up on that report we filed," says Graham.

Oh, right. I start breathing somewhat normally again.

"They've found a witness," he continues. "A neighbor across the street was taking out her trash when she heard the glass break. It was dark, but she saw a golf cart in front of the house and she caught the vanity plate. Guess what it said?"

"I don't know," I say. I'm really not in the mood for guessing games.

"Zumba God. "

My jaw drops. "*Flavio?*"

Graham nods.

"Flavio is in love with me?"

"Close. Flavio is in love with *me*."

I just stare at him, speechless, for a few seconds. Then I burst out laughing. "How does he even know you?" I ask. "Have you been going to secret Zumba classes without me?"

"No!" says Graham. "I only went that one time, with you and my mom. It was love at first sight, I guess. Remember when he flung his sweaty towel and you freaked? Well, he told the police that he was aiming for *me*."

My eyes widen. "So now he's *stalking* us?" An image of Graham and I being gunned down by a Zumba instructor in a neon spandex bodysuit flashes through my mind. What a depressing way to go.

Graham shrugs. "He's been arrested and charged with criminal mischief, which should nip things in the bud. We're leaving soon, anyway. If he turns up in Boston, then we'll talk restraining orders."

"Criminal charges?" I say, shaking my head. "Restraining orders? I can't take you anywhere."

Graham smiles. "So, do you think that maybe you owe Francine an apology?"

Ugh. He's right. I acted like a total monster. Not that I'm convinced she's innocent of *everything,* but I suppose I should be the bigger person.

"I'll track her down tomorrow," I say, "I'll tell her I was—" I'm interrupted by my phone ringing.

"Hello?"

"Summer? This is Nadine."

"Hi, Nadine." I give Graham a confused look. "What's up?"

"I'm sorry to bother you, but I was going over the binder for the *other* wedding that I'm planning, and I realized that—silly me—the person who called the other day, you know the one who wanted to change her colors to bubblegum?"

"You mean the same one who wanted to replace her band with a bassoon trio?"

"Yes, that's the one! Well, it turns out that it wasn't *you* after all. It was the *other* girl."

"The other girl?"

"Yes. Silly me! It's quite the juggling act planning two weddings at once! I do apologize."

Two weddings at once? Right. Odd that she should call tonight, full of excuses about some mysterious *other girl*, right after my run-in with Francine. It's almost as if she was warned that I was onto her. I can tell you one thing, that apology to Francine is off the table.

"Summer? Are you there?"

"I'm here," I sigh. "It's fine, Nadine. Thanks for the call." I hang up and lean back against the couch.

"She called to apologize," I say to Graham. "She says that she changed all that stuff because she had me confused with some *other girl*." I air quote the words.

"That was nice of her," says Graham, smiling at me. "So, everything's good now?"

"Yeah," I lie. "Everything's good."

Okay, maybe it's not a total lie. I mean, Francine knows that I'm onto her and seems to be nervously attempting to cover her tracks. Maybe everything really is good now. Maybe from this point on the wedding will go off without a hitch.

Graham puts his arm around my shoulders and I let myself sink into him. "You know what I think we could use?" he says. "A break from Sunset Havens. A reality check. Every so often you need to drive through those gates and see that the rest of the world is still out there. You need to see *children*. You remember children, don't you?"

"Vaguely," I say. "What's your point?"

"My point is that we should all take a little day trip tomorrow to have some fun and clear our heads."

"That is a good idea," I say. "And my parents would probably like to see more of Florida than just golf courses. Maybe we could take them to the beach?"

"The beach is nice," says Graham. "But there are beaches everywhere. No, I'm thinking about the one place that is unique to Florida."

My eyes widen and I suck in my breath. He can't mean—

"I'm just so excited," he whispers.

And he is. That's the thing that I both love and hate about Graham—that he really, truly is.

22

The Hartwells are going to Disney World!

The Blendermans are going too, of course, but they've already been about a billion times so I didn't think it warranted an exclamation point. Graham is manic over Disney. It's not like he wears Donald Duck sweatshirts or anything, but he loves the whole magical theme park vibe. So do his parents. The three of them could have their own show on the Travel Channel where they go on all the rides wearing Go-Pro cameras and give each other high-fives. They actually spent a few minutes discussing the idea before we got on the highway.

Eric and I never got to go to Disney when we were kids. I have a feeling that Dad would have liked to, but Mom always seemed to have some personal vendetta against it. When asked why we couldn't go, she always said that Disney World was full of "man-made crap." Fair enough, if we were seasoned travelers who spent their summers at the Grand Canyon or Yellowstone. But, typically, we spent our vacations in New Hampshire, at the same motel Dad used to go to when he was a kid. For fun, we would hike out to this big rock in the woods. Boise Rock, it was called. A man hid under it during a snowstorm about three hundred years ago, after killing his horse and wrapping himself in its hide—kind of like Luke Skywalker with the Tauntaun, but in reality, nothing at all like that. Anyway, the point is that while my friends were going down Splash Mountain, I was having my picture taken in front of a rock.

Mom always liked to tell me that when I grew up and had kids of my own, I could take them on vacation wherever I wanted—a cheering thought for a six year old who can't envision life beyond the next five minutes. To be honest, we probably just couldn't afford to go to Disney World. My mother, feeling badly about that, probably converted her emotions into bitterness and rage against the happiest place on Earth. It makes perfect sense, if you know my mother.

Shortly after we started dating, Graham found out about this transgression of my youth and had tickets to Orlando booked the next day. Eric still hadn't been either, so we brought him and Tanya along too. It was the most amazing week of man-made crap that I've ever experienced. After the trip, Graham vowed that we would someday return with the entire family in tow.

I also made a vow, which was for that day to never, ever come.

But my luck has run out—made evident by the eight of us crammed into Eric's Escalade, headed straight for Orlando like a guided missile. John and Babette are seated in the back row wearing fluorescent yellow t-shirts that say *Blenderman Family Magical Reunion 2012* (don't ask) across the front. John's also wearing a baseball hat with Goofy ears flopping out the sides. I point this out for descriptive purposes only, and not to poke fun, since Graham and I are wearing a matching set of bride and groom mouse ears.

Mine are white with a little tiara on top and a short veil in the back. His are black with a tiny little top hat between the ears. Tanya's wearing Little Mermaid themed mouse ears complete with dinglehopper, and I won't even tell you what Eric's wearing because it's just *that* lame. Okay, fine. It's a full-on Captain Jack Sparrow hat with braids. I've been staring at the back of it the entire time we've been driving, and it hasn't gotten any less weird.

Ironically, the only normal looking people in the car right now are Mom and Dad.

Dad is completely giddy over this trip. Ever since Graham pounded on Mom and Dad's bedroom door at five o'clock this morning, announcing that we were hitting the road in exactly one hour, he's been totally onboard. He's already agreed to go on Space Mountain, Thunder Mountain, and have his picture taken with Cinderella. So far, Mom's mentioned heatstroke, sunburn, and diarrhea. The only ride she's picked out of the brochure is—insert eye roll—the Hall of Presidents. Graham has this delusion that by the end of the day he'll have converted my mother into a Disney fanatic. I think he'd have better luck getting her to attend Comic Con dressed as Darth Maul.

Time will tell.

Eric parks the car, and we all walk to the bus stop where a tram will pick us up to drive us to the transportation center. Once we're at the transportation center, we can take either the monorail or the ferry to the main gate of the Magic Kingdom. I haven't conveyed any of this information to Mom and Dad yet. They know that a tram is coming, but that's it. I have a feeling that the words "transportation center" might throw them into a tailspin. So, one thing at a time.

There are kids *everywhere*. We're at Disney World during school vacation, so I knew what we were in for. But still, it's shocking to the system to actually witness it for myself. I try not to laugh as a child, standing directly behind Mom, lets out an ear-piercing shriek. She doesn't even have time to give the child a dirty look before another one plows into her calf with a baby stroller. She steadies herself on Dad's arm. Poor Dad. He's carrying the backpack equivalent of The Duffle. It's filled with bottles of sunscreen and water and basically the same supplies needed to colonize Jupiter.

Once we're on the tram, Graham puts his arm around my shoulders and gives me a squeeze. I smile up at him. We look like absolute fools, but I couldn't be happier. After last night, I've come to realize that no matter what anybody says or does, they're not going to stop me and Graham from getting married this weekend. They can change my colors and cancel my band. They can even burn down the venue if they want to—we'll just get married out on the town common. After a good night's sleep, everything just seemed so much simpler this morning. There are logical explanations for all the bad things that have happened, so there's no reason for me to keep obsessing over these old women. I'm going to stop assuming the worst about everybody, and I'm going to try my hardest to be a better person. And I'm doing all of that starting right—

Hang on a second.

"Mom, what are you doing?"

"What?"

"I'm not putting on a *sweater*!"

"But your arms are bare!"

"Because it's ninety degrees outside!" I push the cardigan roughly back into my mother's lap.

Starting right now.

***

Well, here we are. The Hartwells, together as a family unit, on Main Street USA. I never thought I'd see the day.

Mom and Dad are staring slack-jawed up at Cinderella's castle like it was dropped out of the sky by extraterrestrials. I think that despite all of her complaining about Disney and its "man-made crap," Mom's actually impressed by the place. I had no question that Dad would be. I mean, as soon as we walked through the gates he was blown away by a group of guys dressed as maintenance workers who spontaneously broke into song and dance. He kept saying, "I thought they were janitors! I thought they were taking out the trash!" about a hundred times. It was adorable.

"Let's get a photo!" says Babette, dragging all of us into the middle of the road where a Disney photographer is waiting with a camera. We all cram into an awkward clump with Cinderella's castle in the background.

"Where are you guys from?" asks the photographer.

"Boston," answers Graham.

"They're from Boston," clarifies John. "My wife and I live down here now, at Sunset Havens."

The photographer moves the camera away from his face. "Sunset Havens, huh? I hear that's the second happiest place on Earth!"

"Damn right it is," says John, with pride. "Twelve championship golf courses, thirty-two executive courses—"

Here we go.

"—and as a resident you receive *free* lifetime membership at all of the country clubs."

"I hear you guys have a huge problem with sexually transmitted diseases. That true?"

My jaw drops and several families turn to look at us. Are employees allowed to ask that kind of thing at the Magic Kingdom? I glance over at John. He looks irate.

"That is absolutely not—"

"Stellar," interrupts the photographer, no longer listening. "Okay, everybody say *mouse ears*!"

"Mouse ears!"

We take one more picture in which all of us are forced to give a thumbs-up sign, before dispersing back to the sidewalk. I have a feeling John made a slightly different gesture at the camera.

"Unbelievable," he mutters. "That photographer should be fired. I'm filing a complaint as soon as we get home. Ridiculous. *One* study by the Department of Health and Human Services and the whole place gets a bad reputation."

"What's he talking about?" asks Mom. "Sexually transmitted *what*?"

"Diseases, Mom," says Eric. "You know—the clap, the herp, cra—"

"Eric!" I shoot him a look, willing him to shut up. But it's too late.

"Oy! Richard! They have sexually transmitted diseases where we're staying!"

"Where?" asks Dad. "Here? There are *sexually transmitted diseases* here?" He says the words in the world's loudest voice, and starts looking wildly up and down Main Street. A woman standing about twenty feet away quickly leads her daughter in the opposite direction.

"Sshhh!!" I say. "Will you keep your voices down? He was talking about Sunset Havens. But it's not even true. Is it, John?"

"Absolutely not," says John. "People just make those thing up because…because they're jealous. That's all."

"The Department of Health and Human Services makes up statistics because they're jealous?" asks Mom.

"Well, no," says John. "Not exactly. I just meant that—"

"I really wish you had disclosed this information to us before we came down here, Summer," says Mom, giving me an accusatory look.

"Why would this even matter to you? Aren't you and Dad in a monogamous relationship? Or is there something I should know?" I cough the name *Roger* into my hand.

"Of *course* we are," says Mom. "But what if we catch something from a toilet seat?"

"You've never sat on a public toilet seat in your life, Mom."

I really can't believe we're having this conversation right now. In the Magic Kingdom.

Mom, unable to come up with a rebuttal to my point about the public toilet seats, digs a large bottle of hand sanitizer out of the backpack. Her and Dad start applying it liberally, slathering it on all the way up to their elbows. There will be, without a doubt, some seriously offensive Lysoling of the Blenderman's toilet seats when we get back to The Havens tonight.

"So," says Graham, unfolding and shaking out a park map. "Where to first?"

23

We're slowly working our way counterclockwise around the park. There's zero chance that we'll make it all the way to Adventureland before one of us murders the other and/or collapses from heat exhaustion, but we're making a noble effort. Even Mom.

We've temporarily split up the group so that Graham, John, and Eric can take Dad on Space Mountain, while Tanya, Babette, and I take Mom on some of the tamer rides. Basically, we bought her coffee and a muffin at Starbucks, force-fed her a few motion sickness pills, and then dragged her on Dumbo. And you know what? She *loved* it. She said she felt like she was flying! Seriously, has Mom never gone on an amusement ride before?

Don't answer that.

After Dumbo, we took her on Peter Pan's Flight and It's a Small World. Peter Pan she was okay with, but It's a Small World—with its psychedelic array of multi-cultural dolls, singing in gleeful harmony—was more man-made crap than she could handle. By the time we step off the boat she's rolling her eyes and saying *Oy, please* so much that I consider calling an ambulance.

"I'm supposed to enjoy watching them sing and dance, while they're busy stealing all of our jobs?" she asks. "Oy, please!"

I'm not even sure which country she's referring to, but I give my most apologetic, *She's from a different generation*, smile to all of the families around us.

"The point of the ride is to celebrate diversity," I say. "To show that we're all people, no matter what country we're from."

"And that *song*," she continues, ignoring me. "Couldn't they come up with any other words?" She starts singing, *It's a small world after all*, in a high-pitched, mocking voice. A little boy looks at her and starts to cry.

I start leading us more quickly toward Space Mountain where we're meeting the guys. We only have to wait a few minutes before Dad steps through the turnstile with his white hair standing on end, and a euphoric look in his eye. He's fist pumping the air and letting out these weird primal screams.

"Dad!" I say. "How was it?"

"Incredible!" he says, breathing heavily. "Incredible! It was incredible!"

"Incredible, huh?"

"That's the word I was looking for!"

"He did awesome," says John, clapping him on the shoulder. "He's a seasoned professional now."

"I always knew you had it in you," says Eric. "Mom, you want to give it a go?"

Mom staggers back a few steps, shaking both hands in front of her.

"Where to next, Rich?" asks Graham.

"Millennium Force!" yells Dad.

I laugh. How does Dad even *know* about that ride?

"Wrong park," says Graham. "Maybe next vacation. How about we hit Thunder Mountain after lunch?"

"Yes! Yes!" Dad says. Now he's pacing back and forth like a caged tiger. Geez. I guess that's what happens when seventy years of built up adrenaline finally gets released into your blood stream.

"Let me get you some water," says Mom. She's been looking at Dad like he's some sort of hero back from war. She leads him over to a bench, and makes him lean back while she pours water directly into his mouth. Half of it runs down his chin and onto his shirt. After he drinks, he grabs Mom by the shoulders, giving her the most passionate kiss I've ever seen in my life. At least between my parents.

Speaking of which, gross.

When they finally pull apart, Mom is staring at him all starry-eyed and giggly, like she's seeing him for the first time. Is that really all it took to put the spark back into their marriage? I don't even want to think about what would happen if Dad ever parachutes out of an airplane.

"My life flashed before my eyes, Joanie," says Dad, water still dripping from his chin. "And you were there, right at the center of it. You were all there!" He motions to me and Eric and Toto and Auntie Em. "You've made me the luckiest man on Earth."

"Oh, Richard," sighs Mom.

"I know that things have been a little dull between us lately," he says, squeezing Mom's hands. "But that's all going to change, starting right now. It's going to be like our honeymoon all over again!"

Once again, gross.

"I never thought *you* were dull," says Mom. "I just have no interest in any of your boring hobbies."

"Well, that's going to change, too," says Dad. "We'll find more hobbies that we can do together, you name it! But first, what do you say we kick off our honeymoon with lunch at Cosmic Ray's Starlight Café? It'll be just like our first date."

I'm not sure why Mom and Dad's first date would have been at an intergalactic hamburger joint, but hey. I just like to see them happy.

***

After lunch, we take a break from the heat in The Hall of Presidents, which is basically a fifteen minute educational film followed by speeches from the animatronic doppelgangers of all current and former Presidents of the United States. I've already fallen asleep twice. I'm awakened the second time by Dad attempting to climb over me.

"What are you doing?" I whisper.

"I need a men's room," he says, not at all in a whisper.

"Right *now?*"

"It's an emergency! I should never have eaten those galactic cheese fries!"

Oh boy. I sink down in my seat as I hear Dad trip over the rest of the people in our row. Then there's a brief flash of light as he finds an exit and opens the door.

"How long is this thing?" I whisper to Graham.

"Just a few more hours."

"Very funny."

The film finally ends, and the curtain goes up to reveal all of the robotic presidents sitting and standing onstage. They're very realistic looking, especially from far away.

"George Washington," reads the voiceover. "John Adams…Thomas Jefferson…"

My head is starting to nod again when I hear a door open and shut. I lift my eyelids halfway, and see one of the presidents walking slowly across the stage. Weird. I don't remember that part the last time I was here. I suppose they may have made some updates. The animation certainly looks state of the art.

But…why is he wearing shorts and a fanny pack? I force my eyelids all the way open, just as he stops in front of Abraham Lincoln and turns to face the audience.

"Joan?" he calls out, shielding his eyes. "Summer?"

Shit.

He may have hair like Martin van Buren, but that's no president. That's my father.

"Richard?" shouts Mom. "What are you doing up there?"

"Joan?"

"Over here!" Mom stands up and waves her arms in the air as Dad tries to squeeze behind Barack Obama.

"I can't see you!" he yells. "The lights are too bright!"

We watch in awed silence as President Obama topples into Ulysses S. Grant, who is seated at the table beside him. As Grant falls to the ground, he takes the table along with him, and all of the plates and cups that one would assume were bolted down, slide onto the floor with a tremendous crash. The table also takes down Zachary Taylor, who lands with a sickening thud just before his head rolls off.

In one fell swoop, Dad's assassinated three presidents.

I feel like one of us should go up there and try to help, but I'm frozen to my seat. We all are. As the house lights come up, Graham is the first to snap out of his trance and starts making his way toward the stage. He's quickly overtaken by several Disney employees rushing the stage like Secret Service.

"Sir! Step away from the presidents!"

"You are not allowed up there, sir!"

"I don't even know how I got here!" says Dad, throwing his hands in the air and sending John Quincy Adams' head ricocheting off the back wall. "The doors outside the men's room aren't marked properly!"

"Sir, there is no entrance to this area located near any of the restrooms."

I bite my lip. Where exactly did Dad go to the bathroom?

It's then that the curtain, which had begun lowering from the ceiling in order to hide the carnage unfolding onstage, lands directly on Dad's head, engulfing him in folds of red velvet. He flails his arms around, adding Millard Fillmore to his list of casualties, before pulling the entire curtain down from the ceiling.

Amidst cries and shouts from the audience, a voice comes over the loudspeaker—*Due to technical difficulties, this attraction is temporarily closed. Please exit the theater now.*

"Don't have to tell me twice," says Eric. He grabs Tanya and hightails it to the exit. I hang back to assist Mom, carefully avoiding eye contact with John and Babette. A classic attraction for over forty years, and Dad's destroyed it. Perhaps it's best that the Hartwells hadn't made it to Disney World any sooner.

We exit the theater along with the other guests who are excitedly throwing around phrases such as *Probably on drugs* and *Millions of dollars in damages*. I try my best to ignore them. What do they know? Dad was only on drugs that one time in Bermuda. Speaking of which, when I see Dad on a bench outside, answering questions from security, I'm reminded of the time cruise security thought he was a terrorist trying to blow up the ship. This is almost becoming a Hartwell family tradition. Maybe next year we can go to Washington D.C., and Dad can hop the fence in front of the White House.

We keep the rest of the day pretty low-key, since Dad is understandably shaken up. I would have been okay with heading straight home, but the Blendermans insist that we stay and go on some more rides.

Once we've squeezed in the Jungle Cruise and the Haunted Mansion, it's close to dinner time and we all finally seem ready to call it a day. Only, Graham keeps looking at his watch and seems to be herding us further into the park, rather than toward the exit.

"Maybe we should get something to eat before we leave," I say. "It's going to be a bit of a car ride, and I don't want to have to stop for fast food. You don't want to know what happened the last time Mom and Dad ate at Sonic."

"Uh, yeah," says Graham, distracted. "Mom, what do you think about having dinner here tonight?"

Babette clears her throat.

"That sounds lovely," she says. "Like something out of a *fairy tale*." She shoots Graham a look filled with so much meaning that she may as well have given him an exaggerated wink.

Graham looks at his father. "What about you, Dad?"

John clears his throat. "I think that it sounds like a *tale as old as time*."

I raise my eyebrows. Since when does John say things like that? Why are they acting so weird?

"Summer, dear," says Babette. "How would you like to *be our guest* for dinner tonight?"

"Um, yeah. Sure," I say. "I could eat."

"No, really," says John. "We'd love for you to *be our guest*."

"You're paying? Great. Let's go."

"Summer," says Graham, holding out his elbow. "I would really love it if you would *be our guest*."

Okay, this is getting ridiculous.

"Yes, I get it," I say. "I heard your parents, and I'm totally onboard with consuming some food. Let's *go*."

But the three of them just stand there looking at me. I can tell Graham's trying his hardest not to laugh. That's when it hits me.

"Wait a minute. Be our guest? As in—" I stop mid-sentence and let my jaw drop open. "Are you serious?"

The Be Our Guest restaurant is themed after Beauty and the Beast—my all-time favorite movie—and takes reservations six months in advance. Last time we came to the Magic Kingdom it was still being built.

Graham smiles and I give him a gentle shove.

"I thought this trip was spontaneous!"

"It was," he says. "It's just that the grandmother of the General Manager happens to live in—"

"Sunset Havens," I finish for him, laughing. "I should have known."

"Reservations for eight. Six o'clock. Happy wedding, Sum."

GRAHAM

24

So, maybe I didn't exactly plan this day trip on the spur of the moment. Maybe I didn't contact the General Manager's grandma this morning. Maybe I contacted her six months ago because I needed to arrange slightly more than a dinner reservation for eight.

I needed to arrange—

Well, let's just say that Summer is going to kill me. First she's going to refuse to marry me, *then* she's going to kill me. Then she's going to find herself a nice, quiet bookworm of a husband who never forces her into embarrassing situations.

But, on the off chance that she doesn't end our relationship, it's going to be completely worth it. This is going to become one of those moments that go down in family history. The descendents will still be talking about this over Thanksgiving dinner, 2066.

It's going to be epic.

Not a lot of fiancés would go through all of this trouble. I hope Summer keeps that in mind when she's the center of attention and wishing I would drop dead.

In any event, it's show time.

The costume is a lot hotter than I thought it would be. Heavier too. And it's damn near impossible to see anything on the ground in front of me. I'm being led into the ballroom by Candlestick and Teapot. Candlestick is friendly enough, but Teapot seems a little put out. Not that I can see his face, but I didn't like the way he bumped me with his spout a minute ago. As long as he doesn't push me down a flight of stairs, I'm not too worried.

Summer thinks I've gone to the men's room.

As we step through the ballroom doors, I can already see Mom and Dad smiling at us. They're in on the whole thing since I needed to make sure this trip was set firmly in the itinerary for this particular day. Beauty and the Beast is Summer's favorite movie of all-time and I've had this idea brewing in my head ever since I heard that the restaurant was being built. Actually, it's been brewing ever since we watched the movie together and Summer remarked that the Beast gifting Belle with her own private library was the most romantic gesture she'd ever seen. At that very moment I vowed to one day show up that hideous man-beast by gifting Summer with something even better than a fictitious library.

Unfortunately, I never came up with a better idea. I mean, I did come up with some ideas that would have blown any woman right out of the water, but none of them were very *Summer*. Even if I flew her by helicopter, Christian Grey style, to some remote, tropical location, it still wouldn't have equaled the Beast and his God forsaken library. So I did what any loving boyfriend would do—I decided that I would simply *become the Beast*. All I needed to do was pull a few strings, zip into a costume, and take her for a spin around the ballroom in front of a few hundred strangers. And what better time to make it happen than three days before our wedding?

Summer's staring at her menu and hasn't even noticed us yet. I wonder what she thinks I've been doing in the men's room all this time. As I walk across the dance floor, I wave to the other guests who assume that I'm a regular part of the entertainment.

It's pretty fun.

I start off with a very regal, kingly sort of a walk—the way I imagine a bad ass Beast might strut around his castle, in his killer blue and yellow tuxedo (I've got to get me one of these). But then, about halfway across, I do a spontaneous hop-skip in the air which brings a wave of laughter from the kids. Encouraged, I do a spin and then the Moonwalk. Then, because I've never before Moonwalked in enormous furry feet and a twenty pound head, I trip. But, I recover. I steady myself. I give a big, furry thumbs-up to the crowd and they respond with applause. Maybe I should consider a career change.

Teapot doesn't seem to agree. He turns to me and shakes his entire body back and forth.

Right. There were a few rules I had to agree to before the higher-ups granted me permission to step inside a Disney costume, and I suppose I must be breaking a few of them. I leave Teapot and Candlestick on the dance floor, and make my way over to Summer's table. I thought the out-of-character dance moves might have given me away, but she checks the time on her phone and glances toward the ballroom doors. She's either wondering where I am, or doing everything possible to avoid eye contact with the costumed character heading straight for her. As I continue forward, I finally catch her attention. My beastly eyes lock onto her face and I can sense that she's getting nervous. She looks down. She opens something on her phone. I can almost hear the words *Go Away* broadcasting out of her head.

I stop behind her chair and put my furry paws on her shoulders. She laughs nervously and shrinks down into her chair.

Did I mention that she hates being the center of attention?

I put a furry paw on top of her head and gently pat it, messing up her hair a little.

She shrinks down some more.

I tap her on the shoulder. She turns her head left to look at her mother. I tap her on the other shoulder. She turns her head right to look at Tanya. I put both my paws on her shoulders again, and give her a little shake.

"I think he likes you," says Mom. "Maybe you should turn around."

There's a short delay, in which I imagine Summer shot my mother a filthy look, before she gives in, turns around, and looks up at me. It's hard not to laugh at the look on her face. But I can't. Rule number one of getting into a Disney costume is that you must not speak. Not ever. So, I watch in silence as Summer looks up at me with the same expression of disgust that Belle gave to the Beast when she thought he was merely a repulsive, terrifying monster with no redeeming qualities.

I hope she appreciates the irony, once she's speaking to me again. Whenever that is.

I hold out my paw, and she reluctantly takes it. I lead her—sorry, *drag* her—out onto the dance floor where a waiter hands me a small tiara. The lights are dimmed, and the classic song from the movie begins to play. I plunk the tiara awkwardly on her head, pushing the combs down into her hair. Then I step back and take a low, beastly bow.

Summer's face is quickly progressing from light pink to beet red, but at least the look of disgust has melted into a nervous smile. I still have no idea if she realizes that it's me in here. Judging by the fact that she hasn't yet punched me in the stomach, I'm thinking that she hasn't. I hold out my paw again, and she takes it. Then we start to waltz around the room. She falls right into step because we took ballroom dance lessons only last month.

She thought we were preparing for the wedding.

As we spin around the room, she still looks self-conscious and embarrassed, but at the same time, I can tell that she's enjoying herself. The ballroom is an exact replica of the ballroom from the movie—above us hang three crystal chandeliers and a vaulted ceiling painted to look like the sky. And even though it's still daylight here in Florida, the floor to ceiling windows present an evening view of mountaintops and falling snow. Mission to create a moment that Summer will never forget—complete. When she smiles up at me, she looks more beautiful than any Disney princess I've ever seen.

Even Jasmine.

As the song ends, we come to a stop in the center of the dance floor. I take a step back and give her another deep bow. I can tell that she's eager to return to her seat, probably dying to tell me about the horribly embarrassing thing that happened to her while I was enjoying myself in the men's room. As she turns to leave, I put a paw on her shoulder and spin her back around.

Then I take my head off.

"Hey, Sum," I say. "Surprise."

Summer just stares at me, wide-eyed. Then she covers her mouth with her hand.

As I put the Beast head down on the floor, one of the waiters hands me a microphone.

"Testes, testes, one, two, three?" I tap the microphone and clear my throat. "Hi, everybody—parents, kids, anthropomorphous teapot and candlestick. You probably think that I'm about to propose right now. But, the truth is, this lovely lady and I are already engaged. We're getting married in three days, actually. She thinks I'm in the men's room right now."

The audience applauds and laughs in a nervous, *I hope this isn't going to involve us*, sort of way.

"When I did propose," I continue, "I kept it very low-key, because I knew that would be the only way to actually catch Summer off-guard. I knew that she'd be expecting some big, showy, extravaganza of a thing, because that's the kind of guy that I typically am. And you might think that I'm doing this now because I'm trying to make up for that. While that's ninety-five percent true, it's not the whole reason."

I walk over and put my arm around Summer's shoulder. She looks warily down at my furry paw.

"Summer here, she loves books. She's a lot like Belle in that regard. She particularly loves stories that take place outside of our world, be it the Shire or Hogwarts or the Planet of the Apes— which I didn't even realize was a book until Summer and I started dating." I clear my throat. "Anyway, I've never fully understood the fascination—and seriously, Summer, it's a lot of pressure always having to compete with Time Lords and wizards and beasts with intimidatingly large libraries—" I nudge the Beast head with my foot and Teapot lets out an audible sigh.

"—but, what I do understand, is that her fantastic imagination is a huge part of what makes Summer the woman that I want to marry. And because of that, I wanted to give her a wedding present that she would remember for the rest of her life. Not just a fancy honeymoon, or an expensive piece of jewelry, but something surreal. Something magical. So, Summer, while I may not have the largest library of any man on Earth, for a short time today, you get to dance with the Beast at the most magical place on Earth."

The audience applauds.

"I'm just sorry it had to be in front of so many strangers," I add.

Summer laughs and wipes the tears from her eyes.

"Shall I put my head back on now?"

She nods.

If I'm not completely misreading the situation, it appears that she might still be planning to marry me. I drop the mike, put my head back on, and take her for another spin.

25

Like I said, this trip to Disney was not quite as spontaneous as I made it out to be. It was so un-spontaneous, in fact, that we ended up spending the night in a block of luxury rooms at the Grand Floridian that I've had reserved since January. It was so un-spontaneous, that I had our bags Federal Expressed to the hotel so that Summer wouldn't suspect anything.

Graham Blenderman is full of surprises, and the Beast thing was only half of it. The second half involves our bachelor and bachelorette parties. Well, our *second* bachelor and bachelorette parties. We already had our first ones back home last month—I had the classic bachelor party in Vegas, while Summer and her friends took off to Miami. When we returned home, we confirmed that we were both in one piece and no further questions were asked.

But why stop at one? Why stop at one, when we're this close to the—

Epcot

World

Showcase

If you are unfamiliar with the Epcot World Showcase—first, my condolences—and second, it is a beautiful thing. Surrounding the World Showcase lagoon are eleven pavilions representing eleven different countries. When one sets out to "Drink Around The World," they are in for tequila in Mexico, sake in Japan, a pint in the UK…you get the picture. It's the perfect place for a bachelor party with one's parents and parents-in-law. You get the security of Disney World, but with plenty of booze. And no threat of strippers. Not that I'm averse to strippers. It's just that Summer's dad is going to be with us this time around. Not that *he's* averse to strippers. We just never need to see them together at the same time and in the same place. Even my own father didn't accompany us to Vegas, which is why I thought a second bachelor party would be a nice gesture.

Summer wasn't totally onboard with the second bachelorette party idea, but she'll come around. Sometimes she needs a little push—just ask her about that tattoo on her ankle.

Anyway, I've worked the details out with Eric and my mom. I even arranged to have Summer's bridesmaids fly in a few days early to surprise her. Dad's invited a few of his golf buddies, who offered to give Francine and Janice a ride out here—Summer invited them, if you recall. So, we've got a decent sized group.

Dad and I are meeting his golf buddies in the parking lot of the hotel this morning. As a bus with the words *Sunset Havens* on the side pulls in—and Dad starts flagging it down—the words, *we've got a decent sized group,* start to sound a little ominous.

"Um, Dad?" I ask, as the bus lets out a loud whoosh and pulls to a stop beside us. "Did the casino bus make a wrong turn or something?"

Dad snorts and shields his eyes. With a loud screech, the front doors to the bus fold open "Nope. This is them. There's Roger behind the wheel. Hey, Rog! You old dog! I didn't know you had a license to drive a bus!"

"License?" Roger shrugs.

My eyes widen as Dad lets out a loud guffaw.

"Dad, I thought you invited *a couple* of guys?"

"I did. And then, you know, a couple of guys invited a couple of other guys and then those guys invited a couple of the girls. Then word got around all the clubs. You know how it is at The Havens."

He's right. I *do* know how it is at The Havens, and I should have made it clear that it couldn't be that way this time. This was supposed to be a subdued affair. Summer in no way, shape, or form wanted her mother attending her Miami bachelorette party. Like I said, the reason for having this second round of parties was for our parents to be included in what they missed out on the first time around—only here, in Epcot, where there couldn't possibly be anything to cause embarrassment. But now—

"You're telling me that bus is filled with people?" I ask, pointing at the tinted windows. Outlines of curly hairdos are visible, bobbing around above the seats.

Dad shrugs. "The more the merrier, right?"

I take a deep breath. *Breathe, Blenderman.* Maybe it isn't so bad. If we didn't want our parties crashed by a bus full of retirees, then we shouldn't have had our wedding at a retirement community, right? What did Summer expect? True, she didn't actually want this party at all. But, on the other hand, if she'd just sucked it up and had the wedding back home, Francine wouldn't be stepping off of a bus right now wearing a necklace made out of plastic penises and a pair of New Year's Eve glasses that spell out the year two thousand.

And…is she already sauced?

She's wearing a pair of pink, knee-length shorts with high heels, and she looks a little wobbly. She's followed off the bus by Janice and Gloria. Nadine is there too. All of them are smiling and waving at me, wearing these shirts with rhinestones smattered across the front. *Why limit happy to an hour?* it says across the front of Janice's. *Grandma's Sippy Cup,* says Francine's, underneath three wine glasses. *One tequila, two tequila, three tequila, floor,* says Nadine's. Nice. There's also a whole slew of women I don't even recognize.

"Um, Dad?"

"Yeah?"

Before I figure out what exactly I should even say to him, I notice that all of the men getting off the bus are wearing blue shirts. I watch as Roger pulls a pill bottle out of his back pocket, puts a tablet into his mouth, and pops his collar. He shakes the bottle in the direction of the women, like a Cialis maraca. That's when I realize that Dad is also wearing a blue shirt.

"Dad," I continue, "you didn't take any…"

"What?"

"Never mind."

I stop myself again. It's none of my business. What's done is done. The more the merrier is the only attitude to take right now—although I'm not sure I can instill the mantra into Summer within the next hour.

"Thirty minute bathroom break!" shouts Roger. "Then it's back on the bus, party people! We'll meet you over at Epcot," he says to Dad. Then they do this bizarre sort of grunting chant, grabbing each other by the shoulders, and bobbing their heads in opposite directions.

"What the hell was that?" I ask, as Roger heads off in the direction of the restrooms.

"Rog and I were in the same fraternity back in college!" says Dad. "I was at UMass and Rog was down at Penn State, but we were both Pi Lambda Phi's. Remember how I told you they used to call me the Blendermeister? Well, he was the Chugmeister! You know, because his last name is Chugstein? Small world."

So, here's the thing.

Summer has probably led you to believe that I have no qualms about her parents and my parents spending a week together. And up until about five minutes ago, she would have been right. Up until five minutes ago, I'd always found my parents to be relatively normal people. A little heavy on the cocktails and the golf, but for the most part, normal. Then Roger got off of that bus and Dad morphed into the Blendermeister, and it suddenly hit me that while I may find Summer's parents amusing—and under normal circumstances I might feel that a strand of plastic penises around the neck would do Joan a world of good— I actually have an overwhelming desire to impress my future in-laws.

I had the same odd feeling in my stomach when Eric handed out the *Wanted: Free Shots and Lap Dances* t-shirts that he made for all of us. I've been so damn nonchalant about everything—constantly rolling with the punches and reassuring Summer that everything is no big deal—that I didn't realize until about five minutes ago that I would very much like to appear worthy of their daughter. No, I don't want to just *appear* worthy of their daughter, I want to *be* worthy of their daughter.

Which, deep down, I know that I am. But do *they* know it? I always assumed that they did. Summer's always claimed that her mother is half in love with me. But wishing that she were thirty years younger so that we could date, is different than finding me an acceptable match for her daughter. I heard Joan used to have a thing for Marlon Brando, but I'm pretty sure she wouldn't have wanted him taking Summer out for drinks.

Besides, we're in the home stretch now. These last few days before the wedding could change everything. I know that it *shouldn't*. But, we're talking about the Hartwells, here. Joan Hartwell, who thinks that only assholes get tattoos and that only moral degenerates ride motorcycles. And Richard Hartwell, whose craziest life story involves crashing a scooter into a flock of chickens. Why I couldn't have had this epiphany earlier, I don't know. All I know is that I don't want them thinking their daughter is marrying into a family of moral degenerates. A family of—

Oh, Jesus.

Nadine's pulled something obscene out of her purse. She puts the end of it into her mouth, puffs her cheeks out, and blows. My eyebrows are sky high before I realize that it's a party horn. A flesh-colored party horn in the shape of a—

Breathe, Blenderman.

Thirty years of nonchalance, down the drain. I can feel it all unraveling. Every senior citizen that steps off that bus is like another nail in my coffin. And it's all my fault. I could have ended on a high note, waltzing their daughter around the Beast's castle last night like some sort of superhero. But no, I was wooed by the World Showcase, and look what happened.

I take a deep breath and stare up at the sky. It's a beautiful day here at the happiest place on Earth. I couldn't have picked a better place to have my first nervous breakdown. Maybe this is just part of my initiation into the Hartwell family. Maybe after this disastrous party is over, I can look at Joan and say, "I may be a moral degenerate, but I had a nervous breakdown this morning!" Then Joan will say, "Me too!" and we'll high five each other. The thought calms me down some.

It'll be fine. As soon as I say the words to myself, a very simple solution comes to me. The Sunset Havens bus is meeting us at Epcot, and since the rest of us are taking the monorail directly from the hotel, I simply won't tell Summer until we get there.

26

"Try the grey stuff, it's delicious!" says Eric. Then he bursts out laughing. He's never going to let me live that Beast thing down. Never.

"That's not even a Beast quote, dumbass," I say, leaning against a post and checking the time on my phone. "That was the candlestick."

We're at the monorail stop outside our hotel, waiting for our ride. Summer is giggling on a bench with Tanya and her friends, blissfully unaware that half the population of Sunset Havens will be meeting us shortly. Richard and Joan are nearby, dressed more for a day of hiking the Sahara Desert than a day at Epcot Center. Joan even has one of those battery operated fans hanging from a cord around her neck.

Me? I'm wearing a bright pink *Wanted: Free Shots and Lap Dances* t-shirt. Eric had them made in an assortment of colors which, when we were in Vegas, would have been awesome. But here in front of Richard and Joan, I feel like a major tool. Needless to say, the ladies aren't too happy with the shirts, either. I've been reminding them at regular intervals—first every thirty seconds, and now down to a sparse twenty minutes—that none of us are likely to find a lap dance anywhere in Epcot Center, even if we were actively looking. Which we're not. Every time I say the word *lap dance,* Joan looks at me like I've bashed her across the face with a shovel.

Of course, now that the Sunset Havens bus is here, the chances of each of us receiving a lap dance just skyrocketed. But, it's too late to change clothes now. We're going to split up anyway. The men and the women, I mean. Not me and Summer.

I hope.

Summer looks over at me, and I give her a wink.

Who ever thought I would get married, anyway? Graham Blenderman was never the marrying type. I dated a supermodel once, did you know? She's married to Tom Brady now. Those were the days. Party all night, sleep all day. Rinse, repeat. I never used to be involved in these situations. The kind that belong in some sort of ridiculous goofball comedy. How did this *happen*?

I take a deep breath, and I smile as I look at Summer. Who am I kidding? I know exactly how this happened. Even at my most carefree, I wasn't as happy as I am with her. I wouldn't trade these goofball scenarios for anything. This family is the spice of my life. I knew it back in my party days, too, when I'd bring assorted girlfriends over to the house during the holidays, and spend all of my time watching Summer out of the corner of my eye. I lived for the times her parents said or did something bizarre, and she'd give me that *look*. She may have regretted never moving out of that house, but I sure didn't. I liked that she was always there, always drawing me back home. And without Eric, I most definitely wouldn't have her. So, I owe him, I suppose—

embarrassing neon t-shirts and all.

"*Tale as old as time…*" sings Eric in a falsetto. He's leaning on the other side of the post, quickly losing all of his brownie points.

"Teapot."

"So does the Beast actually say anything?"

"Of course he does."

"Well, what does he say?" asks Eric. "I need something to work with here."

"I don't *know*. I've seen the movie *once*. You realize I did that whole thing yesterday for your sister, right? I don't have some bizarre sort of Beast fetish where I've been waiting my whole life to dress up in his clothes."

There's a short pause.

"But you liked the blue and yellow tux, right?"

"Obviously. I custom ordered one last night."

Eric settles back against the post, satisfied that all is once again right with the world.

If only that were true.

***

I need to pump some drinks into the entire Hartwell family, and fast. That's the other solution that I've come up with. It seems like a decent one. We've just arrived at the World Showcase and are hanging around Mexico while Dad waits for notification that the bus has arrived. I keep meaning to tell Summer before they get here—I really do owe her the heads-up—it's just that your fiancée is supposed to be mad at you *after* the bachelor party, not before it even starts.

That's where the drinks come in.

"Why are you *looking* at me like that?" asks Summer, shrinking back a few inches. I've just bought everybody a round of frozen margaritas and have been casually—or at least I thought it had been casually—encouraging her to take larger and larger sips.

"Like what?"

"Like you're deranged. Like you're a murderer waiting for his victim to swallow the poison."

I clear my throat and try to relax my face. "I just want to make sure you're having a good time."

"We just got here. Take it easy."

"It's never too early to start." I look around for Joan and Richard and find them sitting on a bench, each holding an untouched frozen margarita. "Joan! Rich! Drink up!"

"Oy, please," says Joan.

I turn to Summer. "Why did your mother just 'oy please' me?"

She shrugs. "She probably thinks you're peer pressuring her to drink. She *hates* that. And she has a point. What's wrong with you today?"

"Nothing. I'm just excited to get my bachelor party started."

"Clearly." She eyes me suspiciously over the rim of her drink as she takes another sip. I look down at my watch, and with my other hand, gently tip up the bottom of her glass. She shoots some margarita out of her mouth as she laughs.

"Ole!" says Eric, plunking a huge sombrero onto my head. He walks off again, plunking two more onto Dad and Richard.

"He must have spent over a hundred bucks on sombreros," says Summer.

"Can't say that's the worst way he's ever spent his money."

"At least the outfit is complete now," she says, looking me critically up and down. "That's for sure."

"Believe it or not, the shirts are a bit much, even for my taste."

"You can't mean the colors?"

"No, the colors are amazing. It's the saying that's borderline juvenile."

"Borderline?" Summer snorts out some more of her margarita. "Will you look at my father? He looks like a complete lunatic."

"Blame your brother."

"Oh, I do," she says. "That's why I need you to please watch out for my father today. I know it didn't go so well the last time I asked, with the golf cart ending up in the lake and everything. But please, don't let him do any shots. Eric is useless. Everything's a joke to him. He'll think it's funny seeing Dad drunk. But I don't want him to end up in the ER again. I need you to fling Dad's shots over your shoulder when nobody's looking, if that's what it comes to."

"You want me to babysit your father?" I ask. "This is my bachelor party, Sum."

"Actually, this is your second bachelor party," she says. "The one you decided to have so that our parents could be included. So, yeah. You need to babysit my father. You know how he gets when he's had a few drinks or is, you know, high on medical marijuana."

"Oh, I know," I say. "I've seen his tattoo."

"Exactly," says Summer. "And I think that experience back in Bermuda gave him a taste for the wild side. It wasn't two months after the cruise that he got pulled over for his first speeding ticket. And you saw him yesterday after Space Mountain."

"He's a wild man, Sum." I smile. "Okay, fine. I'll do my best. I planned this party at Epcot for a reason, though. What's the worst that could happen?"

She doesn't respond, but I can almost hear the whoosh of a hundred different disasters running through her mind.

"Never mind," I say. "He'll be in good hands. Trust me."

"Thank you," she says. "And you're right. A least we're away from Sunset Havens and all those crazy old people."

"Gang's here!" announces Dad, holding up his phone. Half his margarita is already gone and his sombrero is on crooked. I look over at Richard and Joan. They still haven't had a sip, and Joan has pushed Richard's sombrero way too far back on his head, yarmulke style.

Okay, then. It's happening. They're coming.

I'm reminded of a scene from *The Lord of the Rings*. The fellowship is deep inside the Mines of Moria, when they hear the distant sound of drumbeats. *They are coming,* says Gandalf. He is, of course, speaking of orcs coming to kill everybody—not a bus full of frail elderly people hopped up on erectile dysfunction medication—but the similarities are there.

"Gang?" asks Summer, looking at me questioningly. "What's this about a *gang*?"

"Dad's golf buddies," I say. "And, you know, Francine and Janice."

"I wouldn't exactly call that a *gang*," she says, crinkling her nose.

Oh, Sum. If you only knew. Which you will, very soon.

I see them now, over Summer's shoulder. They're coming through the crowd, and the crowd is parting like the Red Sea. But instead of Moses leading the way, it's Roger in khaki shorts and New Balance sneakers, and a pair of sunglasses that look like two plastic pineapples. He's also wearing one of those helmets with the cans of beer on either side of his head. Only, he's made his own labels for the cans, so that they both say *Fart Juice*.

In one last attempt to delay the inevitable, I pull Summer in for a kiss.

Too late.

"Where's that bride?" barks Francine.

Summer pulls away from me, eyebrows raised. She turns around, prepared to find only two, relatively manageable old ladies. Instead, she's met with a mob of at least forty men, women, and fart juice. Without another word, she turns back to me. She opens her mouth to speak, but is interrupted by Roger. He's grabbed a pair of maracas off of a display rack and jumped into the center of the group. He throws his arms out and shakes his shoulders from side to side.

"Which of you assholes is ready to *party?*"

"I am!" shouts Richard.

Joan's margarita crashes to the ground. Summer's face has frozen into an expression of surprise and horror. *Surprised horror* is how I will refer to it later, when we're all having a good laugh about this. Tanya clamps a hand over her mouth.

"You heard the man!" shouts Eric. "It's party time!"

Roger and Dad start up the fraternity grunts again, sloshing Dad's margarita all over the ground and knocking into the display of sombreros. Then Eric grabs Richard and *they* start doing something similar—bobbing their heads back and forth over each other's shoulders, until Richard loses the rhythm and cracks his forehead square into Eric's.

I flash Summer what I hope is an innocent, *what are you gonna do?* kind of a smile. She flashes me a Joan Hartwell look of death. I'm also getting one from the original Joan Hartwell, so it's pretty safe to say that my time in this world may be coming to an end.

27

Fortunately, Summer and I don't have much time to argue before Mom whisks all of the women off toward Canada, and Eric starts leading the guys in the opposite direction toward Norway. Summer's still giving me the look of death as Nadine drapes her in rainbow colored boas and they're swallowed up by the crowd.

Once she's out of sight, though, I start to breathe easier. The fact that my future father-in-law seems excited for the day takes a load off my mind. Summer was right. Under his timid exterior, and with a couple of sips of frozen margarita under his belt, Richard's a wild man. As long as he takes it slowly, this could end up being a bonding experience for us.

I walk up beside him and throw my arm around his shoulders.

"So, Rich," I say, "what do you want to do first?"

"Shots!" he shouts.

"Excuse me?"

"You asked what I wanted to do first. I want to do shots."

Shots. Great. It's not like Summer asked me to do *one* thing.

"Why would you want to do shots?" I ask.

"Because Roger said that I haven't lived until I've tried a flaming Dr. Pepper."

I roll my eyes. "Roger is an idiot. You don't want to be like him."

"But he's so *tanned.*"

I shake my head and press the palm of my hand into my forehead. "Look, Rich. I don't think shots are such a good idea. Especially flaming ones. Why don't you stick with mixed drinks? I'll buy you a Canto Loopy in China."

"A canto what?"

"A Canto Loopy. Cantaloupe juice and vodka. You'll love it."

"Lame!" shouts Roger, wedging himself between me and Richard. "What kind of a *man* drinks cantaloupe? More like canta-*nope*! Am I right?"

"I think he's right," says Richard, nodding in agreement.

"Damn straight I'm right! Now, let's get us men some shots!"

"Shots! Shots! Shots!" We're suddenly surrounded by a pack of chanting blue shirts.

"Roger, it's still early. It's like—" I check my watch, "It's *twelve o'clock*. The park doesn't close for nine more hours. We've got to pace ourselves. *We've got to pace ourselves!*" I shout that last part to the pack of blue shirts, but they can't hear me over the chanting.

"Pace ourselves?" says Roger. "Pacing is for puss—"

"*Thank* you, Roger," I cut in. "It's just that not everybody here has the same tolerance as you."

He looks at me blankly.

"You know about tolerance, right?" I ask. "Low tolerance, high tolerance—"

"Low tolerance is for puss—"

"Okay! Never mind. Look, my point is that not everybody here is going to last the day if they don't pace themselves."

Roger rolls his eyes and points to his helmet. "Tell it to the fart juice!"

I shake my head. "Why would I tell it to the fart juice? What does that even *mean*?"

He looks at me as if the answer were obvious. His eyes, at least what I can see of them through his plastic pineapple sunglasses, are bloodshot. Then he turns, lifts one leg in the air, and lets one rip. "Any questions?" He throws his head back and laughs. "A round of Aquavit for everybody!" The pack of blue shirts cheers.

This is going well.

"Hey, Graham! Take our picture!"

I take my eyes off Roger and Richard and turn around. It's Eric, standing with his arm around a tall, blonde woman in Norwegian costume.

"Not a good idea, man," I say. Eric's no cheater, but cameras and bachelor parties are never a good mix. I learned this in Vegas after a photo of myself, backstage at the Britney Spears show at Planet Hollywood, made its way onto Summer's Facebook feed.

By the time I turn back, Richard's holding a shot glass up in the air and Roger's chanting *Chug, Chug, Chug!*

Shit.

I leave Eric, jog over, and grab the shot glass out of Richard's hand. Then I down it. Then I take the shot glass that Roger was holding out to me, and I down that one too. Well, Sum, I might end up flat on my face tonight, but at least your father will be feeling good in the morning.

"You like?" asks Eric's Norwegian friend, coming up beside me.

"Nydelig!" I say.

She smiles approvingly and heads back into the crowd.

"I can't believe you still speak Norwegian," says Eric, looking wistfully after the girl. "How long ago were we in Oslo? Six years?"

"Seven," I say, fond memories washing over me as the two shots of Aquavit start working their potato-y magic. I briefly wonder how I'm supposed to watch out for Richard if I'm drunk off my ass.

"Remember that night at Kokkos?" asks Eric.

"How could I forget?"

"Hvor er toalettet?" he says in a falsetto, and we both laugh. I check one last time that Richard is shot-free, before wandering off with Eric toward the World Showcase lagoon. We lean on the fence and look out over the water.

"This place is completely bananas," I say.

"Epcot?"

"Sunset Havens."

"Oh, yeah," says Eric. "That place is a shit show."

I laugh. "The funny thing is that that's the reason I usually love the place. But, with your parents here, it's like I'm seeing it from a totally different perspective."

"Mom and Dad are having a blast."

"You sure? Your mom's already been to the hospital, and your dad crashed a golf cart into a lake."

Eric looks at me funny. "Weren't you the one that put them on jet skis way back when?"

"That was different. Back then, I wasn't a week away from marrying their daughter. I don't know. I feel like maybe I haven't been taking all of this seriously enough."

"You are who you are, man, and we all know it. Including my parents. If you think they're suddenly judging you based on your parents' retirement community, you're nuts."

I don't typically take life advice from Eric, but he makes a valid point.

"Look," he continues. "Before Tanya and I got married, I introduced them to her father who's on his third wife and has grandchildren older than his step-kids. Mom and Dad survived, and they still love Tanya. This isn't any different."

I look over my shoulder at Roger, who's standing on a bench thrusting his hips.

"It's a little different."

"It'll be fine," laughs Eric. "Let's just focus on the weirdness of the fact that you're marrying my sister. You ready?"

I smile. "I'm ready."

"I don't have to give you the speech about how if you hurt her, I will hunt you down and kill you, do I?"

I look at him, surprised. "No offense, but I never took you for that kind of a brother."

"What? Protective?"

"Yeah."

Eric shrugs. "Summer and I have had our differences, but she's still my little sister. And the way she's stuck it out with Mom and Dad all these years, watching out for them after I left, I have a lot of respect for her."

"Have you ever told her that?"

Eric snorts. "She's my *sister*, I'm not going to talk to her about my feelings. Gross."

"Right. Well, you don't have to worry," I say. "You know I would never hurt her. Summer is it for me."

"I know," says Eric. "But I also know *us*, back before we were two old married men. I know about Oslo, and Amsterdam, and Rio. And then there was that time in Tokyo—"

"Tokyo. Ya." I rub the back of my neck. "That was a rough night. But hey, we were young. We're better people now. Tanya and Summer are no small part of that."

"Here, here!" says Eric, as we clink our empty shot glasses.

We stand in silence for a few moments, bidding farewell to my bachelorhood, and watching the ducks paddle peacefully around the lagoon.

"What are you two girls giggling about?" asks Roger, wedging himself between us and handing me another shot. "Comparing pantyhose brands?"

He bursts out laughing, and the ducks scatter.

"Nope," says Eric. "We were just discussing how many women a guy like you probably gets in a month. At a place like Sunset Havens, it's got to be up there."

"Oh, hey now," says Roger. "That there is private information between myself and Mr. Tambourine Man." He motions to the lower half of his body.

"You call it…Mr. Tambourine Man?" I ask, before realizing that I never should have asked.

"That's right," says Roger. "*In the jingle jangle morning I'll come…*"

"Got it, thanks," I say, drinking the shot. "That's…very clever."

"Did you know that I'm the only one of my friends—my *single* friends, might I add, so you don't get the wrong idea about your dad—who hasn't had an STD?"

"Wow," says Eric. "You and Mr. Tambourine Man must be so proud."

"We sure are. Though, that might change by the end of the night." Roger lets out a long whistle as a gray-haired woman in denim short shorts walks by.

Mr. Tambourine Man, Eric mouths to me. *What?*

I shrug and shake my head. Strangely nicknamed genitalia or not, the alcohol I've consumed is filling me with a fair amount of regard for Roger. Here is a man enjoying life to the fullest, up until the not-so-very-far-away end. I can only hope to have that same amount of vitality when I get to be his age. I hope that I'm not widowed, of course. But if I am—God rest Summer's soul—what better place to be widowed than Sunset Havens? Roger and Mr. Tambourine Man are living the dream down here, crashing bachelor parties, popping Viagra, thrusting their strangely named geni—

Man, I'm pretty buzzed.

What was that about pacing ourselves? Did I really say that? Where did all of these *ducks* come from, anyway?

Okay, maybe buzzed isn't the word. Whatever. Focus, Blenderman.

I clamp a hand onto Roger's shoulder, about to openly express my admiration for his lifestyle, when he turns and belches directly into my face.

And just like that, the moment's gone.

SUMMER

28

I stare Graham down with my mother's look of death until he's swallowed up by the crowd. Then I turn around and take inventory.

Francine

Janice

Nadine

Gloria

Lorraine

Babette

Tanya

Mom

Plus half the female population of Sunset Havens.

All here. All at my bachelorette party. My *second* bachelorette party. To be honest, I was perfectly happy just having one. As I said, we spent a weekend in Miami, and it was a blast. The best part? My mother did not attend. I know, that sounds mean. But my mother isn't exactly the bachelorette party type. Shocking, right? Joan Hartwell, who has never in her life used the proper terms for the male and female anatomy. Joan Hartwell, who simply calls them "your business," as in, "Come any closer and I'll kick you in the business." Needless to say, *Small Business Saturday* has taken on a whole other meaning for me.

Anyway, the thought of having an Australian beefcake shake his business in my face while my mother stood by draped in cheap, plastic, penis-shaped necklaces, was horrifying beyond all horrors. So yes, it was a relief when she didn't join us in Miami. But leave it to Graham to feel *bad* about that. Leave it to my thoughtful, empathetic fiancé to consider that maybe our parents felt left out of the whole thing.

So, he went and arranged this little do-over that he thought would be cute and safe and would make everybody feel happy and included. He's definitely going to be one of those soccer coaches that has to give *everybody* a trophy.

"Get it *off!*" I say, shrugging off the rainbow boa that Nadine's been trying to drape across my shoulders. "That's the last thing I want to wear in public."

As Nadine removes the boa, Janice steps in and replaces it with what is truly the last thing I want to wear in public—a battery-operated plastic penis that flashes (or as Janice loudly announces, *throbs)* from blue to pink to purple.

Mom and I lock eyes as Janice drapes the cord over my head—like the recipient of an Olympic medal—and then drapes another one onto my mother.

There we have it, folks. Mom's received her trophy. Can I let you in on a little secret?

Not everybody needs to get a trophy.

When everybody gets a trophy, your father ends up wearing a t-shirt with the words *Wanted: Free Shots and Lap Dances* across the front (about to get peer pressured into binge drinking with Rodney Dangerfield), and your mother ends up at a bachelorette party with a pulsating penis around her neck. When everybody gets a trophy, a situation that involves two very different families suffering through a week together at Sunset Havens—a week that was *very* close to being over—gets about a million times worse than it needed to be.

I love Graham. I love how thoughtful he is, and how he even arranged for my bridesmaids—Sarah and Amber—to arrive this morning, rather than tomorrow when I was expecting them. And I love what he did for me yesterday, with the whole Beast thing. That was *amazing.* Nobody in the world does a thing like that. Nobody except for him. It's an incredible feeling to have a man like Graham. Only, the feeling is dampened—dampened just a *smidgeon*—by the fact that he didn't give me a heads up about one tiny little thing.

That bus.

That bus full of women who would like nothing better than to send me packing up north, while they form a conga line into the sunset with my fiancé. Oh, I know what you're thinking. You're thinking that we already sorted all of that out. You're thinking that we already established that it was Flavio who threw the brick through the window, and that it was Flavio who had the crush on Graham. That may all be true, and we may even have the police report to prove it—*but,* something's still not sitting quite right with me. Not quite right at all.

"What is *this*?" asks Mom, grabbing the necklace by the shaft. She holds it up in front of her face and peers at it through her bifocals.

"Oh, you poor, dear," says Gloria. "Has it really been that long?"

"Or that short?" adds Francine, and all the women start to laugh.

After a few seconds of staring at it, Mom's face lights up with recognition.

"Oy!" she shrieks. "Is this...somebody's *business*?"

"I don't know if it's any of *my* business," says Francine. "But I'd sure like it to be."

"It looks so real!" says Mom. "Summer, look! Look how real it seems!"

"Mom!"

"What? Look at the veins!" She holds it out so I can feel the veins.

"Gross, Mom! Stop! I don't want to touch your business!"

"Where did they *get* these from?" she asks.

"On the Internet, Mom. Or at the mall."

"The *mall*?"

"Yeah, like at Spencer's."

Mom looks at me blankly.

"That store that you never go in?" I say. "With the lava lamps and the Bob Marley posters?"

"Oh, *that* store," she says. "I'm not surprised. That place smells like drugs."

"I'm pretty sure it's just incense."

"You know, you ladies shouldn't be swinging those things around in public," says a man, passing by with his family. Both me and his wife give him a disgusted look, but the Sunset Havens women start whistling and swinging their necklaces over their

222

heads like lassoes. Mom included.

I take that as my cue to turn Sarah and Amber in the opposite direction, and lead them quickly toward a bench. They both look a bit shell-shocked, which is the same expression that I wore the first time I stepped inside Sunset Havens. I like to call it *surprised horror.*

"I'm sorry," I say. "As horrifying as this must be for you, I've been dealing with it for weeks now."

"I don't know," says Sarah. "Those women seem like fun. Maybe you should give them a chance."

"I've been giving them a chance for *weeks*!" I shriek. "I'm done giving them chances! Did I mention that they're trying to sabotage the wedding? See that one, with the orange hair? That's my *wedding planner.*"

The girls follow my finger to Nadine, who's dragged Mom over to pose for a picture with a Canadian Mountie. They're standing one on either side of him, holding something flesh-colored in their mouths. They look just like—

"Are those party horns?" asks Amber, squinting her eyes.

I let out a defeated sigh.

"How much stuff did they *bring*?" asks Sarah. "I mean, I've never seen so many varieties of—"

She trails off as two latecomers arrive, each carrying a life-sized male blow-up doll. Each of the dolls have been outfitted in a pair of yellow Speedos and a set of mouse ears. We watch in silence as Gloria hoists one of them up and onto her shoulders. Francine does the same with the second doll.

"How do you think they got *those* past security?" asks Amber, and the three of us start to laugh.

"It does feel good to laugh," I say, sinking back into the bench. "I'm glad you guys are here."

"What about *me*?" asks Tanya, leaning over the back of the bench and shaking me by the shoulders.

"*You*, too."

"Good," says Tanya. "I was starting to worry that I'd been pushed out by *these two*, who just showed up out of nowhere. No offense."

"None taken," say Sarah and Amber.

"I'm glad that *all* of you are here," I say. "Can you guys even believe that I'm getting married in a few days? I mean, at one point I thought I was going to die alone in my parents' basement."

"Graham knows about your Harry Potter fan fiction, right?" asks Sarah. "Because that could still be a deal breaker."

I laugh. "No worries. I showed him the manuscripts after our third date. That's when I knew we were meant to be."

"Okay, good," says Sarah. "In that case, *yes*. I can totally believe that you're getting married in a few days. Bring it in, girls."

The three of them wrap their arms around me and squeeze until I can hardly breathe, my plastic penis necklace flashing between us like an S.O.S.

***

Things have been going fairly welf.

Welj.

Well.

Sorry. I've had a few drinks. A few in Canada, a few in Italy, a few in—

Buuuuurrrrp!

Excuse me. Hee hee. I'll tell you what, Mom has been a riot today. They *all* have. All of these women are *amazing*. I love them. I take back everything negative I ever said. I don't know why I didn't give them a chance before. I love Sunset Havens. And I love Walt Disney. What a great man. What a *genius*. What a—

Hang on, I have to pee.

Sorry. As I was saying.

Hi.

What? WHY ARE YOU STARING AT ME?

Oh, right. As I was *saying*, I love these women. Even Francine and Janice. They did this hilarious thing in Germany with a couple of bratwursts. They were standing in the fountain, and then there were these college guys, and one of them *picked up* Mom and swung—

Good God it's hot. What was I saying? I don't remember. Something about Francine and Janice? Speaking of those two…where the heck did they *go*?

GRAHAM

29

We make it through three more countries before Roger passes out on a bench in front of—

Where are we?

America. The American Adventure. That's right. It's hard to keep track. It's just been country, shot, country, shot, country—

What were we talking about?

Roger. Right. He's passed out on a bench in front of The American Adventure, which is just as well because ten minutes ago he got all of us kicked out of the theater for shouting profanities at an animatronic Ben Franklin. Maybe now that he's out of the game, I can ease up on the booze, and—

Man. Is it always this *hot* in Florida?

—and pull myself together.

If I run into Summer like this, I'm a dead man. Not that it's my fault, per se. If anything, it's *her* fault. Because…see…hang on a minute.

Sorry, had to pee.

It's totally her fault. As soon as I stepped away to use the restroom in Germany, Richard and his new best friend Roger ordered a round of Jagermeister. I barely had time to vault a bench, two flower beds, and a small child, in order to bump Richard from behind and make him spill his drink. Then I offered to buy him a new one, drank it myself—gagged, because Jagermeister is disgusting—and replaced it with a few ounces of Dr. Pepper.

This is the most exhausting bachelor party I've ever been on.

Anyway, Roger's unconscious now, and I've sent Eric to the front of the park to rent him a wheelchair. I'd go myself, but I doubt they'd rent me anything in my condition. Once he gets back, we maneuver Roger into the wheelchair and start pushing him toward the parking lot and the Sunset Havens bus. I bring Richard along for safekeeping. Dad decides to come along too, since he feels partly responsible for Roger being here in the first place.

Partly?

Twenty minutes later, Eric and I carry Roger up the steps of the bus and lay him across the bench seat in the back. I fish the keys out of his pocket and toss them to Dad, missing him by about a mile.

"You okay?" asks Dad, picking up the keys.

"Fine, fine. I'm fine. Fine."

"You sure?"

"Yep. So, Dad. Who was planning on driving this thing back to Sunset Havens tonight?"

"I assumed they had a designated driver," says Dad, with a shrug.

I shake my head. "Remember when I was a teenager and you and Mom would lay into me for doing stupid, spontaneous things without any thought about the consequences?"

"And that was darn good advice. What's your point?"

"Never mind."

It's a long, hot walk back to the World Showcase. I'm glad I have the wheelchair to hold onto, even if I have steered it into the shrubs a couple of times. We're just walking through the gates, when Richard suddenly stumbles into the path of a woman pushing a stroller. He does a bit of a pirouette as the woman veers around him. I let go of the wheelchair and catch him before he falls. Too bad nobody caught that on video; I *told* Summer I'd watch out for her dad.

He's a lot heavier than I thought he'd be, though. So, now we're both on the ground and my elbows might be bleeding.

"You okay?" I ask. At least I stopped him from smacking his head on the cement. I maneuver the both of us into seated positions. I don't think I can stand up just yet.

"I think so," says Richard. "I just got a little dizzy there for a minute."

"Here, have something to drink." I grab a bottle of Gatorade out of the back pocket of the wheelchair.

"Why doesn't he just ride in that?" suggests Eric. "We rented it, we may as well use it."

Eric helps Richard up off the ground and into the wheelchair. I slowly stand up—fighting back a wave of nausea—and we start on our way again. As we enter the World Showcase, we take a shortcut through the countries we haven't been to yet—the ones where Summer's bachelorette party started out. We're just entering Morocco, when Francine and Janice step into the path directly in front of me. I'm barely able to stop the wheelchair from plowing into them. When I do stop, Richard comes knee to knee with Francine. She gives him a wink. Slightly behind Francine and Janice, is a very familiar looking blonde in a Hooters tank top.

It can't be. I know that I'm drunk and dehydrated, but I don't think I'm hallucinating. No, it's definitely her.

It's Lana. Lana from the Bermuda cruise.

You've probably only heard Summer's side of that story, but I swear, nothing serious ever happened between us—just some PG-13 making out while Summer was busy trying to marry herself off to a racist hipster and a womanizing activities director. Just the same, Summer hated her guts. Especially that time we all ended up in the hot tub together.

Anyway, it all worked out in the end, with Summer and I sailing off into the sunset, and Lana left behind like a bad plot device. But now, two days before our wedding, she's inexplicably here.

"Graham!" she says, stepping towards me and pulling me into a hug. "I can't believe it's you! Jessica and LuLu are *never* going to believe this!" She whips out her phone and starts texting.

I look at Janice who's glancing eagerly back and forth between Lana and me, and suddenly I'm feeling much more sober. Pieces are falling into place—granted, they're falling much more slowly than they normally would—but they're falling just the same. For years, Janice has been talking up this niece of hers. A niece who used to work at Hooters and used to be married to a no-good bum of a fry cook. A few years later, she told me that she had finally gotten a divorce. Janice was ecstatic. Her niece was single again and looking for love, and was I interested? A nice young man like myself? I told her I'd think about it. Then I started dating Summer and informed Janice that I was off the market. Only, I don't remember the niece's name being Lana, I think it was—

"Svetlana!" says Dad, stepping forward and pumping her hand up and down. "It's so nice to see you again! Graham, Eric, Richard, this is Janice's niece, Svetlana. Now, I don't want embarrass her, but Svetlana's made a pretty famous video that's been circulating all over the Internet, isn't that right?"

A...*video*?

Lana nods her head. "No worries, Johnny. You're such a sweetheart. I made a workout video for the mature woman! It's huge on YouTube, and Auntie Janice says everybody is watching it down here at Sunset Havens. It's called *Perk Up Your Hooters!*" She spreads her hands in the air as she says the words, then she motions to her tank top. "I wear this for the publicity. They haven't even sued me yet!"

A workout video...right.

Eric pushes in front of me, staring at Lana's chest. He sticks out his hand. "Eric Hartwell. You two have met before?" He seems to be asking the question to Lana's left and right breasts, but I assume that he's speaking to me.

Eric doesn't know Lana, since he never actually came on the cruise. The cruise that Lana/Svetlana must have come back from and told her aunt all about. The cruise on which she met this great guy named Graham, who wore vibrant clothing and slinked away into the night, never to be seen again. Not that I slinked away, exactly. Summer and I just avoided her for the rest of the cruise by eating dinner at four o'clock. We never did see her again, which was perfect because, like I said, Summer hated her guts.

Janice would have known that was me in a heartbeat. How easy it would have been for her to invite Lana to Epcot today. How easy to innocently introduce us, and to feign surprise when it turns out that we've already met. How easy to stand back and watch while Summer chops off my head with an axe.

"Uh, yeah," I say. "We met on the cruise to Bermuda. Right before Summer and I got together. You remember Summer, don't you Lana? Summer's my fiancée. This is my bachelor party."

"Of course I know *that*," says Lana. "That's why I'm here. It's a funny story. Auntie invited me today because she said it would be my last chance to—"

Janice whacks her on the arm before she can finish. Lana gives her a look and clears her throat.

"—my last chance to spend some *time with her*, before I head out on tour. I'm making appearances at every Planet Fitness in the Northeast! God, it is so good to see you again, Graham." She gives my left bicep a squeeze. "*So* good."

"Is this true?" asks Dad. "You two have already met?" He nudges me suggestively with his elbow.

"It's true," I say. "It's a pretty crazy coincidence. Don't you think so, Janice?"

Janice looks up from inspecting a liver spot on the back of her hand. "What's that, Graham?"

"I said that it's a pretty crazy coincidence that Lana, from the cruise, turned out to be Svetlana, your niece."

Janice lets out a wheeze of a laugh. "Small world, ain't it?"

"Did you say you were on the cruise?" asks Richard, finally joining the conversation and attempting to get out of the wheelchair. "You do look a little familiar."

Yes, of course she looks familiar. She was suctioned to my face during karaoke night, while Richard sat about two feet away at the same table. This was the same night Summer took off with the racist hipster because she didn't want to watch Lana hang all over me. It's not exactly something I want my future father-in-law remembering two days before my wedding to his daughter.

"Rich, why don't we get you out of the sun?" I grab the handles of the wheelchair, scoop him back in, and zigzag him over to a shady spot. "And here, have some more to drink."

I grab the bottle of Gatorade from the back pocket of the wheelchair and hand it to him. Once he's situated, I head back over to the group to find Francine holding her cell phone in the air. She's pulled Lana's video up on YouTube and has turned the volume to full blast.

"Dad, what's going on?" I ask. That's when I see Lana shaking her hips in time to the music.

"She's putting on a demonstration," says Dad, clapping me on the shoulder. "Too bad Roger's unconscious. This is turning out to be quite the bachelor party."

SUMMER

30

The wedding is off.

The wedding is off and I'm going to be single forever, and I'm actually okay with that. I mean, I used to think that Graham was the one, but now I know the truth. We're all entitled to be wrong once in our lives. Sucks that I had to be wrong two days before my wedding, but so goes life.

Oh, I'm overreacting, am I?

I'll tell you what happened and then you can decide for yourself based on the facts. (The facts being that Graham is a sneaky, no-good cheater.)

After having a few too many drinks, Tanya decided that I needed a cup of coffee if I was going to make it through the rest of the afternoon. The two of us were heading off toward Morocco, in search of a Starbucks, when we saw Graham, Eric, and John standing by a fountain watching a stripper.

We skidded to a halt several feet behind them, too shocked to even ask them what was going on. We just stood there, taking it all in. The stripper wasn't topless or anything. Not *yet*, at least. But from the way she was gyrating, she was well on her way. She was wearing a Hooters tank top and looked, in my opinion, a lot older than someone Eric would have normally chosen. I suppose he just picked her randomly out of the phonebook, or out of a stripper-locating app that he and Graham probably invented. I should really start paying more attention when Graham talks to me about work.

That was when I formed Theory #1—that Eric hired a stripper to come to Epcot Center and dance for Graham.

That's also when I figured out where Janice and Francine had gone off to. There was Francine, standing off to the side holding her cell phone in the air with Britney Spears music blasting out of it, and Janice standing next to her taking pictures.

Suddenly, the middle-agedness of the stripper made a bit more sense, and I moved on to Theory #2—that Francine and Janice hired a washed-up stripper to come to Epcot Center and dance for Graham, so that they could send me incriminating photographs.

But Summer, you're thinking, *It's a bachelor party! Let the man enjoy his stripper! Who cares who hired her?* To that I say, 1) Graham already had his chance for a stripper-filled bachelor party when he went to Vegas, and 2) We're at Epcot Center. *This is not normal.* Where the heck is park security, anyway? The whole point of coming here was to provide our parents with an innocent alternative to coming to our real bachelor and bachelorette parties. Graham should have nipped these shenanigans in the bud. But no, there he was, falling right into Janice and Francine's trap.

And then, things got even worse.

Once I stopped staring at the stripper's jiggling body parts, I was able to take notice of her face. And once I was able to take notice of her face, the more familiar that face began to seem. And then, all at once, it was like one of those Magic Eye pictures coming into focus, and I let out the kind of shriek that I typically reserve for when a spider lowers itself into my face.

In my mind, I was no longer at Epcot Center. In my mind, I was back on the Bermuda cruise—squeezed into a two-person hot tub with that very same woman—while she held a martini glass up in the air and called Lulu and Jessica on her cell phone. It was *her*.

Lana.

Lana from the bloody cruise. Of all the strippers, in all the world, they had to go and hire that one. No, not *they*. It couldn't have been Eric or Janice or Francine. That's when I moved on to Theory #3—that *he* hired her. He as in Graham—as in the only person here who could possibly know her. But why? I mean, I know that I sometimes refer to Graham as a complete psychopath, but I never actually meant it. I can't even wrap my head around this. It's like I'm in a Lifetime movie and I just found out that my boyfriend is the Craigslist Killer.

"Why would he *do* that?" I shriek.

"I…I don't know," says Tanya. "I mean, he's a guy, so…you know how they get…sometimes Eric likes to—"

"No, it's not just that," I say. "That woman, he *knows* her, she was—"

That's when something catches my eye directly behind her.

Dad.

My father is sitting in a wheelchair, under a tree, and he looks unconscious. Let me repeat—my father is unconscious in a wheelchair, while my fiancé, brother, and future father-in-law stand by watching a stripper.

"Dad!" I yell, and take off towards him. He's slumped over in the chair with a bottle of Gatorade in his lap. I shake him gently. No response.

"Summer?" Graham finally runs over, drawn away from the strip show by the sound of my screams. "What happened?"

"How much has he had to *drink?*" I yell. "And why is he in a wheelchair?"

"He was using it to rest!" shouts back Graham, who is totally slurring his words, by the way.

"Resting?" I yell. "You mean like his *final resting place?* Look at him! Dad? Wake up!" I shake the chair again, with more force, and his head flops over to the side. He mumbles a few words. I breathe a bit easier as I realize he is, at the very least, still alive.

"I swear, he's barely had anything to drink!" says Graham. "I've been drinking everything for him, just like you asked! Rich? Come on, man! Wake up!" He shakes the wheelchair again, even harder. This time, Dad falls out of it and onto the ground.

I dial 911.

***

Have I told you about my first bachelorette party in Miami Beach?

It was perfect.

My girlfriends and I spent a relaxing four days and three nights lounging on the beach and partying at the hottest night clubs in the city. I returned home relaxed, mildly tanned, and ready to move on to the next chapter of my life as Mrs. Graham

Blenderman. I was perfectly satisfied to leave it at that.

Then came bachelorette party number two or, as I like to call it, the one where Dad ended up severely dehydrated with a blood alcohol content of .14.

He's going to be fine, although I'm still quite shaken up by seeing him that way. He's at the hospital right now, hooked up to an I.V., and resting comfortably with Mom by his bedside. The rest of the family is sitting around the waiting room, each with our own degree of dehydration and blood alcohol content.

As soon as the paramedics arrived at Epcot, we all attempted to leave the park to drive to the hospital—only to realize that we'd taken the monorail from the hotel and that none of us had a car. There was also the little problem of all of us being too drunk to drive, even if we did have a car. Graham ended up calling us a couple of Ubers, and so here we are. Graham also still has the keys to the bus, so we've left about fifty residents of Sunset Havens behind with no way of getting home.

I'm sure they'll figure something out.

Once we got the report from the doctor, we all sat around the hospital waiting room trying to figure out how Dad could have possibly become so intoxicated. Graham continued to insist that he didn't let Dad drink too much, and that the reason he was so hammered was because he drank all of Dad's shots. The only reason I leaned toward believing him was because he reeked of Jagermeister, and I know Graham wouldn't normally touch that stuff with a ten-foot pole. Then Graham mentioned how he even made sure Dad kept drinking Gatorade in order to stay hydrated. That's when the light bulb turned on in John's head, and he asked if it was the same bottle of Gatorade that had been stuck in the back pocket of the wheelchair. When Graham said yes, John said that Roger had been carrying around a bottle of Gatorade mixed with vodka, and that he'd stuck it in the back pocket of the wheelchair after Roger had passed out.

Mystery solved.

"You gave my father a half-empty, old bottle of Gatorade to drink from?" I ask. "Didn't you see Roger drinking out of it? What is *wrong* with you?"

"What's wrong with me is that you told me to make sure your father stayed sober! Of *course* my judgment was going to suffer!"

"Oh, so this is all *my* fault?" I ask. "I never told you to *drink* all of his shots! I told you to dump them in the bushes!"

Graham shakes his head. "One doesn't simply walk around Epcot Center, pouring drinks into the bushes. It's not *done.*"

I can't even argue with him. Not in front of his parents and all of these waiting room strangers. But I know, deep down, that this isn't my fault. This whole second bachelor party thing was his idea—hence, all his fault. And let's not forget about Lana. I haven't even had the time to yell at him about that little issue yet. I wonder if he thinks I didn't notice. Ha! There is no way he can charm himself out of that one.

"I'm gonna go find some coffee," says Graham, standing up and leaving the waiting room.

Yeah, you do that, Graham. You go find some coffee. Maybe Lana can make you some, and then she can pour it for you while she shakes her big, fake boobs around.

The wedding is *so* off.

31

I run my hands over my face and stare at the hospital ceiling. Graham never came back from his coffee run, so I've just been sitting here thinking. John, Babette, Eric, Tanya, and my bridesmaids have barely said a word to me. I think they're afraid I'm having a nervous breakdown. In reality, I've simply come to the conclusion that, unlike vodka and Gatorade, Graham and I just don't mix. I mean, how could we if he'd stoop so low as to contact Lana? Graham's poor judgment today is nothing compared to how bad mine must have been these past two years, when I thought that we should actually be together. The thought that things could change so quickly brings tears to my eyes.

"Hey," says Graham, coming back into the waiting room. "Mind if I sit?"

I quickly wipe my eyes and give him what I hope is an indifferent shrug. He sits down on the couch beside me.

"That was some bachelor party," he says.

I don't respond.

"Gatorade?" He holds a bottle of red Gatorade under my nose.

He actually went and bought that thing just to make a bad joke. I close my eyes, count to three, and then don't respond. We sit in silence for a few minutes.

"Still want to marry me?"

Ah. The big moment has arrived. What I like to call, the time I canceled my wedding in a hospital waiting room while watching reruns of *Roseanne*. And it's that weird episode where Darlene gets her period. Great.

I shift on the couch so that I can look him in the eye when I ask the question that needs to be asked. I need to be able to tell if he's lying to me, because simply reeking of Jagermeister isn't going to get him off the hook. Not this time.

"Tell me, Graham—because I can't even begin to imagine what the answer is going to be—what *Lana* was doing at Epcot today? Hmm? Normally I would have blamed Eric for hiring the stripper. But *Lana*? That was no coincidence. *You* must have called her. *You* must have hired her. Why would you *do* that?!" I'm holding a hospital copy of the *National Enquirer* in my hand and using it to smack him on the arm. I don't even care that everybody is watching. If the wedding is off, they're going to want to know why. This way they get to hear the explanation straight from the horse's mouth. The horse being Graham.

Only, the horse doesn't look nearly as guilty as I expected. He looks more stressed than I've ever seen him, sure. But for Graham, that's not saying much.

He plucks the newspaper from my hand and places it calmly back on the coffee table.

"First of all," he says, "Lana isn't a stripper. She was just demonstrating her workout video."

"Are you *defending* her?" I shriek, earning a shush from the nurse at the nurse's station. I lower my voice. "Because you've already defended Francine and Nadine this week, so I don't have a whole lot of patience left if you're going to start defending the woman you did God knows what with on that cruise ship!"

An audible gasp comes from our family and friends. Eric snorts. Okay, maybe I shouldn't have said that much out loud. But, whatever. If Graham is the Craigslist Killer, everybody has a right to know.

Graham's face clouds over.

"*Second* of all," he continues, "Anything that happened between me and Lana on that cruise ship, was because *you* were too busy hitting on sixteen year old boys to notice what was right in front of you."

Another gasp from our family and friends. And me.

"He looked much older!" I cry. "And that it *so* not the point. Jackson wasn't here today at Epcot, was he? Jackson wasn't shaking his big boobies around for me, was he? No. Lana was! So, I'll ask you again. *Why* was she there?"

"She was there, Sum, because…you were right."

"I knew it!" I say, slapping myself on the thigh. "Wait, what?"

"Lana is Janice's niece," he says. "*Janice* invited her, not me. Janice has been trying to set the two of us up for years, and then she found out that we'd actually met on the cruise. So, you were right—they're not all sweet innocent old ladies. Some of them are pretty damn manipulative, and some of them might, just like you said, be trying to keep us apart."

"If you think that's bad," chimes in Babette, "you should see what happens when you Electric Slide next to one of their boyfriends."

John looks at her with his eyebrows raised. I do the same. Then I look back at Graham.

"So...you didn't call her?" The huge knot in my chest is tentatively starting to loosen.

"Of course not. Why would I do something like that to you? I *love* you. What kind of a person do you think I am?"

I probably shouldn't mention that thing about the Craigslist Killer.

"I'm sorry," I say. "I shouldn't have assumed the worst. I mean, I shouldn't have assumed the worst about *you*. I should have stuck to assuming the worst about Janice and Francine. I never should have pressured you into babysitting my father, either. He's an adult and this was your bachelor party."

"No," he says. "It was my second bachelor party. I should have listened when you told me that one was enough."

"Your heart was in the right place," I say. "If not for you, my mother would never have known that flashing, plastic penis necklaces existed."

Graham smiles. "I'm sorry that I brought up that thing about Jackson, by the way. That was low."

"It's okay," I say. "I can admit that I was a mess on that cruise."

"You really were," says Graham, pulling me over for a hug. "So...are we still getting married?"

The whole room seems to be waiting in anticipation of my answer. And by *seems to be*, I mean they are all leaning forward in their seats and staring at us.

"Of course," I say, feeling the relief wash over me. The tears that I've been struggling to hold back, start flowing down my cheeks. Only now, they're happy ones.

Graham keeps his arms around me, and we finish watching *Roseanne.*

***

The wedding is back on.

Granted, it was never officially off—that was all pretty much in my head—but still, it feels good. You know what feels even better? That the wedding is tomorrow!

That's right, tomorrow. We've made it through the week!

Of course by, *we've made it through the week,* I mean Mom and Dad have each been to the emergency room, Dad has crashed an insanely expensive golf cart, and Mom and I were nearly eaten by an alligator. But that's just life at Sunset Havens—never a dull moment.

We picked up Dad from the hospital this morning, and we're all piled once again into the Escalade, heading back toward Sunset Havens. Mom and Dad are sitting in the back row, fussing over each other. Dad's life flashing before his eyes on Space Mountain, mixed with his near death experience at Epcot, seems to have solidified their marriage in a way that no amount of couples therapy could ever have achieved. I think they're going to be okay.

Graham and I are going to be okay, too. With both of us finally on the same page, there isn't anything these nutty old women can do to further ruin our wedding. They tried, and they failed. Better luck next time, ladies. Better luck with a different guy, I mean. Obviously, Graham isn't going to be attempting to marry anybody else at Sunset Havens ever again. He's even offered to speak to them privately tonight to make sure that *they* know that *he* knows, and that all of this nonsense is over with.

Life is good, and there are only two things left on the agenda—the rehearsal and the rehearsal dinner. Both are taking place tonight at The Lakeview. Most of the relatives that we invited to the wedding either flew in last night or are arriving today, and since we couldn't invite all of them to the rehearsal dinner, we had to narrow it down to an even more select few.

Graham's Aunt Jo-Ann and Uncle Chuck have made the cut—mainly because they're the folks John has been trying to convince for years to move to Sunset Havens. He's basically using our wedding as one of those marketing ploys where you give away a free stay at a nice hotel, dinner included, and then try to sell people a crappy time-share. I should probably be more offended by this, but considering that Graham and I had sex in Aunt Jo-Ann and Uncle Chuck's rental home, and John still hasn't disowned us, I'm going to let this one slide.

Also making the cut is Dad's brother, Eddie. Eddie Hartwell lives in Iowa where he's been studying and teaching Transcendental Meditation for the past thirty years. He's very calm, cool, and collected. In other words, the polar opposite of my father. Graham has been dying to meet him.

And then we have Mom's sister, Mary. Mary and her husband own an antique shop in Provincetown. In her spare time, she dresses up as Dolly Parton and performs at nursing homes. Whenever we get together, she's full of positive energy and uplifting stories about the people she meets at her shop or through her volunteer work. It's fun to watch her and Mom go head to head, with Mom trying her best to inject negativity into the conversation, and Mary shooting her down with one *Chicken*

Soup for the Soul style anecdote after another. I still don't think Mom has recovered from the time Mary said she let a homeless man spend the night in her guest bedroom.

Dad and Eddie. Mom and Mary. I don't understand how my grandparents managed to raise siblings on such opposite ends of the spectrum. Actually, I kind of do, since I wrote a research paper on it for my abnormal psych class back in college. Mom and Dad were not amused.

But I digress.

It's going to be an interesting mix tonight. It'll be good practice for the wedding, which is going to be an even bigger, even more interesting mix. Whenever I picture our wedding reception, I think about this time that I looked out the front door of the Blenderman house and saw about six million bugs gathered on the ceiling of the front porch. It was a really hot night, and the lights were on, and the bugs were just going ballistic. There were big ones, small ones, slow ones, fast ones— all kinds of species just thrown together and forced to interact. Some were sitting and kind of bobbing their heads to the music ("What Is Love" was playing in my head), while others raced drunkenly around, bumping into everything. A couple of bugs were attempting to swing dance to rap music.

Don't get me wrong, they looked like they were having a blast. It was just chaotic, and trippy, and not the sort of thing I would ever want to find myself at the center of. But guess what? I'm the bride. I'm the center of attention. All of those drunk, psychotic bugs, who may or may not be our metaphorical relatives, will be buzzing around *me*.

And I think that it's going to be okay.

As long as that one tall, blonde bug stays by my side, and then flies me off to Jamaica, I think that everything is going to be just fine.

32

Our Justice of the Peace is ancient.

Like, he looks too old to even live at Sunset Havens. But he was hired by The Lakeview, so they must have been keeping him around here somewhere. Certainly not on the golf course where they like to keep all the energetic, young-looking old people. Those are the ones they want you to see when you drive by on your trolley tour. Not Arthur Spanley. This guy is just... prehistoric.

He's pulled his golf cart right up to the curb in front of The Lakeview—the place where you're supposed to park long enough to drop someone off—and just left it there, with the right blinker flashing. One of the doormen started to say something, but Nadine rushed outside and waved him away as she helped Arthur out of his cart. I'm more shocked by the fact that Arthur is still driving, than I am by his illegal parking practices. Back in Massachusetts, elderly drivers plow through the fronts of Dunkin Donuts on a weekly basis, so I'm just glad we're standing well away from the front windows.

We all watch as Arthur pulls a wooden cane from the

passenger seat and starts the long, five-yard shuffle toward the sliding doors, with Nadine hovering nearby as if expecting him to drop at any moment. He's wearing these huge, black Orville Redenbacher eyeglasses, with shorts, black knee socks, shiny dress shoes, and a tan Members Only jacket. I feel sort of terrible for being disappointed that this is the man performing our marriage ceremony—but in my mind, I was picturing more of a Matthew McConaughey or a Ziggy Marley type. I was picturing someone who would give a really cool, laid back sort of ceremony. Once again, it's my own fault. You get what you pay for, and I opted to pay nothing.

Before Nadine can even introduce us, Arthur excuses himself to use the restroom. We watch as he shuffles right past the restroom and into the coat closet, closing the door behind him. After a couple of seconds, he comes back out and one of the women at the front desk directs him to the restroom.

"Arthur's great," says Nadine, while we wait. "He doesn't let anything stop him. He lost his driver's license ten years ago because of his glaucoma. That's when he decided to move to Sunset Havens, so he could still get around by golf cart."

I raise my eyebrows. "They let you drive a golf cart with *glaucoma*?"

"Sure do," says Nadine. "That's half the draw of this place!"

I make a mental note to be extra careful the next time I cross any streets down here, and also to possibly call in a tip to the police.

Arthur finally returns from the men's room, digging around in his pants pockets and extracting a hard candy. He unwraps it and puts it into his mouth.

"Where is—" He pauses, makes a face, and spits the hard candy back out. He re-wraps it, puts it back into his pocket, and fishes out a different flavor. Pleased with his new selection, he continues.

"Where is—" He pauses again to clear some phlegm from his throat. "Where is the bride?" He has this very raspy, Gandalf-y kind of a voice.

"Right here," I say, smiling and stepping forward.

"And is this the young groom?" asks Arthur. He walks up to Dad and puts his hands on his shoulders. "The young man on the eve of his wedding? Do I need to give you *the talk*?" He gives Dad a wink.

"That's my *father*!" I say, horrified. I take a step closer to Graham. "*This* is the groom."

Arthur looks over at Graham, then back at Dad, then back at Graham again. He shrugs, as if seeing no difference at all, and shuffles over to shake Graham's hand.

"Let us begin then," he says, and begins leading us in the direction of the coat closet.

"*This* way," says Nadine, gently steering Arthur in the correct direction. The rest of us follow behind at a snail's pace.

***

Arthur has our wedding ceremony printed out on a stack of yellowed, stapled pages, from probably the first wedding he ever performed. Or, more likely, from the first *wedding* ever performed.

Every time he turns a page, he pauses for a really long time before starting to read again. I don't know if it has something to do with his glaucoma—like, maybe it takes his eyes a while to refocus on the words—but, it's pretty awkward. I'm holding out hope that he'll have the whole thing memorized by tomorrow afternoon, but I'm guessing that his memory is about as sharp as his eyesight.

Graham and I look at each other and smile. Sure, it's a little weird to read from a bunch of stapled pages and have awkward pauses all over the place, but what's the alternative? That he forget the lines and start reading us our Miranda rights? Or the Pledge of Allegiance? Let the man have his script, I say. As long as he makes it to the end, where Graham and I are pronounced man and wife, bound together for all eternity, who really gives a fig? The man is no Ziggy Marley, but that's okay. I've become much more accepting over the past twenty minutes.

"And this is the part where you shall exchange the rings," says Arthur.

I choke back a laugh. He really does sound like Gandalf, especially with all this ring talk.

"*Does anybody have the rings?*"

I jump. He's quite loud, too. I think there might be something wrong with his hearing aid.

"We, um, we didn't bring the rings to the rehearsal," I say.

"*What's that?*"

Backing up my theory that something must be wrong with his hearing aid, is the fact that he's barely heard a word I've said all evening. It's starting to get on my nerves.

"*I said we didn't bring the rings tonight!*"

"Oh," says Arthur, looking concerned. "You're going to want to purchase those soon. The wedding is only a few weeks away."

"No, the wedding is *tomorrow*. And we *have* the rings. We just don't have them *here*."

"*What?*"

Okay, I can't do this. At any moment he's going to call me sonny and give me a nickel to shine his shoes. I look to Graham for assistance, but he just makes a hand motion indicating that I should speak up. I return his suggestion with a dirty look, and walk over to where Mom is sitting and holding my purse. I fish out my keys, pull apart two key rings, and walk back to the front.

"Here," I say. "We can use these for now."

Arthur studies the key rings. One of them still has my Stop & Shop rewards tag dangling from it.

"Oh, my. You're going to want to resize these," he says. "They're much too big."

"Yes," I sigh. "I'll do that."

After Graham and I pretend to exchange rings, Nadine directs us back down the aisle and into the outdoor area where we'll have our pictures taken after the ceremony. Lake Fillmore might be man-made, and it might be full of fake sunken pirate ships and the missing bodies of a few Sunset Havens residents—but at this time of the evening, it's absolutely beautiful. I wrap my arms around Graham's waist as we look out at the water. I can't imagine what a relief it will be tomorrow, to be standing here with all of the stress of the wedding behind us, and ten days of relaxation in Jamaica ahead of us.

"Now, Summer," says Nadine. "Will your mother be joining you in the family pictures?"

"Of course," I say, glancing at Mom. "She's my mother."

"I just wasn't sure," says Nadine. "with all of the *personal family matters* we talked about the other day. I wanted to be able to clue the photographer in ahead of time."

"We did not talk about any personal family matters! I told you, my mother just lives far away. That's the only reason she wasn't involved in planning the wedding!"

"If you don't want me in the photos, Summer, you can just say so," says Mom, pulling a tissue out of her purse and blowing her nose. "Your father can take a few photos of me in the parking lot, so you'll at least remember that I was here. You know, *after I'm gone.*"

"Don't be morbid, Mom. Of course I want you in the photos. Nadine is just trying to cause unnecessary drama."

"She's right," says Nadine. "I must be watching too many soaps! They put all sorts of crazy ideas into your head!" She laughs loudly and takes off toward the reception hall. Great. Nadine's hooked on soaps. She'll probably kidnap me on my wedding day, surgically swap our faces, and trick Graham into marrying her instead. I can only hope that her turkey neck and liver spots clue him in before he goes through with it.

Aside from that, I leave the rehearsal feeling slightly more than fifty percent confident that everything is on the right track. One of my small, nagging concerns is that Arthur Spanley isn't going to show up tomorrow—you heard him, he thinks the wedding is in a few weeks. I can't exactly trust Nadine to remind him. If I mention that he might have mixed up the days, it could give her a whole new idea on how to screw with the wedding. Besides the simple surgical swapping of our faces , she'd probably break into Arthur's house and erase the wedding from his calendar.

I certainly can't call to remind him. I mean, if he can't hear me in real life, he'll never hear me over the phone. I don't know that he could hear anybody over the phone, even Graham. He could probably hear Mom. She's got one of those voices that can cut through anything—like Soundwave from the Transformers—but I don't want to listen to her tell me how she could have found us an awesome Justice of the Peace if only I'd let her help plan the wedding. She probably knows one who almost won *American Idol* or something.

No, I just have to hope for the best. I just have to drink a lot of wine at the rehearsal dinner, and hope for the best.

GRAHAM

33

Summer's been signaling to me for a while now.

We're having a little cocktail hour before the rehearsal dinner, with some of the family that have flown in for the wedding. Summer's standing across the room in this sexy little white cocktail number, champagne glass in hand, talking to my Uncle Chuck, who is already seriously sloshed. I don't know why Dad's been having such a hard time convincing him and my aunt to move down here. Uncle Chuck seems about as ready for Sunset Havens as they come.

He keeps leaning in real close to Summer's face, like he's telling her a juicy secret, and Summer keeps taking more and more steps backward. Unfortunately, she's taken so many steps backward, that she's backed herself right into a corner—which, I believe, is how he and my aunt first got together. Now she's trying to catch my eye over one of Chuck's beefy shoulders. Every time she does, she jerks her head toward the exit. She's blinking a lot too. I hope she hasn't gone through the trouble of learning Morse Code.

If all she had in mind was for me to rescue her from Uncle

Chuck, I'd have been over there in a heartbeat. Obviously. But she has a little bit more than that in mind, so I admit that I've been dragging my feet.

"So, man, it was like this," says Eddie, holding his hands out in front of him in a frame shape. "We were all at Club 44, watching the tribute show for Artie Mendelsohn. Great guy. Passed away last month at ninety-four, halfway up Kilimanjaro. Anyway, we're all at Club 44, when in walks David Lynch."

The other reason I haven't come to Summer's rescue, is that I've been standing here talking with Richard's brother, Eddie. The man is fascinating. How the two of them are even related is beyond me.

I raise my eyebrows. "*The* David Lynch? The *Twin Peaks* guy?"

"The one and only," says Eddie. "It turns out that he and Artie met years ago at a retreat in Rishikesh. That's India, you know? Same place the Beatles went to learn transcendental meditation."

"I had no idea."

"Yeah, back in the sixties. Anyway, we talked with David all night. He's a cool guy. He's doing a new season of *Twin Peaks* for Showtime. Says he's got a small part for me if I'm interested. I've never seen the show myself, but he said he's looking for someone to play a guy named Bob. Ever heard of him?"

My eyebrows go even higher. Below them, my eyes flicker to Eddie's shoulder length gray hair. He could totally play Bob. Summer's uncle is going to reprise the role of one of the most evil characters in television history. I've got to go tell her. I've—

I glance across the room again, only to be hit with the

Summer Hartwell Look of Death. Uncle Chuck has one hand on each of her shoulders, and as soon as she catches my eye, she starts up again with the head jerks and the blinking.

I sigh. Bob or no Bob, I'd better get over there before she breaks out in hives.

"You'll have to excuse me," I say. "But my blushing bride has been trying to catch my attention for a while now. She misses me when I'm gone for too long. We'll have to finish this conversation later."

"No problem," says Eddie, giving me a slight bow. "Namaste, man. Na-ma-ste."

"And a Namaste to you, as well."

I return the bow and make my way over to Summer. She immediately ducks out from under Uncle Chuck's grip and drags me toward the exit.

"Geez, Sum, the man flew all the way out here for the wedding. You could at least let him squeeze your shoulders."

"I've been signaling to you for like *thirty minutes*!" she hisses.

"Were you?" I nonchalantly rub my hand over my face. I allow a couple of veins to pop out of her neck before I break into a smile. Sometimes she's just too easy to tease.

"I'm sorry," I say, putting an arm around her shoulders. "But did you know your uncle might play Bob on *Twin Peaks*?"

"Did you know that *your* uncle has extreme halitosis?"

"*Bob*, Summer. He's a major character."

She looks up at me blankly, then shrugs out from under my arm. Now I know how Uncle Chuck must have felt.

"Look," she says, shaking her head. "You need to hurry if you want to catch the both of them together."

"Okay, sorry. I'm going." I hand her my drink and slip out of the dining room. I cross the lobby of The Lakeview and head out into the parking lot toward my golf cart.

Earlier today I made the mistake of promising Summer that I would speak to Janice and Francine to ensure that they aren't planning to pull any more funny stuff. I figured I'd run into them at some point today and casually bring it up. Or maybe I wouldn't end up running into them at all, and the whole thing would blow over without me ever having said a word.

But, when three o'clock rolled around and I still hadn't seen them, Summer whipped out an activities schedule and told me that both Janice and Francine regularly attend Friday night beer pong. Then she pulled out a map and a highlighter and showed me that beer pong is located at a rec center only five minutes from The Lakeview. She then told me that she wants this taken care of tonight, in case they have any last minute desperate attempts up their sleeves.

If it weren't for the fact that I recently—as in yesterday—landed her father in the emergency room, I don't even know that I would have agreed to it. I understand her concerns. And, like I said in the hospital, I believe her that some of these women aren't as innocent as I'd originally thought. It's just that I still don't have any solid proof that Francine is some sort of criminal mastermind. And sure, Janice did a lousy thing by inviting Lana to Epcot, but she did it out of a desire to have me marry into her family.

Come on. Who can blame her? I think that my reaction to seeing Lana yesterday was confirmation enough that I wasn't happy about it. Bringing it up again today just seems like unnecessary overkill.

Then there's the misconception that just because I'm an outgoing, lively guy, I don't have a problem with confrontation. I most definitely have a problem with confrontation—particularly awkward confrontation between myself and women who are a quarter of my size and three times my age. I don't enjoy it. You know what I do enjoy? The fact that everybody down here loves me. The fact that I took Francine to the Senior Prom and I made her night. The fact that when I walk into Starbucks, I'm like some kind of local celebrity. There are so many levels as to why I love this place—from the superficial to the Freudian to the fact that I just really, really like driving around in a golf cart—that I really, really don't want to ruin it.

I'd do anything for Summer. You know that, right? But what, exactly, am I even supposed to do in this situation? Pull two old ladies into a darkened parking lot and…what? In my head, I keep hearing myself speaking in this corny mobster voice while pointing a soda bottle at them from beneath my trench coat, asking how they feel about cement overshoes. I don't know, man. Like I said, if I hadn't just landed Summer's father in the hospital, I might never have agreed to this.

I take a deep breath of the warm, night air, and bring the golf cart up to its full speed of twenty-six miles per hour. I have to make this quick. I only have about thirty minutes before our families sit down to dinner. Summer's all ready with an excuse if I'm not back in time—apparently I left Eric's Best Man gift back at the house and needed to go get it. Note to self, buy Eric a Best Man gift.

I park the golf cart at the Sea Breeze Rec Center and head into the lobby. *Beer Pong, Cypress Room, 6:30pm* it says on a chalkboard easel. It's not too difficult to find the Cypress Room, as I just have to follow the sounds of all the whistling and cheering. Several long, metal tables are set up with red plastic cups on either end. Each table has a small crowd gathered around it. The table closest to the door has four cups left on one end, and only one cup on the other. A tiny woman with pinkish, cotton candy hair, is setting up her shot. She shoots. She scores! Her teammates go wild and I high-five her as I pass.

"Graham!" shouts a woman from the other team. "Everybody, Graham's here!" Several other people, both women and men, step over to high-five me and clap me on the back. "Are you joining us for beer pong night?" Another cheer goes around the room and I suddenly feel like Norm walking into Cheers.

"Yeah!" I say. "I mean, maybe. Not tonight, though. I was just looking for…I'm here to…I'm just checking it out. For now." I look around at all the smiling faces and somebody thrusts a can of Coors Light into my hand. How is it that I never came to beer pong before? What the heck have I been doing with all my Friday nights when I'm down here? I used to be a beer pong champion back in college. I could teach them so much. I wonder if they know about Flip Cup? Or Quarters? Or—

It's at that moment that I decide not to go through with it. I know, it didn't take much.

I'm going to *pretend* that I went through with it, of course. It's too late to just leave, since Francine and Janice have already spotted me from across the room—my entrance wasn't exactly subtle—and they know that I'm supposed to be at my rehearsal dinner right now. I'll just tell them that I came by to give them one last kiss on the cheek as a single man. That'll make their week. Then I'll head back to the rehearsal dinner, tell Summer that everything's been taken care of, and we can get on with this wedding.

I'm a firm believer in mind over matter. A positive attitude and a sunny disposition have served me well in life, and I believe it can work for Summer too. It worked on the cruise, didn't it? Once she stopped worrying and started seeing her parents from a different perspective, her life took a major step forward. Similarly, once she thinks I've laid down the law with Janice and Francine, her whole outlook will improve and things will naturally start to fall into place.

It's just the way the world works. Mind over matter.

Trust me.

34

"I'm really looking forward to checking out that Hospice Thrift Shop," says Summer's Aunt Mary, taking a sip of wine and flipping her scarf over her shoulder. "I saw it on the way here. We have one back in Provincetown where Barry buys his shirts. You fill a trash bag and they charge you by the pound. It's the only way to shop."

Joan eyes Barry's shirt distastefully, and shudders. "But aren't they—" She makes a motion with her hands, attempting to get the words *contaminated by the germs of the dead* across without actually speaking them. You have to appreciate her tact.

"A loving tribute to those who have passed?" finishes Mary. "I couldn't have said it better myself. They allow our living, breathing bodies to become walking celebrations of the deceased. Where do you think I got this scarf?" Mary shakes the end of her scarf out over the table, while Joan throws herself across the plates of appetizers like a human shield.

Summer nudges me under the table and I snort back a laugh. I've been back in her good graces since returning from the rec center, and we've been enjoying our rehearsal dinner. It's been basically an endless exhibition of conflicting lifestyles, morals, and political opinions. Eric's sitting to my right, so I've been getting nudged from both sides pretty much non-stop.

"Chuck, Jo-Ann," says Dad. "What do you guys think about Sunset Havens so far? Not bad, huh?"

Uncle Chuck leans back in his chair and tips the last of his beer into his mouth. "I could live here," he says. "It's *her* you need to convince." He jerks his thumb toward Aunt Jo-Ann who's wearing an *And I thought my husband was gross back home* sort of expression.

"It's very nice," says Jo-Ann. "From what we've seen so far. Which hasn't been much." She grimaces as Uncle Chuck whistles for the waitress and orders another drink. "I have to say though, whoever they've got doing the housekeeping in the rental homes should be *fired.*"

"Why's that?" asks Dad.

Jo-Ann leans forward and says, almost in a whisper, "When we were unpacking this morning, I found a pair of *black lace panties* in the living room, just sticking out from under the couch! *Real* trashy stuff."She bats her hand in disgust.

And…Summer's choking. I pat her gently on the back while Dad's face turns beet red. Mom takes a long gulp of wine and gives me a wink.

"Sorry," says Summer, clearing her throat. "Choked on a…" She looks around the table before realizing she hadn't actually been eating anything yet. "Ice cube."

The conversation returns to relatively safe topics—sports, the weather, golf—as our soups and salads are served.

"I can't wait to see that golf cart of yours," says Uncle Chuck, stabbing his fork into a ranch dressing covered crouton. The rest of his salad has been pushed to the side of the plate, half of it spilling over onto the tablecloth. "Is it in the parking lot?"

Dad cringes. "It's, um, it's actually in the shop right now."

"Is that the name of the lake?" asks Eric. I kick him under the table and glance over at Rich, who meets my eye with a slack-jawed look of horror. He must still feel terrible about what he did to Dad's golf cart. Although, I've seen him with a similar expression after winning three hundred bucks on a scratch ticket, so maybe he hasn't even been listening to our conversation. He is all the way down at the other end of the table.

I'm about to dive back into my salad, when Richard suddenly stands up, Manhattan in hand, looking like he has something important to say. He clears his throat. Summer hits me hard in the leg. I look over at her and shrug. My father already gave the rehearsal dinner toast right after our drinks came out, and he made sure to ask if anybody else wanted to say anything. Richard didn't speak up at the time. But, maybe he's changed his mind.

"I have a few things I'd like to say," says Richard. "I know that John has already made a toast, but this…this is different."

Different than a toast? Suddenly my hands are feeling clammy. What if this is his speak-now-or-forever-hold-your-peace moment? He had all those life and death revelations the other day, maybe he's decided to revoke the permission he gave me to marry his daughter. No, he wouldn't do something like that in front of everybody.

Would he?

"Graham," says Richard, looking right at me. I've never seen him so serious before. Now my back is starting to sweat.

"Yes?"

Now we're just staring at each other. He looks like he's about to speak at a funeral.

"I don't know how to say this," he continues. "I…I've never had to do this before. But I just can't allow—"

"More bread for the table?" The waitress has chosen this moment to place six additional baskets of bread, one at a time, onto our table.

"Thank you," says Richard. "Could we also get some fresh butter? The ones on the table have been sitting out."

"They're *soft*," says Joan.

The waitress leaves, and Richard takes a sip of his Manhattan. Then he puts it down, pulls out a bottle of hand sanitizer, and squirts it into his palms. He rubs his hands together, then selects a piece of bread. He takes a bite. He does all of this while standing at the head of the table.

He wouldn't recant his permission while chomping on a dinner roll, would he?

"As I was saying," he finally continues, between bites, "I simply can't allow this wedding to go on."

The entire table gasps.

"Your butter, sir," says the waitress.

"Thank you," says Richard. He opens up a packet of butter and spreads it on his bread. "Oh, Joan. This bread is out of this world. Try some."

"Um, Rich?" I say, looking nervously around the table, trying not to sound rude. "What do you mean?"

"Well, it's sort of like a challah, but it has *seeds* on top, which I've never seen done before on a—"

"Not about the *bread*," I say. "About not allowing the wedding to go on?"

"Oh, right," he says. "I mean that I can't allow this wedding to go on…without saying a few words about this wonderful, young man, Graham Blenderman."

The entire table lets out a collective sigh of relief and Summer mumbles a few choice words under her breath.

"I see that everybody here agrees," says Richard.

"We thought you were calling off the wedding!" says Summer.

"Why would I do that?"

"Maybe because you look like somebody died?" says Summer. "And because you already said you didn't want to give a toast?"

"That's because this *isn't* a toast," says Richard. "It's a poem."

"You wrote a poem?"

Richard wrote me a poem?

He fishes around in his pants pocket until he locates a folded scrap of paper. I thought the man was going to disown me, when in reality, he wrote me a poem. I lean back in my chair, taking a long sip of scotch, feeling kind of like Clark Griswold after he got his Christmas lights to work. Maybe I should actually listen to the poem first, before I start to celebrate. It could still say *Roses are red, violets are blue, over our dead bodies will our daughter marry you.*

Richard clears his throat, and begins to read.

"When Summer was a little girl, her very favorite things,
Were stories about castles, and fairies with bright wings.
And as she changed into a teen, her favorite things changed too,
To wizards, Hobbits, orcs, and elves, and even Doctor Who."

Summer laughs and looks admiringly at her father.

"At age fourteen she told us, she would never date Prince Charming,

She found his lack of personality, more than a bit alarming.

And then again at twenty-four, she rejected Edward Cullen,

She found him too controlling, too boring, and too sullen."

"Still do," says Summer, nodding along.

"Her mom and I had our concerns, that she'd never find The One,

And live down in our basement, until all our lives were done."

Everybody at the table laughs, and Summer's jaw drops open. That was unexpected. And awesome.

"And even though we always hoped, she'd find one worth a damn,

We never thought we'd have the luck, for that one to be Graham."

Richard pauses for a moment and holds a hand out in my direction. Everybody at the table lets out a collective *awww*. Summer squeezes my hand, smiling up at her dad. I smile at him too. Richard P. Hartwell, Poet. Who knew? He continues.

"Graham took us out on jet skis, and even for tattoos,

He taught us how to take some risks, on that special Bermuda cruise.

But life is full of ups and downs, it's not a vacation every day,

You need someone to be by your side, who makes everything okay.

He looks lovingly down at Joan, and squeezes her shoulder. Then he folds up the piece of paper and puts it back into his pocket.

"That's all I wrote," he says. "I'm not much of a poet. But Joan and I wanted to make sure, in our own way, that you know how happy we are that our daughter is marrying somebody like you. We know that you'll make a wonderful husband, father—"

Joan holds both hands up in the air with her fingers crossed, and everybody laughs.

"—and son-in-law. Welcome to the family, Graham."

There is a brief moment of silence before the table breaks into applause. Aunt Mary whistles. I jump up, walk to Richard's end of the table, and pull him into a hug.

"You don't know how much that means to me," I say, patting him heartily on the back. "For a minute there I thought—"

"Don't mention it," says Richard, sniffling a little, and hugging me back. "It was nothing. We're just so happy to have you in the family. Take good care of her, that's all I ask. Better care than you took of me this week, am I right?" Richard gives me a wink.

I knew someday we'd be able to laugh about all of this.

"I promise," I say. "Your daughter will never end up at the bottom of a lake."

Okay, that may have come out wrong. Richard's face may have turned briefly back into the slack-jawed look of horror, but only for a second. Then I'm being pulled into another hug by Joan, who's joined us at the head of the table.

"Welcome to the family," she says, squeezing me tightly.

"It's an honor," I say, squeezing her back and lifting her slightly off the ground.

And I mean it.

SUMMER

35

It can't possibly be six o'clock already.

I feel like I slid into bed mere minutes ago. It can't have been more than a millisecond since my head sank into the pillow and I blissfully lost consciousness. I would give anything to be able to hit the snooze button right now. *Anything.* But I can't.

Would you like to know why?

Because instead of a simple alarm going off—one that I could smash with the palm of my hand, and then roll over into a deep, glorious slumber—I have Graham's mother pounding on my bedroom door. She's pounding on it, and she's *singing.*

Good morning! Good morning! Good morning to you!

The woman is completely insane. I mean, I love her and can't wait to be a part of the family and all that. But let's face it, she's nuts.

"Summer? Are you up?"

Bang! Bang! Bang!

"Yes, yeah…I'm up," I mumble into my pillow.

"Summer?"

Bang! Bang! Bang!

"Yes! Yes! I'm *up!*" I scream, before she has a chance to start banging again. Or worse yet, singing.

Yes, I'm up. At least I don't have to shower. Zumba class at Sunset Havens doesn't exactly require one to look her best. That's where Graham and I are right now—

Wait a minute.

I roll over and look at my phone. As the fog slowly clears from my brain, I stare up at the ceiling. A smile slowly spreads across my face as reality sinks in. Babette's not waking me up early for Zumba class. Those days are finally over. Babette's waking me up early because—

"Summer? Are you in there? It's your *wedding daaaay!*"

Because it's my wedding day.

"I'm up! Thank you!" I shout, making sure she hears me. I sit up in bed and shake Graham. "Hey, wake up! It's the big day!"

"You think I slept through that?" he asks, rolling over and smiling up at me. "Come here, Mrs. Blenderman." He pulls me down for a kiss.

"Right now, the only Mrs. Blenderman in this house is out in that hallway," I say. "Let's not jinx anything."

"There's nothing left to go wrong, Sum," he says. "We're getting married in, like, ten hours."

"You're right," I say, rubbing my hands over my face. "And if I didn't already say it, I'm *so* glad that you talked to Janice and Francine last night. I really do feel so much better about everything. So, thank you." I give him another kiss.

"It was nothing," says Graham. "Oh, hey…I almost forgot. I made you something." He grabs his phone off the nightstand and flips it around so I can see the screen.

Wedding Countdown – 9 hours 55 minutes 16 seconds

We smile giddily across the bed at each other.

Bang! Bang! Bang!

"We're making everybody breakfast!" shouts Babette. "Come on out when you're done!"

Done? Ew. I quickly jump off the bed and throw open the door to prove that nothing sinful was happening on the morning of our wedding. Days and months before the wedding, sure. Just not the morning *of.*

Graham follows me into the kitchen where Mom and Dad are already seated at the table, sipping coffee. Babette and John are both buzzing around, scrambling eggs and cooking bacon. Thankfully, there is no kale to be seen. Just a normal, old-fashioned, pre-wedding breakfast with our loving parents. Maybe it's me, but there's a general sense of happiness and well-being in the air today.

Also in the air, the approaching sound of sirens.

"Those sound close," says Babette, over her shoulder.

"Sure do," says John, dumping a pile of bacon onto a plate and bringing it to the table.

I pick up a slice and start nibbling on it. Despite the incoming food, I feel a small pit starting to form in the bottom of my stomach. Wedding day jitters, I suppose.

"Should we be concerned?" I ask anyway. Just to be safe.

Babette looks over her shoulder at me. "Don't worry. Ambulance sirens are nothing new around here."

That's when several fire trucks drive by, laying on their horns.

"Somebody probably burnt the toast over at Marmaduke's," says John.

He and Babette laugh as the small pit in my stomach increases to more of a medium-sized pit. I stand up and walk over to the window. I'm not expecting to see much, since the Blendermans live on a residential side street, so I'm surprised to see a large column of thick black smoke rising in the not so distant distance.

"Oh!" I say, stepping away from the window. "Something *is* on fire! Something close!"

"Is it a wildfire?" asks Mom. "Should we evacuate?"

"I'll pack the underwear!" says Dad, heading down the hallway faster than I've ever seen him move in his life. "Joan, grab the canned goods! I'll get The Duffle!"

Mom's breakfast plate clangs to the floor as she jumps up to join Dad. I don't even bother trying to stop them. I'm too distracted by the medium-sized pit in my stomach turning into something straight-up gnawing at my guts.

"Canned corn? Will that work?" shouts Mom. She's in total panic mode, ransacking the Blenderman kitchen, while everyone else has joined me by the window to watch the smoke.

"Beans! Get beans!" shouts back Dad.

Mom pulls down a can of string beans, and then sweeps a bunch of forks into a plastic bag.

"That does look like it's coming from Duke's Landing," says Babette, a slight waver to her voice.

"Like I said," says John, "it's probably Marmaduke's. Or maybe Starbucks. No big loss. There are still seven thousand nine hundred and forty-six of those left!"

He chuckles and looks around the room for recognition of his joke, but none of us respond. I barely even realized he'd been speaking. All of the voices in the room seem to have faded into the background and all I can process is the sight of that black smoke, curling up, up, up. Up from where? Not from Marmaduke's. Not from Starbucks.

No.

There is only one place that could be on fire this morning. On *this* morning. Don't ask me how I know, I just do.

That's when my cell phone rings.

I walk back into the kitchen like a zombie, and am not at all surprised to find that it's Nadine.

"Hello?" I answer. I listen for a few moments, close my eyes, and swallow hard. "Okay. Thank you."

I hang up and walk back into the living room.

"That was Nadine," I say, sinking onto the couch. "The Lakeview caught on fire this morning. It burned. It…it burned to the ground." I choke on those last few words and cover my mouth with my hands. Babette lets out a loud gasp, clutches her hair with both hands, and starts walking in frantic circles around the living room.

Mom freezes in the kitchen with a can of tomato soup in her hand. Dad, oblivious to the news, comes back into the room holding beach towels and a hairdryer.

"What is it?" he asks. "Is it the neighbor's house? Once the neighbor's house goes up, it's too late!" He staggers backward into the counter, knocking a frying pan full of eggs onto the floor. Mom shushes him and pulls him into the other room to explain.

Graham just looks at me, seemingly at a loss for words. His face looks more ashen than I've ever seen it; except for maybe that time we climbed the lighthouse in Bermuda.

"Oh, Summer," moans Babette, sitting down next to me on the couch. I'm expecting a comforting hand on my shoulder, but instead she flops back into the pillows with her hand across her forehead. "I can't *believe* this."

"Is this it?" I ask, through my sniffles. "The wedding's off? After everything? After all that? It's…it's *off*?" I burst into tears again. This is all my fault. If I'd just had the wedding back home, none of this would have happened. I'm being punished, that's what it is. It wasn't enough that I apologized to Mom. No. God, or Zeus, or whoever is in charge up there, decided that instead of ending juvenile diabetes, they were going to make damn sure Summer Hartwell paid in full for planning a wedding without her mother.

Thanks, guys. I get it. Lesson learned.

"I think I'm having a nervous breakdown," I moan into my hands.

Graham takes Babette's seat on the couch—she's already gotten up and wandered off somewhere in hysterics—and puts an arm around my shoulders.

"It's going to be okay," says a voice that doesn't belong to Graham. Another arm comes around me from the other side, and I realize that it's Mom. She's put down her sack of canned goods and forks, and is looking at me through tear-filled eyes.

"How, Mom? The wedding is in nine hours and we have no venue. We have no venue, no tables, no chairs, no *food*."

"One way or another," says Mom "my daughter is getting married today. It may not be the wedding of your dreams, but I don't think any of this was ever going to be the wedding of your dreams."

I give her a weak smile. How was I the only person who didn't know what a mistake all of this was?

"It may not be the wedding of your dreams," she continues, "but there will *be* a wedding. Isn't that right, Graham?"

I turn and look at Graham. He really doesn't look well. I mean, none of us do. We all just received some terrible news. But still, I've never seen him looking so…what is it? The word *guilty* flickers through my mind. That's silly. What would Graham possibly have to feel guilty about? It's not like he burned the place down.

Oh.

It's as I'm looking into his eyes, and the synapses in my brain are beginning to form connections between thoughts of Graham and thoughts of arson, that a montage of Francine images starts running through my mind. In each image she's holding a cigarettes in one of her shaky hands. She's flicking ashes on the ground. She's blowing smoke in my face. And then, like a geriatric Vin Diesel, she's driving calmly away in her golf cart as The Lakeview goes up in flames behind her.

Graham never talked to her.

That's why he looks so ill right now. He thought he could get away with not saying anything, and now he thinks that this is all his fault. I open my mouth to accuse him, when another thought stops me in my tracks. What if he *did* talk to her? What if talking to Francine pushed her over the edge, making her so angry that she decided to set fire to the place? Then this would all be *my* fault.

Maybe I don't ever want to know whose fault it was.

Graham and I look at each other in silence for a few more

seconds, telepathically communicating that we shall never speak of what may or may not have happened last night—not to each other, not to anyone. It will just stay buried for all eternity, 'til death do us part, forever and ever.

Amen.

"Graham?" says Mom, still waiting for a reply.

"Yes," he says, jumping a bit. "Of course she's getting married today. This is just a minor setback. This is nothing, Sum. Venue? We don't need no stinking venue!"

Dad returns to the living room, beach towel and hairdryer free, and sits down on the coffee table across from me. He squeezes my hand. I smile, and look back and forth between him and Mom. Ironically, John and Babette have both disappeared, while my parents are the ones still here, holding it together. Sometimes I feel like my parents were simply constructed with some of their wires crossed. Like, this one time when Dad fell off a ladder, they were totally calm about the whole thing. But then, this other time, I forgot to bring my car in for an oil change and they totally lost it.

They're stronger than you think. The words Graham once said to me come floating back.

So, here I am. Back to square one. Back to square one with the two people who should have been here all along. Lesson learned.

God, or Zeus, or whoever, sure works in infuriating ways.

36

"Seventy-five," says Graham, into his cell phone. "Seventy-five chairs, that's right. And tables to match. And a tent. And we need it all delivered and set up by two o'clock. Yep, two o'clock *today*. Whatever it takes. Money's no object." He gives me a wink. "Thanks."

I smile and turn back to surveying the charred remains of The Lakeview. The fire trucks and police cars are still there, probably searching for signs of arson.

I'd point you right to her if I had any proof, fellas.

But the longer I sit here looking at the extent of the destruction, the more I start to doubt that Francine could have done this. I mean, she *could* have. It's not hard to start a fire, and fires certainly like to spread. But seeing the reality of it, laid out in front of me with its smoky tendrils curling up toward the sky, it seems too insane. Even for her.

I stand up to stretch my legs, and suddenly feel the oddest sensation beneath my feet. It's a light vibration—almost as if a train were about to whiz through town—only, there aren't any trains around here. It's weird, but I shrug it off. It's probably just pins and needles from sitting here so long. I've been sitting on the fountain, across the street from The Lakeview, staring at it with a dulled sense of loss, for the past half hour. I know my wedding was supposed to have been in there. And I know that it would have been beautiful—as long as Nadine took care of those bubblegum table linens—but, like Mom implied, how much of it would have actually been *mine?* That wedding was more Babette's than it was ever mine. I see that now.

Graham's been on the phone for the past thirty minutes trying to order last minute supplies for our suddenly outdoor wedding. Judging by the thumbs-up he just gave me, the chairs, tables, and tent shall indeed be here. And by "here," I literally mean *here.*

We're getting married right here in Duke's Landing. On the town common.

The town common, you say? Isn't that where retirees drunkenly line dance, night after night? Isn't that where the daring ones get frisky, get arrested, and get drinks named after them? Why, yes. Yes it is. In a few short hours, I shall walk down a makeshift aisle in my wedding dress—the real pretty one that wasn't eaten by an alligator—and begin the next chapter of my life. I shall begin the next chapter of my life five hundred feet from the blackened heap that was once The Lakeview.

I know, I cried about it too.

At first, saying our vows directly across the street from a smoldering graveyard of wedding decorations and filet mignons seemed like a bad omen—like a black cat crossing your path, or seeing a single crow. I even called the Sunset Havens Recreation Department to check on the availability of the other town commons, but Duke's Landing was the only one not hosting a special event tonight.

Then, as I dejectedly hung up the phone, I thought of how well-done our filet mignons must be by now. I mentioned it to Mom, and we laughed about it for a long time. After that, I felt a little better.

Now, I'm fully onboard.

In other words, I've come to accept that I have no choice. It's make the best of a bad situation and get married out here at Duke's Landing, or postpone the entire wedding. And while I see now that I should have involved my parents all along, there's no way that I can go back home and start over from scratch.

I'm tired.

I want to get married—today. I want to go on our honeymoon—tomorrow. I don't care how it happens. I just want to be Mrs. Summer Blenderman more than anything else in the world. Besides, it's a well known fact that if you hit rock bottom and manage to survive, things can only get better.

***

I take back what I said.

Things *can* get worse. Things can *always* get worse. Even when you've hit rock bottom, someone can come along with a stick of dynamite, blast through that layer of rock you've been resting comfortably upon, and push you further into the Earth's crust. That's where I am right now. Crust bottom.

"How is he *dead?*" I screech into my phone.

"Well," says Nadine, her voice shaking. "He was quite old. I…I don't know the exact *cause.* I suppose I could find out. We may need to wait for the autopsy—"

"No," I interrupt. "I don't want any autopsy results. It was a rhetorical question, Nadine. I'm stressing out here."

Arthur Spanley, our pre-historic Justice of the Peace, died in his sleep last night. Nadine called while I was having my hair done to tell me the news. I'm not trying to be disrespectful. I understand that a man has lost his life and that this shouldn't be all about me...*but.*

I'm getting married in—I glance at the clock—five hours. I'm getting married in five hours and our Justice of the Peace is as dead as a door nail.

"Can you get us somebody else?" I ask. "Who's next on the list?"

There's silence on the other end. All I can hear is a light shuffling of papers as Nadine digs through her binder.

"Oh," she says at last. "Oh, my."

"What?"

"Well, one of the others is up north for the summer, in Massachusetts. He's usually *fabulous.*"

Perfect. The fabulous, totally alive Justice of the Peace is back home in Massachusetts.

"Are there any others?" I ask.

Nadine clears her throat. "Well, there was a third, up until this week. But we've since been forced to sever ties."

"Why?"

"He got into a bit of trouble with the law. Do you know Flavio? From Zumba?"

"*Flavio* was a Justice of the Peace?"

"Oh, yes. A lovely one, too. *Very* handsome."

An image of Flavio performing our marriage ceremony in one of his neon, nineteen-eighties aerobics outfits flashes through my head. Maybe it was a blessing that he threw that brick at us.

"Okay," I say, my head swimming. "Where does this leave us?"

"I'm afraid I'm out of ideas," she says, flatly.

"But you're our wedding planner! You're supposed to be there to solve any problem that comes up!"

"I suppose you could get married at City Hall," she says. "But you'd have to wait until Monday."

I don't even say goodbye. I just click off my cell and scan the rest of the faces in the room—Tanya, Babette, Sarah, Amber, and a bunch of hairdressers. The one person that I need right now isn't here. She's outside calling every restaurant in Orange County, looking for someone to cater a wedding on short notice. I told Mom that she should let someone else handle that—God knows Babette's been totally useless since The Lakeview burned down—and that she should just come inside and have her hair done. She replied by saying, *Oy, please. Who's going to look at an old lady's hair?* Her response made me smile at the time. Now, my smile is gone and I stand impatiently by waiting for her to get the hell off the phone.

"I'm not having any luck with *any* of the local caterers," she says when she finally hangs up. "I hope you don't mind, but we're going to have to consider—"

"Mom," I interrupt, "that's going to have to wait. This is more important. Arthur Spanley is *dead.*"

Mom drops the phone into her lap. "Oh, no! Your father will be devastated. Dr. Spanley's been his proctologist for more than thirty years."

"What? How would I possibly know that dad's proctologist

died? No, Arthur Spanley was our Justice of the Peace."

"Oh, thank God."

"Mom!"

"What? Your father's proctologist is very gentle," she says, with a shrug. "You'll understand when you're older."

"Focus, Mom. *Please.* What are we going to do?"

She looks at me thoughtfully for a few seconds. Then, in the most deus ex machina moment ever, she says, "I'm an ordained minister. I suppose I could marry you."

I didn't exactly expect her to have a nervous breakdown at the news about Arthur Spanley—since this morning, I've become accustomed to this new, less-stressed, version of my mother. But I was in no way expecting those words to come out of her mouth. *I'm an ordained minister.*

"You're a *what*?"

"An ordained minister," she says. "I became one on the Internet."

"But *why*?"

"I was on AOL," she says. "checking your father's email, and this ad popped up on the screen. Universal Life Church, it said. So, I clicked it, like I always do, and it took me to this website."

"Didn't we tell you to never click pop-ups?"

Mom shrugs. "The next thing I know, I'm an ordained minister!" She takes her wallet out of her purse and hands me a folded up piece of paper. I unfold it.

Joan Hartwell, Certificate of Ordination. Universal Life Church.

Well, I'll be damned. Mom's either an ordained minister or she's been scammed out of a lot of money. Either way, her computer is filled with spyware.

"Hang on a minute," I say. I take out my phone and google the Universal Life Church. I scroll through the page, noting that Conan O'Brien and Benedict Cumberbatch are also ordained ministers. Seems legit. I put my phone away and smile at Mom.

"You're an ordained minister!" I throw my arms around her neck and bounce her up and down. "Wait a minute. If you're going to be performing the ceremony, *everybody* is going to be looking at your hair!"

I turn and start marching her back toward the salon. I pull open the door, then I pause and close it again. "Hang on a minute. I have one more thing to say to you."

Mom looks at me hesitantly, like she thinks I'm going to say something snarky, which makes me feel awful. It also makes what I'm about to say even more important.

"I love you," I say. "And I'm sorry that I planned my wedding without you. And I'm not just saying that because you keep swooping in and saving the day. I'm saying it because not including you was an extremely shitty thing for me to do."

"Summer!"

"I'll be a married woman soon, Mom. Let me swear. Just listen. I'm sorry about the wedding, and I'm sorry that you've been lonely living in the house with just Dad. When I moved out, I thought you'd be obsessing over whether or not I knew how to turn on the heat in my apartment, but I never considered that you would *miss* me. I want to fix that. I want us to spend more time together—as friends."

Mom's face lights up. "You want to be friends?"

I nod.

"That would be nice," she says.

"Maybe when we get back home, we can plan a little shopping trip, or go out for lunch or something."

"Or I could teach you how to knit!"

"Uh, sure," I say. "Like, a scarf?"

"Or a sweater! I can teach you how to knit your own cardigans!"

"That would be great," I say. "A married woman can never have enough cardigans."

I suppose I can use them to cover my old, married bosom.

Okay, so being friends with Mom is going to take some getting used to. I'll just have to work on my patience.

"And you can teach me how to use Facebook!"

Nope. Nobody has that much patience. Least of all, me.

"One thing at a time, Mom," I say, pulling open the door to the salon. "One thing at a time."

37

Typically, when a woman is about to walk down the aisle—her arm hooked through her father's elbow, the butterflies in her stomach beginning to stir—she finds herself adrift in the scent of roses, lilacs, or Chanel No. 5.

Not, typically, McDonald's French fries.

That unmistakable scent—the one that lingers in your car for weeks after hitting the drive-through—is wafting all over the town common. Ground zero is the back of John's Lexus, where Dad's stuffed about three hundred bags of the stuff. Dad's tuxedo reeks of it too, since he's been driving from McDonald's to McDonald's all afternoon, gathering up enough Chicken McNuggets to feed seventy-five people. The downside of finding out that Mom is an ordained minister, is that it somehow fell to Dad to finish up the business of finding a caterer. But, he did the best that he could on short notice, and he did it all out of love.

What more could a girl ask for on her wedding day?

Don't answer that.

I take a deep breath. It's all good. My wedding is just one more scene in this comedy of errors that I call my life. I'd be a fool to have thought there wouldn't be McNuggets involved. And while the old Summer would have walked down the aisle hoping this to be the *final* scene in that comedy of errors—

Wait. That makes it sound like I wished I were dead. Not true.

While the old Summer would have foolishly hoped that once she were married she would no longer be subjected to these types of bizarre situations, the new Summer realizes that the old Summer was kind of an ungrateful little shit. The new Summer—the one who now appreciates her mother and father, despite their eccentricities—is learning to *embrace* this comedy of errors that is her life.

Besides, trying to avoid it has only made things worse.

"Dad?" I whisper.

"Yes?"

"How many tubs of dipping sauce did you get?"

"Thousands."

"Nice work." I squeeze his arm.

"I packed them all into The Duffle," he adds.

And that is how I came to be thinking about The Duffle, as I walked down the aisle on my wedding day.

I smile at Graham, but in my mind I'm picturing The Duffle—stuffed full of barbeque, honey mustard, and sweet and sour sauce, the tubs all rolling around between Mom and Dad's socks and underwear. Then I picture Mom and Dad carrying it out of the SUV, one on each end, like they're moving a bureau. As the great Stephen King once said—*Life is like a wheel. Sooner or later, it always comes around to where you started again.* Indeed, two short years ago, Mom and Dad carried The Duffle through a cruise terminal, and today they shall carry it through my wedding reception.

Life is a wheel.

Graham smiles back at me, naturally assuming that my smile is for him and not for the goofball comedy running through my mind. What he doesn't know won't hurt him. As I walk up the aisle, I look around at the friends and family who have made the journey down to Florida, acknowledging that one good thing about all of this, is that there are very few people here to stare at me.

John and Babette's Sunset Havens friends are taking up two entire rows, and that includes Janice and Francine. It's aggravating that they're here after having—with ninety-five percent certainty—burned down my wedding venue, but what could I do? Sometimes there is no justice in the world. Sometimes, the only way to get justice, is to make it yourself. But, seriously. What woman wants to make justice on her wedding day? Instead, I simply avoid eye contact as I pass by their row.

As we reach the end of the aisle, I give Dad a kiss on the cheek before he hands me off to Graham. I hand my bouquet to Tanya. It's a bit bizarre seeing Mom standing there in front of us, in the officiant's spot, but she does look beautiful in her mother-of-the-bride dress with the shoulder pads. She's holding a familiar stack of stapled pages; somehow she got the copy of our ceremony from the late Arthur Spanley. I wonder if Nadine went over to his house? Hmm. Maybe she wasn't such a bad wedding planner after all. Either that, or she killed him herself.

Anyway, poor Mom. She must be nervous getting ready to

speak in front of all these people. I wonder, briefly, if she's having a nervous breakdown.

"You look beautiful," whispers Graham. "I like the dress and the—" He twirls his hand around the top of his head, indicating my up-do. I remember the first time he did that. I was wearing yoga pants and had my hair in a who-cares-I'm-traveling-with-my-parents kind of ponytail, about to board a cruise ship to Bermuda.

Yep, life is a wheel.

Behind Mom is the Duke's Landing fountain. The water, shooting up in a gentle spray, makes for a very pretty backdrop. With the police and fire trucks finally gone, it's actually very peaceful out here on the common. Beyond the rows of chairs that our guests are seated in, is the bandstand where Tyler Maxwell will be performing. Graham called Squirrelly Dan and The Nuts earlier this afternoon and offered him five hundred bucks if he'd take a hike and let Tyler Maxwell have the stage. We may not be able to keep random retirees from crashing our wedding reception, but at least we'll have control over the music.

Graham and I face each other as Mom begins to speak. He looks so handsome. A part of me was afraid that he'd show up wearing the Beast's yellow and blue tuxedo (I *know* that he ordered one, even if he won't admit it to me). Instead, he's wearing the light gray tux, white shirt, peach tie, and peach boutonniere that we picked out. He looks very Florida cool, although the muted colors must be killing him. Fortunately, he's also got on the world's loudest pair of boxer shorts. The fact that I alone have this tidbit of information makes me smile again.

"Oy," says Mom, into the microphone, as she comes to the

end of the page and turns to the next. "How long *is* this thing?"

A titter of laughter goes through the audience.

"Almost there, Mrs. H," mutters Graham, giving me a wink.

Mom does have a point, this ceremony is taking forever. And it's seriously hot out here. I wasn't even listening to half of what she said.

"…played 'Fur Elise' *so* beautifully at a piano recital…"

Oh, for Pete's sake. Did she really just bring that up during our wedding ceremony? I didn't realize she'd made her own revisions to the script. Maybe I ought to start paying more attention.

"…always hoped he would someday, somehow, become a part of our family. Such a lovely, lovely, young man…"

Geez. With all the old women down here having the hots for Graham, I almost forgot that my own mother's been half in love with him for the past fifteen years. If I'm not careful, she might try to marry herself off to him. I don't think she's even mentioned my name once. I sigh a bit louder than is becoming for a bride, and Mom looks up at me sharply.

"What?"

"*What* what?" I whisper.

"You gave me a *look*," she says loudly, and directly into her microphone, cuing another titter of laughter from the crowd. "And now you're getting an attitude!"

"I am *not*," I hiss. Am I seriously arguing with my mother *at the altar*? Of course I am. "Just finish the ceremony and…and I'll teach you Facebook."

Mom clears her throat, gives me my last Joan Hartwell look of death as a single woman, and continues with the ceremony.

As Graham repeats his vows, my mind drifts back to the old days when he would come by the house to see Eric, and stop by my room just to chat. I think back to the time that I almost took him to my prom, and I wonder if maybe we wouldn't be here right now if things hadn't played out the way that they did. I picture our future Blenderman children, full of blonde hair and energy. Then I picture Mom and Dad as grandparents, and it totally fits. The sweaters and the junk food and the inability to use Facebook. It's the role they've been waiting to play their entire lives.

They're going to be amazing at it.

"And do you, Summer Eve Hartwell, take Graham Michael Blenderman to be your wedded husband to live together in marriage? Do you…oy." Mom pauses again to turn the page. "Do you promise to love him, comfort him, honor and keep him for better or for worse, for richer or poorer, in sickness and health and forsaking all others, be faithful only to him so long as you both shall live?"

"I do."

"To commemorate this union, you may now exchange rings. Let these rings remind you always of your eternal love and commitment to one another," says Mom. "Will each of you please repeat after me?"

We repeat after her. We exchange rings.

"By the power vested in me, by the Universal Life Church and America Online, I now pronounce you husband and wife. You may kiss the bride."

I'm briefly horrified by the thought of kissing Graham in such close proximity to my mother. Graham looks at me and smiles one of his mischievous smiles that means, *I know what you're thinking and I'm about to make things much, much worse.* Then he pulls me in, wraps his arms tightly around me, and kisses me without a single ounce of restraint. To my surprise, I don't even care. Mom melts away, and it's just me, Graham, and the very first moment of the rest of our lives. We did it.

38

"But why does he have to keep taking their requests?" I ask Tanya, taking a sip of champagne. "Can't we do something?"

She shrugs. "It's a public place, and these people were expecting Squirrelly Dan and The Nuts tonight. We had to compromise."

"They're hi-jacking my band," I say, stubbornly. You would think that they'd notice a bride, a groom, and a whole mess of wedding guests standing around and maybe rethink their decision to butt in and request the Cupid Shuffle. But, no. These Sunset Havens residents have paid their monthly entertainment fees, and they want to dance. I chug the rest of my champagne as Tyler Maxwell starts a very Sinatra-y rendition of said shuffle. To be honest, it's not half bad. I can't believe he didn't win *American Idol*.

"What are you drinking?" I ask Tanya. She's holding a large, red plastic cup, like she's at a frat party instead of my wedding.

"I believe it's Babette's famous Rusty Twizzler."

"Oh, boy," I laugh. "Go easy on those."

Since our open bar idea went up in smoke along with the rest of The Lakeview, our only option for booze seemed to be for everybody to purchase drinks from the kiosks that operate every night on the town common. But, Babette had another idea. She's set up a folding table next to the bandstand and is mixing her own drinks, free of charge, and without any sort of permit. She says that if the cops show up, she'll take the fall and that John shouldn't bail her out of jail until Graham and I have left for our honeymoon. So, we've got that to look forward to. In the meantime, there's my mother-in-law, tossing jiggers and shakers in the air like she's Tom Cruise. She's having the time of her life.

"Care to Cupid Shuffle with your hubby?" Graham comes up behind me and slips a hand around my waist. I turn around and wrap my arms around his neck, resulting in a few nosy guests clanging their forks against their champagne glasses—or in our case, hitting plastic cups with plastic forks. It makes an odd sound, but we get the message and give each other a kiss.

"I already told you," I say, pulling back a bit. "I'll Electric Slide or Achy Breaky with you *one* time. No Cupid Shuffle. Besides, it's almost time to cut the cake."

The cake. One of the few things that wasn't destroyed in the fire, as it was still nestled safely across town at the bakery. I'm dying to get something into my guests' stomachs that didn't come out of a fryolator. If you thought serving McDonald's food at a wedding was gross, imagine serving it two hours after purchase. Luckily, at Sunset Havens, paramedics are always on standby.

As we make our way toward the cake table, I take a moment to appreciate everything that my friends and family have done to get the town common ready for tonight. Tanya, Sarah, and

Amber made a run to the dollar store for decorations—resulting in the folding tables being covered with white plastic tablecloths, overlaid with silver tissue paper, and sprinkled with confetti. Granted, the confetti contains the words *Happy Birthday*, but so what? Is this not the birth of a marriage? I might just start wishing brides and grooms a happy birthday at every wedding I go to from now on. Our wedding photos will probably end up all over Pinterest as some sort of sophisticated new trend.

The LED candles that Graham bought for our romantic evening a few nights ago, are now warmly lighting the center of each table. And Eric, my dear brother who I pegged to be sitting by the pool all afternoon not doing a damn thing, actually spent several hours personally winding Christmas lights around the trunks of all the trees. When I saw what he had done, I threw my arms around his neck and told him that I loved him. In return, he told me that the two hundred dollar generator he needed to purchase in order to actually turn the Christmas lights on was doing double duty as our wedding present. And also, that he loved me back. Then we agreed to never speak of any of that again.

Don't tell him that I told you.

"Summer," says Mom, grabbing my arm as we pass her table. "Did you feel that?"

"What?"

"I'm not sure," she says, clutching the back of the chair with her other hand. "Some sort of *vibration*."

I look at Graham. "Did you feel any vibrations?"

I wait a few seconds while he sings part of the Marky Mark song. Then he shrugs. "I don't think so. Mrs. H, maybe you've had one too many Rusty Twizzlers?"

"Oh, stop!" says Mom, playfully punching Graham in the arm. Then she squeezes him around the shoulders. "My *son-in-law!*"

"It's true, Mom. He's ours now. Look, we were just about to cut the cake, can we—"

"Oy! I felt it again!" She stops smiling and squeezes Graham harder.

I raise my eyebrows, suddenly remembering the odd vibrations I felt beneath my feet earlier today, when I was sitting on the fountain. But, we're in Florida. It's not like it's an earthquake. Best not to feed into Mom's paranoia.

"It's probably nothing," I say. "I didn't feel anything. And they don't get earthquakes down here. So, how bad could it be? Dad, you didn't feel anything, did you?"

Dad doesn't respond. He's been muttering to himself and staring across the common at something. I follow his gaze to find Roger, walking rather unsteadily, with a bottle of red Gatorade in one hand and an unfamiliar woman in the other. She has long, blonde hair, similar to Janice. They probably shop at the same hair extension kiosk at the mall. By the look on Dad's face, he hasn't quite forgiven Roger for that spiked bottle of Gatorade; if it weren't for that, he would never have ended up in the hospital.

"Never mind," I say, not wanting to be around when Dad blows a gasket. "Come on, Graham. Cake time."

We wait by the cake table until Tyler's finished with the Cupid Shuffle and receives the cue to start up our cake-cutting song, "Sugar, Sugar."

Ah, sugar…do do do do do do….ah, honey, honey…

"Smash it in her face!" shouts Roger.

I look at Graham and roll my eyes. Roger and his date have arrived front and center of the wedding cake, and now he's egging Graham on.

"Don't you dare," I whisper.

Graham picks up his slice of cake and hovers it slowly in front of my face. Then he jerks it to the left, to the right, then up, then down, making me duck and bob like there's a swarm of bees flying at my head. Then he gently feeds me a bite. Honestly, smashing it into my face would have been less embarrassing. I repress the urge to squash frosting into his perfectly spiked wedding hair, and instead gently feed him a bite in return. Then there's some more tapping of plastic forks against plastic cups, and Graham and I kiss again.

As we make our way from the cake table, I notice a few underdressed, and clearly uninvited, old people slowly moving in the opposite direction. I turn around, and watch in disbelief as a woman in a gold sequined baseball cap picks up our cake knife, and starts slicing off large hunks of cake.

"Margo! Edgar! Free cake!" she calls back over her shoulder. A woman who I can only assume is Margo, pushes past me—literally *pushes past the woman in the wedding gown*—and stuffs a hunk of cake into her gigantic purse.

"Hey!" I cry. "That cake is for the guests!"

The first woman just looks at me blankly. "Guests?"

I motion to my dress. Seriously?

"I think we may have crashed a wedding, Edna," says Margo.

Edna looks at my dress, then looks around at all of the other people who are slightly overdressed for a regular night on the town common. Then she shrugs, picks up our cake knife, and starts slicing off more pieces.

"Hey!" I march up to her and wrench the knife out of her hand. I'm not sure about this, but I might be about to have a knife fight at my wedding. I wonder if anybody has ever been stabbed with a silver-plated Lenox cake knife before. Sure it's got two interlaced silver hearts on the handle, but that doesn't mean I couldn't use it to—

"Okay! Let's put down the cake knife and nobody needs to get hurt," says Graham, gently prying the knife out of my hand and placing it on the table. "Margo, Edna, Edgar, you're all welcome to some cake. There's plenty for everyone."

At the words, *there's plenty for everyone,* Edna puts her fingers into her mouth and whistles. For a few seconds, nothing happens. Then, like a scene from *The Walking Dead,* old people start shuffling in from every direction, some of them seeming to appear out of thin air. They're popping out from behind trees and creeping around the corners of buildings. I swear one even climbed out of a mailbox. All of them are converging on our wedding cake.

"No!" I cry out, but it's too late.

Graham pulls me to his chest and leads me quickly away. I take one last look over my shoulder, and then wish that I hadn't. My cake, my beautiful cake, is being torn apart in large, jagged chunks. Paper plates are being passed overhead, while a pulsing mass of greedy, frosting-covered fingers, reaches up to snatch at them. And then there's Edna. She's laughing. No, *cackling.* She throws her head back, gold sequined baseball cap falling to the ground, yellow teeth smeared with purple frosting from the flowers that had, only moments ago, been cascading down the sides of my cake. Then she turns to me, her eyes two blackened hollows, with maggots crawl—

"You okay?" asks Graham, snapping me back to reality.

Yikes.

I probably shouldn't have read all of those Stephen King novels over the past couple of months.

"Fine," I say, glancing back over my shoulder. Edna, Margo, and the rest of the wedding crashers are standing quietly around, munching on cake. Edna, with her gold sequined baseball cap still firmly in place, smiles at me and nods.

I nod back. I think the stress might finally be starting to get to me.

And on that note, Tyler Maxwell asks the crowd to please gather around for our first dance.

39

"Did you feel something?" I whisper to Graham.

We're slow dancing to our wedding song with all of our guests gathered around in a big circle. Also gathered around is an uninvited horde of gawking retirees (after the cake/zombie incident, I've started referring to them in my mind as *the horde*). After three members of the horde started trying to line-dance to "Can't Help Falling In Love," Tanya and Babette started shooing them off the dance floor.

"Like what?" he asks.

"Like…I hate to say it…a *vibration*."

"Wow," says Graham. "I didn't think it would happen so quickly."

"What?"

"You turning into your mother. I have to say I'm a little disappointed that it happened right before the wedding night."

I gently swat him on the back of the neck.

"Stop it. You're telling me you didn't feel anything?" He doesn't respond. "You *did*! You felt it too!"

He shrugs. "I might have. Maybe it's a sandworm."

"A Dune themed wedding would have been so cool," I say, dreamily. "We could have ridden a sandworm off into the sunset. I could have been Chani, and you could have been *Graham Muad'Dib*."

"You are so lame," says Graham, pulling me close and kissing the top of my head.

"Stuck with me now," I mumble into his shoulder.

After our wedding song ends, Tyler starts up his rendition of "Blurred Lines," which sets off quite a bit of shrieking from Sarah, Amber, Tanya, and the horde. Before long, I'm caught in the middle of a massive, pulsating, throng of young and old, and somebody's shoved a Rusty Twizzler into my hand. I raise the cup over my head, like I'm at spring break in South Padre Island. It's either that or risk spilling Rusty Twizzler all over myself.

"Ah!"

I take that back. Just spilled some on my head.

Then Tyler segues from "Blurred Lines" into "Sexy Back," and suddenly there's Dad, twerking. He's been proudly working on his twerk ever since the cruise—so, for about two years now—but I haven't noticed much improvement. He's bent down to the ground with his tuxedo clad butt up in the air.

VIP…Drinks on me…

"Whoooo!"

And here come Janice and Francine. Poor Dad. He just wants to twerk for the sake of twerking. He doesn't do it for the women.

You see what you're twerking with…Look at those hips…

Janice smacks Dad on the butt, then pulls her long blonde hair extensions out to the sides as she shakes her hips. My word.

"Yee haw!" says Francine. Her short black hair is gelled and spiked for the occasion, and she's put on a slash of hot pink lipstick. She parks herself on the other side of Dad, so close that if he stands up he's going to bang his head right into her—

"*Hello*, Dolly!"

I turn around to see who's addressing me so oddly, only to find that it's Roger, and he wasn't talking to me at all. He's heading straight for Mom, who's been uncomfortably observing everything from the edge of the dance floor. I pull Graham a little closer to where Mom's standing, so we can hear what they're saying.

"You look lovely tonight, Joan," says Roger, taking one of her hands and kissing it. Ew.

"Thank you," says Mom. "And you, as well."

I narrow my eyes. Bullshit. Roger's wearing a bright orange polo shirt with gold chains around his neck, and I distinctly recall Mom saying—on *several* occasions—that men who wear gold chains are assholes.

"Your husband is making quite a splash," he says, motioning to Dad who's now been flanked on his two remaining sides by Nadine and Lorraine.

"Oy, please," says Mom. "He just likes to think he can do that dance. That, what do you call it? Twerping?"

"Are you sure about that?" says Roger. "You know, if you were my woman, I would never twerp with another."

"Huh?"

Roger sidles closer to Mom and puts an arm around her shoulders.

"This might be our last chance, Joanie. What do you say you

and I make your husband jealous with a little horizontal Tango?"

Oh.

My.

God.

Did I hear him correctly? I look up at Graham, who confirms by facial expression alone, that I did.

"I don't know that dance," says Mom. "But maybe we could Foxtrot?"

By the expression on Roger's face, I can tell that he's trying to figure out if *Foxtrot* is code for something kinky.

"Well, I don't know *that* dance," he says, apparently deciding that it is. But maybe you could teach it to me…privately. My golf cart is just over—"

"Excuse me," says an unfamiliar voice.

Graham and I turn around. It's *Dad,* fresh out of his twerk. He's very sweaty and red-faced, and pretty much exactly how you would expect a late sixties-ish man to look after twerking. But his voice seems different. Commanding. All that blood rushing to his head must have caused a similar phenomenon to when he rode Space Mountain. He's determined. He's pumped up. He sounds like he's shoved his head inside a Darth Vader helmet.

"Excuse me," he says again, taking a few steps closer to Roger until he's standing directly in front of him. "Take your hands off of my *wife.*"

Roger takes a step away from Mom and holds his hands up in front of him. "Take it easy, Rich! I was just trying to have a good time." With one hand he reaches into the inside pocket of his suit coat. I clutch Graham's arm. First a knife fight, and now a gun? I relax as Roger instead pulls out the bottle of red Gatorade. He untwists the cap, takes a sip, and then holds it out toward Dad. A peace offering. Dad's eyes bulge.

"*That* thing landed me in the hospital!" says Dad. "I've had it up to *here* with your good times!" He wrenches the Gatorade bottle out of Roger's hand and shakes it out all over the ground, splashing a liberal amount onto my white shoes. "Now I want you to get *away* from my wife, get *away* from my daughter's wedding, and don't show your face around here again until my wife and I are back home!"

With a few heavy buffalo snorts from his nostrils, Dad grabs Mom by the hand and leads her back to the safety of their table. Mom is blushing fiercely and looking very much the giddy schoolgirl.

Roger turns to Graham. "Tell your father I'll be happy to join him again for golf once those *snowflakes* are gone. Come on, Diane. Let's get out of here."

Roger's date, Diane, had been standing next to us the entire time he was hitting on Mom.

"You're still going to leave with him?" I ask, perplexed.

She shrugs. "I'm paid for 'til seven."

***

The next couple of hours fly by, and before I'm quite ready for it all to be over, Tyler Maxwell is announcing that it's time for the bride to toss the bouquet. I grab my bouquet from the table and climb the steps onto the bandstand.

"All the single ladies!" says Tyler. "Come on up front!"

Almost the entire female component of the horde starts

converging on the bandstand, elbowing each other out of the way. That's when I feel it again—vibrations under my feet. I glance at Tyler and can see it on his face that he felt it too. What *is* that? He continues anyway.

"Alright, Summer. Into position. On three. One…two… three!"

I toss the bouquet backwards over my head and spin around fast so as not to miss anything. Francine jumps into the air and grabs for it first, but is quickly tackled by Janice. After Janice has her pinned, Nadine starts prying it out of Francine's fingers. Nadine holds the bouquet triumphantly into the air, only to be side-tackled by Gloria. Gloria hangs onto it for a mere three seconds, after which she's taken down by a woman in knee-highs rolled down to the ankle. After that, it's nothing but a blurry pig pile of white hair, flowered tops, and broken hips. I hold my breath as the pile writhes and twists and the occasional arm or leg shoots out from beneath. Then I see Lorraine crawling out the back. She's got it. She's got the bouquet! She staggers to her feet and holds it up over her head, and then…

Something's wrong.

Lorraine stumbles. In fact, everybody is stumbling. I stumble right into Tyler Maxwell, who catches me and pulls me away from the edge of the bandstand. It's the vibrations. They're increasing rapidly. I look out at the crowd and watch, frozen, as an invisible hand seems to draw a large, jagged circle around the pile of women. Then, the edges of the circle begin to crumble inward, and the pile drops down about a foot. The women are screaming and trying to stand up, but they're unable to gain the footing needed to pull themselves out of the enormous—

"SINKHOLE!" screams Tyler into his microphone.

Florida doesn't have earthquakes. Florida has sinkholes.

My wedding is sinking.

I look desperately through the crowd for Graham, and spot him sprinting toward the bandstand. He runs up the steps and grabs me by the hand. I'm still hanging onto Tyler, so I drag him along with me. Boy, did Squirrelly Dan and The Nuts luck out tonight.

We run across the common, grabbing Mom and Dad along the way, and head for the safety of the sidewalk across the street. Then Graham, Eric, and John run back toward the bandstand to help the others. The women in the pig pile have sunken even deeper into the hole. I watch from a distance as Graham, Eric, John, and several others, lean over the crumbling edges of the sinkhole, and start pulling them to safety. In the nick of time, Graham pulls Nadine out, and hustles her across the street.

With a sound like thunder and suction cups, the hole in the ground widens, and the bandstand collapses into it. A few seconds later, the sinkhole swallows up all of our folding tables and chairs. It swallows up the cake table, the LED candles, the Happy Birthday confetti, and every last McDonald's French fry.

All of it.

Gone.

40

My wedding guests are screaming. The horde is screaming. The sound of sirens is growing closer. God, am I sick of the sound of sirens. Our entire wedding party huddles together on the sidewalk as police, fire, and assorted emergency vehicles arrive on the scene and begin cordoning off the town common. After about thirty minutes, some of the stupider members of the horde start inching their way back toward the hole, cameras in the air.

"We're sure that everybody got out, right?" asks Babette.

"Of course," says Graham. "Lorraine, Gloria, Edna, Margo, Nadine—"

"What about Francine and Janice?"

"I…I don't know," says Graham. "I didn't see them. Somebody else must have pulled them out. Eric? Dad?"

Eric shakes his head. "I didn't see them."

"Dad?"

"I'm not sure," says John, struggling to remember. "I pulled out so many. I lost track!"

"The last time I saw them they were trying to catch the

bouquet," I say. "Francine was the first to get it. Then Janice shoved her. Then…*oh*."

"Oh *what*?" asks Babette.

"Well," I swallow hard. "If Francine was the first to catch the bouquet, and then Janice fell on top of her—" I act the scene out with my hands. "That means they would have been…at the very bottom of the pile."

In other words, ground zero.

Babette's eyes widen. "You don't mean…" She clamps a hand over her mouth.

"No!" I say. "Those two are tough! They probably crawled out and took off before you guys even got there."

"How deep do you think that thing is?" asks Eric.

"Could be fifty feet by now," says John. "Nobody's coming out of that thing alive."

I feel dizzy. I may not have had any love for Francine and Janice, but I certainly never wished a sinkhole to swallow them up. At least not *seriously* wished it.

"It was only three or four feet when we pulled everybody out," says Graham, adamantly. "We worked fast. Nobody got left behind. We *checked*. We checked, didn't we?" He looks desperately at Eric.

"Of course we did," says Eric. "The ground hadn't even caved in yet, it had just sunk a little. There was nowhere they could have gone. Don't worry, man. They're here somewhere."

"There! There they are!" shouts Babette, pointing across the common. "I see them! Oh, thank God!"

We all look to where Babette's pointing. Far away, I see two women from behind—one with short black hair, and one with long blonde hair—heading down the street toward a residential area. Relief washes over me. Everybody got out. Everyone is safe. I close my eyes and put my head in my hands, shivering a bit. Is this what shock feels like? I thought I knew what shock felt like ever since Mom and Dad showed up as chaperones to my prom. Yet, this feels different.

"Summer, Graham," says John. I raise my head at the sound of his voice. "I have a feeling the police are going to want to clear the area soon. Why don't you two head on back to the house? The rest of us won't be far behind."

The words every woman dreams of hearing on her wedding day—*the police are going to want to clear the area.*

"Okay," I say. "Yeah, I think I'd like to get out of here. I don't feel very well." Selfish tears are starting to sting my eyes. Duke's Landing just fell into a sinkhole, and I'm getting teary-eyed because this wasn't the send-off I'd been hoping for. Tanya, sensing my impending breakdown, pulls me into a hug.

"It was a beautiful wedding," she says. "No matter how it ended. We've got the pictures to prove it."

"Actually," says Eric, "I think I saw the camera go down the hole."

Tanya shoots him a dirty look.

"Too soon?" Eric pats me on the back. "I was kidding, Sum. The pictures are fine. You can post them all over Facebook tomorrow and nobody will ever know that it was anything other than perfect."

"Yeah," I snort. "Until they turn on the news."

"Your wedding made the news!" says Tanya, shaking her fists in the air. "Yay!"

"Oh, but wait," I say. "Graham and I don't even have a car to leave in. Or a golf cart." There was supposed to be a limo picking us up tonight, but the orange barriers that the police are hauling into the road say otherwise.

"Not true," says Mom, stepping forward. She and Dad, believe it or not, have been complete rocks throughout all of this. They've been fetching bottled water from Starbucks, and even bought some blankets from the Sunset Havens gift shop to drape around people's shoulders—like the police do at the end of Lifetime movies. Like I said before, when something actually serious happens in life, they're fine. Tell them two inches of snow are coming? Forget it.

"We have a little surprise for you," says Dad. "We made it ourselves. Come on."

Mom and Dad direct us down the sidewalk and over to a parking lot by the public restrooms. Parked in one of the spaces, is a golf cart decorated for a wedding. Two banners are strung across the back, spelling out the words *Just Married* on burlap triangles. The rest of the cart is wrapped in streamers and bows and there are bunches of flowers everywhere. It's beautiful.

"We're on Twitter *and* Pinterest," says Dad, proudly.

I wrap my arms around the both of them, squeezing them tightly.

"Thank you," I say. "If I haven't told you before, I'm glad that you're my parents."

"You don't have to thank us," says Mom, wiping a tear from her eye. "Just enjoy it. Go on home. Babette and I will deal with all of this." She motions carelessly to the geological disaster unfolding behind us.

"We will." I give Mom another hug.

"And make us some grandchildren," she whispers into my ear.

"Mom!" I laugh. "Geez. Give it some time."

Graham and I get into the golf cart and wave goodbye to our guests—many of them covered in dirt and debris. We pull away from the curb to the sound of sirens, horns, and Elvis Presley, trickling perpetually down from the PA system. Mom and Dad wave happily back, ecstatic that their only daughter has been married off at last. It's a pretty antiquated idea. But, then again, so are they.

It's funny to think that I wanted my wedding down here in Florida because I thought planning one with my mother would be the worst thing in the world. Then my entire wedding literally fell into a hole.

So is life.

And so ends another beautiful day at Sunset Havens.

The End

⌘

We're about halfway back to the Blenderman house, when we catch up to Francine and Janice walking down the sidewalk. Graham slows the golf cart down as we pass, and then comes to a stop along the curb. I turn around in my seat to speak to them, to ask how they managed to get out of the sinkhole without anybody seeing, why they didn't—

It's not them.

I'm looking into the face of a short man with dyed, jet black hair, and Roger's paid escort, Diane—Diane with the blonde hair extensions that she probably buys at the same mall kiosk as Janice. My mouth is suddenly quite dry.

"I'm…I'm sorry," I say. "We…I…we thought you were somebody else."

"That's quite alright," says Diane. "Summer, isn't it?"

I notice now that she and this man aren't dressed anything like Janice and Francine. I mean, the guy is wearing a pair of black cargo shorts and his legs are hairy. But, from a distance, we couldn't see…we only saw the backs of their heads and we thought…

Oh, man.

"Summer, yeah. That's me," I mumble. "I, um, I thought you had left a long time ago, with Roger?"

"It's seven fifteen, honey. Roger's time was up. I met Jerry here across the street at the Gator Bar. We're going back to his place."

Jerry pops the collar of his blue polo shirt and gives me a wink.

"Besides," continues Diane, "Roger had this big idea of sneaking back over to your reception, hiding under the bandstand, and surprising all the women who came up to catch the bouquet." She laughs. "I wanted to be far away when *that* happened. Roger can be a little grabby, if you know what I mean." She gives me a wink. "Jerry and I did hear a lot of sirens after we left the bar. Everything alright over there?"

In my head I hear the sound of the bandstand collapsing into the sinkhole, and instead of answering Diane's question, I turn back around and stare out the front of the golf cart. Then I look over at Graham. He's looking back at me, wide-eyed. He presses the gas, and without another word, starts us slowly off again up the street. He reaches over and squeezes my hand. I squeeze back.

I may need to make a few calls.

Join Beth on Facebook:
www.facebook.com/bethlabontebooks

And Twitter:
@Beth_Labonte

You may also visit Beth's website and sign up for her newsletter:
www.bethlabonte.com

Other books by Beth Labonte:

What Stays in Vegas
Summer at Sunset
Down, Then Up (A Novella)

Beth Labonte was born in Salem, Massachusetts and received a B.A. in Sociology from the University of Massachusetts Amherst. She worked as an administrative assistant for fourteen years, turning to writing as her creative outlet in an excruciatingly mundane corporate world. Beth now writes full-time, and resides in Massachusetts with her husband and son.

Made in the USA
San Bernardino, CA
18 April 2017